THE EULOGY

Jackie Bailey

I live and work on the traditional lands of the Wodi Wodi people of the Dharawal nation. I pay respect to Elders past and present and acknowledge Australia's Aboriginal and Torres Strait Islander peoples as Australia's Traditional Owners, Custodians and First Nations. Aboriginal and Torres Strait Islander readers are advised that this novel contains the name of a Yugambeh man now resting in the Dreaming.

THE EULOGY

JACKIE BAILEY

Hardie Grant

BOOKS

Published in 2022 by Hardie Grant Books, an imprint of Hardie Grant Publishing

Hardie Grant Books (Melbourne)
Wurundjeri Country
Building 1, 658 Church Street
Richmond, Victoria 3121

Hardie Grant Books (London)
5th & 6th Floors
52–54 Southwark Street
London SE1 1UN

hardiegrantbooks.com

A catalogue record for this book is available from the National Library of Australia

The Eulogy
ISBN 978 1 74379 832 4

10 9 8 7 6 5 4 3 2 1

Cover design by Akiko Chan
Pressed flowers by Stefan Alfonso, iStock
Typeset in 13/19 pt Adobe Garamond Pro by Kirbyjones
Printed in Australia by Griffin Press, part of Ovato, an Accredited ISO
AS/NZS 14001 Environmental Management System printer.

The paper this book is printed on is certified against the Forest Stewardship Council® Standards. Griffin Press holds FSC® chain of custody certification SGSHK-COC-005088. FSC® promotes environmentally responsible, socially beneficial and economically viable management of the world's forests.

Hardie Grant acknowledges the Traditional Owners of the country on which we work, the Wurundjeri people of the Kulin nation and the Gadigal people of the Eora nation, and recognises their continuing connection to the land, waters and culture. We pay our respects to their Elders past and present.

For Allison

PROLOGUE

It's my job to write your eulogy, but every time I try to think of an amusing anecdote that sums up your life, I find myself asking, *How did we get here?* Not in a general sense, but specifically *here,* with me sitting in a car I have been living in for the last twenty-four hours, a husband on my blocked caller list, an airtight Tupperware container filled with the finely blended powder of three hundred sleeping pills in the glove box; and you, or what is left of you, currently in transit from the Logan Hospital morgue to Angel Companions Funeral Home.

I left the hospital an hour ago and have spent the time since sitting in my car, staring at a blank laptop screen.

It's not as if your death was unexpected. That's not what confounds me.

My mind keeps returning to a study I read years ago when I was a psychology undergraduate. A team of doctors in San Diego surveyed almost twenty thousand adults and found a statistically significant, graded relationship between adverse childhood experiences and cancer. At the time I dismissed it as so much humbug. Without triangulated evidence, the researchers only had people's self-assessment as to whether they had experienced psychological, physical or sexual abuse.

It turned out that I was right to be dubious about the San Diego research: magnetic resonance imaging has since shown that negative events stimulate activity in the emotion-processing regions of the brain that lead to the creation of memory. This may be an evolutionary survival technique – we remember bad things in order to avoid them in the future – but whatever the rationale for the tendency, the fact is that people's memories cannot be trusted.

Yet here I am, trying to work out if the general conflict of 1983 – because there was certainly enough mayhem to go around; I do not claim sole licence to suffering in the Bradley household – was enough to trigger one cell, then another in your brain to turn radioactive? I suppose I am asking – for twenty-five years I have been asking – did you get sick to protect me?

PART 1

CHILDHOOD

As much as possible, include personal
memories to illustrate the deceased's
story. It is the little details that really
bring the past to life.

How to Write a Eulogy

I startle awake, drool sliding down the side of my chin. I must have nodded off for a few minutes, because the hospital day-shift workers are starting to arrive: I can see the pale blue of nurses' uniforms and the bright pink of the maternity unit smocks. I fumble on the seat next to me for last night's coffee. The tepid bitterness of the burnt beans kicks me awake, which is good because I need to get moving, but when I try to sit up, I can't.

This is interesting, the calm part of my brain says, taking mental notes. I have read studies about the physiological impacts of bereavement. They include neuroendocrine activation, altered sleep, immune imbalance, inflammatory cell mobilisation, and changes in heart rate and blood pressure. This explains why I feel exhausted but can't sleep. Why my fuse is short and my heart shivers; why my stomach clenches as if something terrible or wonderful is about to happen, or I am about to throw up. My heart genuinely aches; my body is labouring with less air, under more strain. Waking feels like acclimatising to high altitudes, because I am doing exactly that. These physiological responses are greatest in the early months after bereavement. In some cases of extreme sorrow, survivors have been found to experience increased mortality. In other words, dying of a broken heart is real.

After a few minutes of deep breathing, and before anyone comes to tap on my window and ask why a strange, unkempt woman is sleeping in the hospital carpark, I am at last able to start the car. I head for a playground not far from the hospital. An early morning jogger plods the perimeter, but there are no harassed mothers chasing gleeful toddlers, so I make my way to the toilet block. Technically I am not in breach of the protection order if there are no children in sight. I splash my face, brush my teeth and give myself an all-over spray of deodorant.

The funeral home is situated in a light industrial area of Logan City, just off the southbound freeway. As I take the service road exit, families and young couples stream below me on the A1 freeway, headed for the Gold Coast with surfboards and dreams of sunnier, happier versions of themselves strapped to their roof racks. The A1 highway circumnavigates the entire continent of Australia – an estimated 14,500 kilometres of bitumen, winding ever onwards. You can go anywhere on that road, become anyone you want to be.

I contemplate the prefab building with 'Angel Companions Funeral Home' painted in cursive font on the concrete wall before me. 'Funeral home' is such a ridiculous term. I suppose it would sound a bit too commercial to call it a funeral *shop*;

but *home*? I prefer the old-fashioned term, 'parlour', conjuring images of creaky furniture upholstered in faded velvet where countless bottoms have farted during countless cups of stewed tea and triangular sandwiches. That's my idea of a send-off.

My siblings begin to arrive in their separate vehicles, a horde of Bradleys descending upon the unwitting funeral directors. Here comes Doctor Trish in her ten-year-old Mercedes, the one she refuses to upgrade even though she probably makes more money than the rest of us combined, because it still works, doesn't it? Barb is in her zippy Honda hatchback with the personalised licence plates: 'BARB01' they say, with a little picture of a pink bunny rabbit on the right-hand side. I wonder where she got the money for that; she always cries poor when we pass the hat for Mum's bills. Brian is in yet another of the endless parade of Japanese four-wheel-drives that have passed through his garage since he married into Anglo-Aussie suburbia; and Val is in her sleek white company car. Last but not least, Bev arrives, with Mum in the front passenger seat. I have already heard from Barb all about Bev's car: a metallic-gold Ford purchased with her late ex-husband's life insurance.

Before this morning, I had not seen Bev for eight years; not since Dad's funeral. I watch her alight from the gleaming vehicle and imagine his ghost circling it, kicking the tyres and nodding his approval. Dad had been a Ford man through and through and would have advised me against the nearly new Subaru that Evan and I bought last year. I would not have listened. I had done my research. An image of Evan shaking his affectionate head at me as I trawled the internet for the safest car in our price range pops into my mind, but I block it like his calls.

Val was the one who tracked Bev down. It wasn't nearly as difficult as when we had to track Val herself down, back in 1983, when you had just been diagnosed with cancer and everyone thought you only had a year to live. All Val had to do this time was log on and search for Bev's children on Facebook, and there they all were. 'How r u? Nice to hear from u again ;-)'

Seeing Bev flash a smile with her new dentures, also courtesy of the insurance money, I can't help but feel a tiny bit disappointed. What had I imagined? That miraculously, through a change of location and a failure to share her phone number with the rest of us, she had escaped the mediocrity of her projected life? The babies smelling of air freshener and cigarettes within minutes of emerging from her womb; the ex-husband who finally died of an overdose, by accident or on purpose no one will ever know, although based on my recollections of him, I think I can hazard a guess?

It turns out that Bev and her family left the caravan park they had been living in and drove up the A1, the road where you can go anywhere, become anyone. Our sister stopped in Bundaberg, a small city merely five hours north of Brisbane, and stayed there for the next eight years. What is that, if not a drastic failure of imagination?

Now here she is, the prodigal sister, seated next to Mum with just as much right to be present as any of us, I suppose. I walk over, give her a kiss. She is soft, a black polyester cardigan warming layers of beautiful fat. I am transported to you, Annie. It's her cuddliness, the obliging give of her body in my arms. Flesh of my flesh, blood of my blood.

The funeral director has to fetch more chairs.

'So lovely to see you *all* so involved,' she says.

We blink at her, the Bradleys, glazed and dazed with sleep deprivation and grief, yet still radiating a kind of collective heat, an energy born of being together. It's because we bring out the best in each other. Or the worst, depending on what is at stake.

Packets of tissues have been artfully arranged in a basket at the centre of the meeting table. While the director is out of the room, Barb leans forward. Hand halfway to her handbag, she suddenly remembers that we are all there with nothing else to do but watch her, pocketing the free stuff.

'Look,' she says. 'Tissues.'

'I think they're for people who are crying, Barb,' Val says.

Barb extracts one and dabs at her eyes.

When the funeral director comes back, Val begins talking about buying a new outfit for you to wear. We all agree on a cardboard coffin (which costs $2000 – the nerve of these people), so that we can decorate it ourselves. Val and her kids will paint the coffin in a floral pattern.

'Annie would have loved that.'

'Yes, Annie would have loved that.'

'Whatever happened to Annie's gold crucifix?' I ask Barb.

'What crucifix?' Barb asks. Annie, *you* know the one I mean. It was only nine-carat gold but with a detailed figure of Christ on the cross. Trish gave it to you for our trip to Lourdes in 1988 and you wore it right up until you were moved into the aged care home. The last time I saw it, it was dangling from Barb's neck as she kissed you goodbye. By then, you were unable to make a sound. 'I'm looking after it for her,' Barb told me when I confronted her. 'In case it gets stolen.' Which is ironic, when you think about the tissues.

Now I stare at Barb carefully, searching for her telltale tic: when Barb lies, she can't stop the tiniest of smiles from flitting across her face. But she looks genuinely puzzled. I wonder, is it more galling that she took this most sacred memento of yours, for God knows you had little enough to call your own, or that she cannot even remember doing so?

I take a deep breath. The crucifix is not the priority, I tell myself. The priority is the funeral. There was not much I could do for you when you were alive, but what I can do is this: I can give you the funeral you would have loved.

Val and her family are already doing the decorating and her boys can be pallbearers. Barb can do a prayer of the faithful, brief enough that she can't steal the spotlight from you for too long. I'll let Bev do one as well. I ought to involve her. Her boys can also be pallbearers and her daughter can do the offertory procession with Brian's kids. Each of our siblings has a role, just like you would have wanted.

Brian, Trish and I are doing the eulogy. Trish will open with something about you as a little sister. Brian wants to tell the story of your life in chronological order and I think that is a good idea: it gives us a narrative structure, a spine to which I will add the flesh. I will take the bones and make them giving and forgiving, like you, Annie.

I make myself turn away from Barb and focus on Brian. We agree to meet with the priest to talk through the service, Brian because he knows the priest, and I because I know you, Annie.

Although how well can I say I really knew you by the end? When was the last time I spoke to you and you spoke back? Even before the stroke, the one that landed you in the aged care home, your speech had been getting more and more slurred. It might have been because of the meds that kept your seizures in check, or it might have been the hemiplegia. Whatever it was, I can't actually remember the last time we spoke in dialogue; you know – me, then you. You, then me. I miss that. I miss the sound of your voice.

After the meeting I head to the nearest servo for fuel and a one-dollar cup of coffee. It's one of those modern petrol stations with a swooping roof and a food court. A group of teens loiter in front of the Macca's storefront. They look too old to be covered by the protection order against me, so I should be fine.

I idly scope the carpark but dismiss it as a potential sleeping place tonight. Too many bright lights. I pull out my laptop and stare at the screen.

Childhood. More specifically, 1983, the year it all began.

1983 starts like any other year in Loganlea. Hot and wet.

Our street is flooded as it always is in January, the height of the cyclone season. I stand on the upstairs verandah and watch two entire gum trees float past the house, rushing towards the creek. Our family is like the flood below, each one of us kids a fallen branch that could be smashed to bits any time. Trish, twenty-two, the medical student; Barb, nineteen, the prettiest one; Val, eighteen, who is wild; and Bev, fifteen and so far, so good. Then comes Brian, twelve, the only boy; and then you, seven, and me, four: the accidents. When people ask me how many brothers and sisters I have, I always pause, and not for effect. I just can't be sure I have done the sums right.

You and I are normally already in bed when the fighting starts. I sleep with our parents in the room next to yours, the room you share with Trish. In a month or two, Trish is going to move away for medical school. It's her second-last year and she has to be close to the hospital for student shifts. I will get to share the double bed with you and not be squished between our parents anymore. I am looking forward to that.

I hear your door creak open and I scramble to meet you in the hallway.

'Go back to bed Kathy,' you say, but I trail behind and you are too focused on your mission to insist. As we head towards the living room, I hear the mournful notes of the *Jeff Wayne's Musical Version of The War of the Worlds* record coming from behind Brian's door. He is the only one with his own room because he is a boy. I picture him in there, painting model cars, determined to tune out the shouting with the song that always makes me cry. *Cause you're not he-ee-ere …*

You sidle into the living room; I follow. You clench and unclench your right fist, but I grab hold of your arm so you can't go anywhere without me. I want us to stay near the wall, try to remain invisible.

Barb must be thinking the same thing because she is pushing herself into the green–and–white curtains. She should know by now that she can't hide. 'Why are you so mean to *meeeeee-eee-eee-eee-eee*,' she croons at Mum, over and over and over. It is kind of annoying; but then again, Barb is kind of annoying.

Val, on the other hand, refuses to say *a single word*. She stands as still as a statue.

This makes Mum go completely mental. Thunder judders the house down to its concrete slab; a tree crashes to the ground, its fall vibrating in my jaw. I want to go back out on to the verandah to see if the lightning has started a fire. But I have a job to do. I screw up my forehead, staring at Val as if I could bore holes through her stone–still skin.

Just say sorry, I think at Val with all my might.

But it's Barb, not Val, who starts bawling, 'I'm sorry, I'm *sorr-eee-eee-eee*. I'll kill myself, is that what you want? Is that what you want?' And so on.

'Val, just say sorry!' you shout at Val, as if you could read my mind, but Val has her eyes carefully fixed on a point above Mum's head and refuses to flinch, even when Mum stands centimetres from her. Then, *whack*! The slap sounds like Barb's Holden Gemini backfiring.

Tears glint in Val's eyes but still she refuses to speak. Nevertheless, I breathe out with relief. The hitting means that Mum has almost reached peak fury. The smacks and shouts escalate to the point that I worry that the curtain rods are going to come down, but then the pauses between curses start to lengthen, and we can hear Mum puff from exertion. I don't know exactly how long it takes, but eventually the big kids go to their room. We scurry back to bed in case she finally notices us.

* * *

This is probably not quite the right place to start a eulogy. I sigh, hit backspace. The one-dollar coffee is actually quite good, although that may be because I have only had a few minutes' sleep since I got the call from Val last night, telling me to come. I order another. The lady working the register has lines etched around her mouth into a frown more permanent than the blonde dye in her hair. She reminds me of the sour-faced woman who managed the Woodridge TAB, that mainstay of our childhood, frowning pointedly from us to Mum, but taking Mum's money all the same.

When I was five, I type, *Annie kicked me in the stomach. I asked her why. She said, 'Sorry. I was aiming for your nose.'*

I read over what I have written, select and delete. The entire concept of a eulogy, attempting to encapsulate the story of someone's life, is pointless anyway. My recollections would be different to Barb's, whose memories would be different to Trish's, whose stories would be different to Val's, and so on and so on, ad infinitum. Annie, you'd probably be interested in this little fact I came across in the literature review for my PhD, given the impact of the tumour on your own memory: my 'gist' memory – my memory of the overall tenor, the *vibe* of our childhood – would be, according to the science, coloured by recent life events, which may make me even more liable to focus on the negative aspects of our shared history.

Maybe 1983 wasn't that bad. Maybe I am looking for the root of your death in the past when I am both the cause and the consequence. The Alpha and the Omega. Apparently now I am likening myself to Jesus. Not much of a saviour if I cannot rescue a single half-breathed soul.

Remember the time Val brought the government down on our heads? That was 1983. Maybe it wasn't as bad as I thought it was. Maybe it was worse.

* * *

Unlike Barb's threats to harm herself, Bev goes for straight-up begging: 'Leave me alone! Please leave me alone!' Trish tries to stay calm but sometimes she does yell: 'What do you want? What do you *want*?'

Dad is normally at work when it happens, but if he is at home he sits in his armchair and stares at the blank television, occasionally interjecting, 'Come off it, Madge.' He can't really interfere too much, because Mum would turn on him and he needs his rest. Dad works three jobs trying to take care of all of us: full-time as a nurse in a psych ward, and on his days off driving buses for the school, and clearing the gutters for the priests and nuns at our parish church.

A fighting spate can go for days until it suddenly breaks like a summer storm over the house on Railway Road. Nothing is resolved. It's just that Mum gets tired and needs to regather her strength. Also, I think she likes to surprise the big kids, catch them off guard. She seems to enjoy those fights the most, the ones that no one is expecting.

It's almost the end of summer when a man and woman come to our house, but still too hot for the suit jacket that the man drapes over the back of one of the kitchen chairs. We can see big underarm sweat patches and try not to get too close.

The man and woman wear special badges. They don't drink the tea Mum makes for them. Mum calls Dad at work, and half an hour later he is sitting at the table with a mug in front of him, still in his nurse's uniform, his socks kept up to his knees by special elastic circlets. I've never seen Dad home early before.

While the man and woman talk to our parents, we wait with the big kids in their bedroom downstairs. I am curled up under Val's blankets and you are planted on the floor, hugging your knees, watching the big kids talk.

'Why did you call them?' Trish asks Val.

'Mum is gonna go mental on you,' Barb says to Val, but she sounds sort of glad about it. Bev says nothing, just watches the door as if waiting for Mum, or the government people – because that is who they are, people from children's services – to burst in. Brian is in his room upstairs, probably painting and re-painting a model car.

Val picks at her nails, ignoring everyone.

'What did you hope to achieve?' Trish persists.

'I don't know. I just wanted a break,' Val finally says. She puts her thumb to her lips. Crimson red leaks into her mouth and drips on her leg. You hand her the tissue box.

'Did Dad really do anything to you?' Trish asks. 'If he did, you should absolutely tell them.'

'No.' Val looks at us all, the Bradley girls. 'But, well, I couldn't exactly say it was Mum, could I? They wouldn't have believed me.'

None of us has anything to say to that.

Each of our sisters is called, one at a time, to talk to the government people. Val swears black and blue that it wasn't Mum *or* Dad and that actually she made it all up. Eventually the duo leave with nothing to show for their trouble but a deeper dislike of teenage girls.

After their departure I wait for the screams to begin; the sound of my sisters' faces being pushed into walls. But there is nothing: only a silence that could be either the end or the beginning of something. I can't tell which.

* * *

A billboard outside the servo advertises the Logan Hyperdome, where I will have to go soon to find a crucifix for you. *The largest single-level shopping mall in the Southern Hemisphere*, it reads. It was built on the empty lot in Loganholme, the other side of the railway tracks, where the travelling circus used to pitch its tents each year. Remember, we went that time with Dad in 1983? It was pouring with rain so the tickets were half price. It must have been a few weeks at least after the government people had visited, because Val and Mum were getting along. It was before your diagnosis, before Matthew's visit, before the orange light swaying above me although there was no breeze. The circus was a good memory, Annie. A memory I can recount without shame.

* * *

I am four years old and you are seven, and neither of us have ever been to the circus before. There is hay all over the ground so people can walk around despite the mud, and the air smells of a mixture of fresh straw and horse poo. It smells like what I think the outdoors would smell like if we were in a book like your favourite, *Black Beauty*. I inhale deeply and imagine a life in which we are animals free to roam.

Dad lets us have a turn on a game of clown heads in sideshow alley. I take a ping pong ball and put it in the clown's mouth and jump up and down when I win a green fairy doll stuck to the end of a bamboo stick.

'Well done Kathy!' you clap. I take the stick in my hands and hold the doll far above our heads. The stick makes the fairy seem like it is flying high in the sky, sprinkling good cheer and luck everywhere.

You don't win anything, so Dad has a go and he wins you a fairy doll too. Yours is pink because pink is your favourite colour. Then Dad buys us Dagwood Dogs and fairy floss, the giant cloud of pink sugar spun out and out until it looks like an oversized cotton wool ball. It melts the minute I put my tongue on it. It is the best thing I have ever eaten in my life.

'Yum!' I say, mouth full of deliciousness.

You grin back. 'This is the best, Dad, thanks!'

'Mm yeah fad, fanks!' I say through a mouthful of floss. He laughs and dabs at my sticky face.

I fall asleep on the bench seat of the Kingswood on the way home, leaning against Dad.

When we get back, Mum takes the dolls off their sticks because she says she doesn't want us poking our eyes out. She is in a good mood, helping Val to make a cake for Bev's birthday. You wander off to put our dolls to bed, but I perch on a high stool in the kitchen, eager to be near Mum when she is happy. Mum and Val laugh about something. For the weeks since the government officials' visit, things have been quiet at home. I hang around hoping I might get to lick the spoon when they are done. Then Mum takes the bamboo stick from where she has placed it in the corner of the kitchen and whacks me across both legs.

'Why did you do that?' I ask, tears springing to my eyes.

Mum shrugs. 'Just in case.' She laughs again. So does Val, which somehow hurts more than the sting of the blow. Later, Mum tucks one stick into the couch upstairs and one downstairs, in between cushions. She says she is keeping them handy. Just in case.

I think, *She must not have liked me waiting around for the spoon. I was being greedy. I shouldn't be greedy.* I run to find you and you listen carefully then nod. 'Yeah, that was probably it,' you say, your forehead creased with thought.

Even though I don't deserve it, and even though tonight is not my night, you let me have a turn of the teddy we share, but I still can't get to sleep. Mum gently snores on one side of me, and Dad loudly snores on the other. I slip off the end of the bed and tiptoe out of the bedroom to the loo. As I wash my hands I glance out the window and almost scream. There is a ghostly white figure creeping towards the back fence! Only, it's not a ghost. I hear the faint *crack, crack*, as you snap the bamboo sticks and throw the fragments into the incinerator. I fetch the teddy and place him back on your pillow.

* * *

Jesus Annie, does every memory from our childhood involve someone being hit? Is it just a trick of my memory creating the *before* and *after* of your diagnosis? I wonder again about the San Diego research, the ticking time bomb of your tumour armed by the violence, ready to explode when most needed.

How about some other cheerful anecdotes, like the time you got a bicycle for Christmas, or the time I made you laugh and laugh when I dressed up as a pink ghost, or my first ever birthday party? The problem is that every time I seize upon one of these memories, I can't help but remember what came after: you never rode that bicycle, because of your hemiplegia; I draped a pink blanket over my head because you were weeping in your hospital bed and it was the only thing I could think to do. My birthday party, with the frosted cake, happened because Mum and Dad thought you were dying and wanted to make you happy, and you said that what would make you happy was to make me happy. This may be selective memory, but when I look back, it seems that all the good things in our lives were a result of your gradual dying.

I gather my laptop from the plastic bench I have been sitting at and move to the area reserved for customers of the Coffee Club, one of the fancier shopfronts in the servo's food court. The seats are comfier and the coffee table, I notice, is made from the smoky glass that I once coveted when we were kids, thinking it the height of sophistication. If you wait long enough, everything comes back.

* * *

It is way too hot to be in the Kingswood, and yet here we are: you and me in the back seat, Mum and Dad up front.

When we get to Bev's boyfriend's place, Mum slams the door of the Kingswood and huffs off, Dad following more slowly. You and I struggle with the jammy handle until finally you manage to wrench the door open.

We creep to the house. I can see parts of cars in the tall grass, and a garden gnome with a red hat and blue clothes, its nose cracked off. I wish we could get garden gnomes. They remind me of Papa Smurf, who is always smiling and being wise and making everyone feel better.

The screen door swings shut behind us. The living room has shag pile carpet (I wish we could get shag pile carpet – so soft) and a black leather couch. The TV is way bigger than ours. A low, smoky glass coffee table is cluttered with empty cans and full ashtrays, but the room smells like air freshener.

Bev's boyfriend is in his jeans even though it is already a stinker. These wogs, Dad always says. They don't know the first thing about how to manage the heat. His hair is receding from his forehead like Dad's, but unlike Dad he keeps it long in the back, and even more hair sticks out of his T-shirt. *Yuck, I think. How much is under there?*

'She go, if she like,' he waves his hand. 'No one stop her.'

Bev emerges from the kitchen. She is the smallest and quietest of the big kids, her glasses big and round like her face. Which is why it is even more shocking that she stayed at her boyfriend's place last night. Although today is her sixteenth birthday, Bev looks not much older than you, which makes it hard to imagine how she could have been doing the things with that gross, hairy bloke that Mum has been shouting about.

Mum stomps across the living room but I can't hear her footsteps because the carpet pile is so deep. She yanks Bev by the hair and pinches her hard, raising red marks on Bev's bare arms. 'No shame!' Mum shouts. 'Make me *sick*!'

I cower, even though I am not the target. Mum's voice could squeeze my heart until it stops.

You shove past me. 'Stop it, Mum! Stop it!'

You place yourself between Mum and Bev, both hands raised. Mum reaches around you like you aren't even there and slaps Bev.

'Leave me *alone*,' Bev whimpers.

Dad pulls you out of the way. He hustles the two of us

back to the car and puts us in the back seat, this time locking the door.

'This is all Bev's fault,' you say from your side of the car.

'Then why did you try to stop Mum?'

You pause. 'Mum gets high blood pressure. Bev shouldn't get her worked up like this.'

'Was Bev really bad?'

'Yes,' you say. 'She was living in sin.'

'What's that?'

'You're too little to understand.'

'I am not!'

But you refuse to say anything further. It doesn't matter. I know what living in sin means. I saw it on TV, in one of Mum's shows, *The Young and the Restless*. It's where a man and a lady live together in the same house and they are not married. It's also something to do with boobs and being itchy. At least, that's what Mum yells at the big kids. *So there, Annie Bradley*, I think. *You're not the only one who knows things.*

Back at home the shouting goes on all day, with short breaks for meals during which Bev has to kneel and eat what she is given. I wonder what happened to the cake, but I know not to ask.

It's almost bedtime and Bev is still kneeling at the top of the stairs. Mum is watching TV in the lounge room.

I creep up to Bev and whisper, 'Are you OK?'

Bev tries to smile but her face is too puffy from crying. I circle one more time, then lean under her curtain of hair and give her a quick hug. I hurry back to the living room so I don't get her into any more trouble.

* * *

Was it that night, I wonder? Someone murmuring, *Shh, shh*; a choking sound; orange light swaying above; hands kneading my four-year-old skin? It happened once. Twice. Maybe three times. Maybe not at all. Except that it did; the knowledge came before memory, when my cells were the only available depositories for threat. My body is aware of exactly how much I owe you, Annie, even if my mind is not – you and your cancer.

My phone pings with a text from Val. 'Everyone to wear something pink for the funeral for Annie xx.'

Another thing for the Hyperdome shopping list. It's funny, isn't it, how Val turned out to be the stable one? She has a house, a husband, three kids, her own business in medical supplies. I wonder if that first trip to the hospital put her in mind of a career in the health system. Not your first admission, Annie. Hers.

* * *

The room is decked out in green and white. Even the sheet covering Val is dark green, like the paint Dad bought for the downstairs bathroom because it was on special. Mum is puffing like a horse at the races she bets on. Val is only barely conscious, her face green like the decor, but even so she has her glasses on. They must have let her keep those so she could see who was coming. I think she is smart to keep her eyes closed. The minute she opens them, Mum will be off.

Val is the worst of the big kids. She has tried to run away four times, and there was that time she brought child services to our doorstep.

But this is way worse. Barb says she took too many Panadols and the doctors had to pump them all out of her stomach. I look around the room, but there is no giant tube anywhere. Barb says it was just a stunt to get attention.

Two days later Val is allowed to come home. For some reason Mum is keeping her anger in check, but I wish she would just let it all out. Then it would be over with. I wish Trish was here, talking to everyone in her calm, soon-to-be-a-doctor way, but term has started so she's moved to the medical students' residence, where she lives on scholarships and part-time jobs.

Val still looks sick and weak. Usually she walks around with an energy that sparks, like Rice Bubbles – snap, crackle and pop! Even when I know she is up to no good, I just can't help but follow her lead. But at the moment, it's like all the energy is sunk somewhere deep inside her, if it is still there at all. Maybe the doctors scraped it out along with the Panadol.

Right when I start to think things might just go back to normal, it all comes pouring out, the way I imagine the contents of Val's stomach did when the doctors pushed a tube down her throat and made her vomit her way back to life.

Dad protests, 'Stop it, Madge! Stop it!' but Mum ignores him.

It gets late and the shouting is still going on. We go to bed without being asked. We lie next to each other in the iron-framed double bed that we now share, you on your side of the invisible line and me on mine. When you think I am asleep, you slip out of bed and tiptoe back to the living room.

I can be quiet too. I am just in time to see you inserting yourself between Mum and Val. I know that you don't approve of Val's sins, but I guess you don't approve of Mum's, either. You are the bravest person I know, but sometimes your courage makes us do stupid things.

I join you, raising my hands over my skull to avoid the whirligig of limbs and bodies. The air in here is stale and hard to breathe, as if we are stranded in space with just one oxygen tank between us.

'Stop it, Val, stop annoying Mum!' you sob.

'Stop it!' I repeat.

Mum breathes heavily, ignoring us. Val has already half pulled down the curtains in her attempt to hide.

In the morning Val is not in the big kids' room. More than half of her clothes are gone. My parents leave and don't return until the sun is already well on its way to the other side of the world. They do the same the next day, and the next.

A few days after Val's disappearance, I wake with a start. I go straight to the bathroom and get rid of the rest. I debate with myself for a moment or two but the sheets are too dirty. I rouse Mum.

'Mum,' I say. 'Mum?'

'Hmm? What, what is it?' she asks, voice furry with sleep.

'I pooed my pants,' I say.

'What?'

'I pooed my pants!'

This next bit is hard to tell.

Mum shakes you awake, telling you to go and sleep with the big kids in the room that they share downstairs. She strips the bed of the soiled sheets. Then she gets me to rinse out my purple undies, hand-me-downs from you, and fill the laundry sink so that they can soak overnight. She puts clean sheets on the bed, refusing to let me help. She tells me to wash myself, which I do, crying in the shower, not wanting to take too long but not wanting to get out, either. As I get dressed, she whips me with the sheets she has just removed. It's hard to stay out of reach because I am naked and crying and trying to get dry and pull clean pyjamas and underpants on, so I can't see the next strike coming.

After I am dressed, she tells me to get back into bed. I curl myself up into a ball and face the wall. Our mother shoves her way down the narrow gap between the wall and the bed so that she can place the sheets that I soiled next to my face. So, she says, I can sleep in my own shit.

I hold the clean sheet tight to my chin. I close my eyes but I keep having to open them when the tears need somewhere to go, and so I keep seeing the bunched-up sheets, the yellowy-brown smudges.

There is a rustling sound and a warm breath on my face. It's you, leaning over me, gently placing the sheet on the floor in a tangle that looks as if it dropped there of its own accord. You put a finger to your mouth, *Shh,* then creep back downstairs.

The next morning Dad is back from night shift and he scrubs the sheets while I scrub the stains from my undies. He says nothing, but having him standing next to me allows me to swallow the tears which would have got me into more trouble.

After Dad has helped me hang the sheets on the line, I come back into the house looking for you.

'Annie!' I call, but there is no response.

I find you back in the big kids' room even though it is the middle of the morning now, the sun already beating the sweat out of my skin during my brief trip to the Hills hoist. You are lying down on Val's empty bed. You place your hands over your ears as if trying to stop your brains from spilling out and when I ask you what's wrong, you keep your eyes closed and say, 'I have a headache.'

* * *

30

Don't worry Annie, I won't do it here. I know how terrible it is to be the finder of the body, and I would never want to put the big kids through that. Besides which, the bureaucratic procedures for transferring a body interstate would be a nightmare and I wouldn't inflict the paperwork on anyone I loved, not even Barb.

Much easier to drive back to Sydney after your funeral, where I will head straight out to the Garden of Remembrance.

But first, your funeral. It is time to brave the crowds. The Hyperdome is less than a kilometre up the road, but it is never the right weather in Queensland for incidental exercise. Remember when I tried to get you to go for 'mall-walks' in the Logan Hyperdome? One of my many ideas for trying to get you fitter, more active, more independent. More like someone I did not have to feel guilty about leaving behind.

The Logan Hyperdome has metastasized since I was last here. I attempt to interpret the directions of a touchscreen map, then wander around trying to look like I know where I am going until I stumble upon a jewellery shop not far from the cinema.

A female shop assistant unlocks the cabinet of crosses for me. Her fingers are strewn with cubic zirconia. I sit down, weary at the mere thought of the hours that went into her make-up. She only has two necklaces that have body of Christ figurines fused to the golden arms of the cross. 'This one is $329,' the woman says, indicating the rose gold one. 'The yellow gold one is $249. I can probably do a ten per cent discount if you want to get a good chain to go with it.'

'No, I don't need a chain,' I say.

I prefer the rose gold crucifix because it has a more detailed corpse. I ask if I can take pictures with my phone and the lady nods.

I send Val the images. She calls me. There are outdoor sounds where she is; I imagine sunshine and the quiet satisfaction of getting things done. 'We're just picking up the coffin and taking it back to our place so we can get started. We only have three days and they weren't going to be able to deliver it until Friday so we just got a work van and picked it up ourselves.' Val sounds pleased with her own initiative.

'Oh, good one, thanks for that,' I say. 'Have you dropped off clothes to the funeral parlour?'

'Yes, I did that on the way. I bought a lovely pink frilly top and a nice pale green skirt.'

'Nice. Hey, listen, which crucifix do you reckon I should get? I think the rose gold one is more like the one she used to wear.'

'I agree, I think the rose gold one's more like hers.'

'All right, I'll get that one then.'

'But you said it's more expensive?' I know what she is really asking: *Are you sure you want to spend that much on something that is just going to go into the flames?*

'I want to do it for her. It wouldn't be the same, Annie with no cross on.' My voice wobbles.

Val's voice drops. 'I know what you mean.'

When I hang up, the shop assistant is looking at me.

'It's for a funeral,' I explain.

'Yes, I gathered that.'

'That's why I don't really need a new chain,' I add, probably unnecessarily, because the woman merely nods. As she does so, not a hair on her head moves. I have never, not even on my wedding day, looked as well-groomed as she does.

'I'll take the rose gold one, please,' I say.

I hand over my credit card. The woman places the crucifix in a padded gift box and ties it with white ribbon. She taps numbers into a calculator and mutters to herself. She applies a thirty per cent discount to the purchase and, without meeting my eye, drops a fine gold chain into the bag. She then goes out back and brings back a handful of tissues for the tears that have been sliding down my cheeks since I got off the phone.

I once read that functional magnetic resonance imaging has been used to show that the orbitofrontal cortex and the amygdala, the parts of the brain associated with processing emotions, are more active when processing negative events. In other words, people tend to recall the details of a negative event much more clearly than the details of positive events. This is why I still remember your first hospital admission like it was yesterday; why, despite my best attempts, the memory of the orange light remained buried in my subconscious for twenty years.

* * *

In the weeks after Val's hospital admission and disappearance, the shouting and punishments spread like an ink stain. One night it is Bev, kneeling at the top of the stairs and trying not to cry; the next it is Barb, screaming that she will do something crazy if Mum keeps at her. Even Brian is not immune, copping an earful for being bad-tempered, which is, truth be told, fair, although the way Mum yells, I find myself siding with Brian.

I know Val is bad through and through, but I miss her. Whenever I flop face-down on our bed after a scolding from Mum, I think of Val. The image of my sister, safe and free, balloons in my chest and I can't help but think fierce thoughts. *Next time our mother hits me, maybe I won't just stand there and take it.*

You start complaining every day of headaches, which just makes Mum mad. She hates it when we say we don't feel well. At night in bed, I whisper for you to stop. But maybe you really are sick, because you keep it up until Mum finally takes you to Doctor Lin's surgery, where Barb works on reception. Barb plays the grown-up, smiling and ushering us into Doctor Lin's room. You lie back on the bed as told, covered with a blue paper sheet. Doctor Lin presses your tummy. He tells you to get down and then sits across from Mum.

'There is nothing wrong with her. She's a hypochondriac,' he says, smirking at you.

'Ah, hypochondriac,' Mum repeats, nodding. After that, whenever you complain of any sort of pain, Mum laughs and whips out the new word. Sometimes you cry with frustration right in front of Mum, but she doesn't hit you because she has the word.

There is still no news of Val, but one weekend Trish comes back from medical school for a few days. She even brings her special leather bag so we can play doctors and patients.

'Annie, do you want to lie down and be first?' As the eldest herself, Trish has always had a strong sense of age-based hierarchy.

'No.' You fold your arms. This is weird. Doctors is your favourite game and Trish is your favourite of the big kids.

But I don't waste too much time wondering about your reticence. I seize my chance. 'Do *me!*' I shout.

Trish obliges, putting the stethoscope on my chest and hitting my knees with the hammer that makes my legs twitch. This is called a reflex, Trish tells me. She says it's automatic, which means I can't stop it: if someone hits me in exactly the right spot, my body will kick back. Then Trish makes you lie down and pretends to check your eyes with the penlight and taps your knees too. She watches your right leg jerk, then announces, 'We're going into the city. To see a friend of mine.'

You cross your arms. 'It's past our bedtime.'

'That's OK, Mum will come with us,' Trish replies as she packs away her equipment.

I am excited but you just scowl and shake your head. You always know if something is up, and I assume this is the case now, but I don't dwell on it because we are out, at night, past eight o'clock. I swing my feet, which are not long enough to reach the floor of Trish's Datsun. The street lights flash by the window like fireworks. Mum is in the front passenger seat next to Trish. I am four years old but soon I will be five, which means I will finally go to school with you. I hate having a birthday at the start of the year. Everyone gets you things like pencil cases and erasers, which they would have had to buy you anyway.

We are near the hospital now, but we don't take the turn to the students' residence. You have been silent the entire drive, but now you say, 'I thought you said we were going to see your friend.'

'We just need to make a quick detour first,' Trish says.

The emergency room is glaringly bright. Long fluorescent light tubes line the ceiling and the hall reflects them, so I have to squint no matter which way I look. Doctors in white coats and blue scrubs smile at me in a friendly way, but they are all walking really fast to places I am not allowed to go.

We are directed to a bed behind a curtain and a young male doctor, also friendly, also smiling, tells you to lie down. Trish talks to him, and then he does the same tests that Trish did at home. Trish wears a grown-up smile now. She seems to be a few centimetres taller than she was an hour ago.

'I'm just going to test your muscles,' the doctor says. Even though you still look annoyed, you do what the doctor asks because he is, after all, a doctor.

'What are they doing?' I ask you after the doctor walks away.

'I don't know,' you reply. 'Mum?' you ask, but Trish draws Mum beyond the curtains that surround your bed.

You scrunch your face into a prune. I can see that you are angry, but it feels like your anger is smaller here than when we were at home.

'If the wind changes,' I remind you, 'your face will stay that way.'

You ignore me, scrunching your face even more. You seem a long way away up there on the bed. I don't have our teddy with me, and I wish I had something to hold right now.

'We're going to admit her,' I hear a doctor say in a lowered voice through the curtain. Do they realise these things aren't really walls?

'Mum!' you call, but the curtained area suddenly fills with people. Someone writes on a clipboard and two men in blue pyjamas start wheeling you away. Trish walks alongside the bed, talking to you in her doctor voice, which is meant to be soothing and which you and I usually giggle about, but you are not laughing now.

Mum does not go with you. I wince as she digs her nails into my shoulders, holding me so I can't follow. It is not until the bed disappears through a pair of double doors that I realise I should have waved goodbye.

A few days later I sit in the hospital corridor with Brian and Barb. Bev leans against the wall. Mum, Dad and Trish are inside the intensive care unit talking to the doctor. Only two visitors are allowed in to see you at a time, plus Trish, who is allowed in whenever she wants because she is almost a doctor, so I have spent a lot of time out here over the last week.

It's a wide corridor that we are waiting in – it has to be so the wardens can roll beds up and down. Across from where we sit are two plastic sheets which are like the swing doors in a western saloon, but instead of Clint Eastwood, hospital orderlies push through, rolling trolleys of meals on trays. They give Brian and me leftover cups of jelly. I don't think it would be polite to tell them I don't like jelly, so I swallow the shards of wobbly stuff as if it is medicine, which it sort of is, seeing as this is a hospital.

Brian and I are just finishing our jelly (green today, yuck) when Mum and Dad come out. Because there are only three seats in the corridor, I get up for Mum and try to perch on her lap. She is wearing one of her good nylon skirts, and it is hard for me not to slip right off. Dad remains standing, hands behind his back, as if he is about to deliver a speech. He starts to explain what the doctor told them.

Brian is frowning but I can tell from the red around his eyes that he is actually trying not to cry. Under his grumpiness and boy smells, he is a bit of a softie, really.

Barb doesn't care who hears her: she starts wailing loudly. She says to me, 'Kathy, you know what this means? It means that you won't have a playmate anymore.'

I reach over and smack Barb in the face.

No, I don't; that's just what I want to do more than anything else. I might only be four, but I know one thing as if God had parted the clouds and told me himself: you are much, much more than a playmate to me.

I swivel around and try to climb back up Mum. She does not respond. I could be any of her children, any child at all, and she the statue of any mother.

On the way home from the hospital we visit the police station. Val turns up two days later. She tells us she has been on a 'holiday' to Cairns. She gives me a pair of orange flip-flops, an orange singlet and a matching orange pair of shorts, then sits next to Bev in the corridor and waits.

So here we all are, Annie. You are the only one missing now. I wonder if you did this to bring Val back. To stop Bev from returning to her boyfriend. To stop everyone from fighting.

* * *

After your diagnosis, I have no further memories of swinging orange lights, or hands pressing against my four-year-old skin. I realise this is at best a statistically insignificant correlation, not remotely a causal relationship. I know that a child cannot give herself cancer to protect her sister. Of course she can't.

After walking for at least fifteen minutes past endless rows of boutiques, I find Kmart, where I can purchase an entire pink ensemble for less than $25: top, trousers, even underpants and bra. I am in the change room when my phone buzzes but it is not Val with more instructions, it is an unknown caller, which means it is Evan. Since I blocked his number he has been using a different SIM card to try and trick me into picking up. I consider chucking my phone and getting a cheap replacement, but that would probably raise too many carefully plucked eyebrows among Barb and the others whom I need to call to make all the arrangements for your funeral. So I hit the red button like I did the last ten times, and hope he takes the hint.

* * *

I met Evan in 2004, three years after Dad died and I moved to Sydney. I was working at the Department of Education, where it had swiftly become apparent to the head of HR that I had a special flair for workplace safety and risk auditing. A long apprenticeship in the Bradley family was probably the greatest qualification.

People don't take OH&S seriously, but it's second nature for me. I see danger everywhere. My colleagues at the department call me big sister and don't believe me when I tell them I am the youngest of my family. It's because I am constantly urging them to watch out. They don't know what damage a desk corner can do to a head slammed into it, or what knees look like after tripping over a cord while running away. I wheedle a laminator out of my director's executive assistant, a fuzzy-haired lady who is the true power in the division, and soon the department is plastered with my helpful signs, smiley faces grinning desperately from elevator walls and bathroom doors. I realise they are cheesy, but if something stops even one person from harm, I'll do it.

One morning a tall Chinese-looking man is already inside the lift when the doors glide open for me on the ground floor. I am surprised when he presses the same floor number as me and then walks two steps behind me to my office.

'I'm Evan,' he grins broadly, looking right in my eyes. This is off-putting. In my experience, Chinese men normally hold themselves ready for a blow to the back of the head, but Evan walks with an easy, open stride, taking up his rightful space in the world. Women and men alike look up from their desks as he passes.

I clear my throat. 'Kathy Bradley, OH&S Coordinator, Department of Education,' I reel off as if I am answering the telephone, immediately cursing myself for my nerves. He has put me off balance. I was expecting a hipster with a ginger beard as the new head of digital when I saw the name 'Evan Lee' in the department memo, not this. Evan is still grinning, looking straight at me. I have to stop myself from checking if I have food in my teeth.

'Take a seat,' I say. I hand him the induction kit I give all new staff: a print-out about the training modules he has to complete, a roll of duct tape and a card with CPR instructions. He laughs when I hand it to him. 'Nothing you can't fix with gaffer tape,' he quips. He is looking, possibly pointedly, at the beat-up sneakers under my desk.

'You're a lunchtime walker?' he asks.

'We encourage all staff to take their breaks and get fresh air and exercise. It's very important for mental health and wellbeing,' I say. 'I have a pamphlet—'

I start rummaging on a shelf when he interjects, 'Can I come?'

'Oh. There is a group that meets for yoga on Thursdays, and a lunchtime football game,' I say. 'It's all in this pamphlet—'

'I can't really do those sorts of activities. Old war wounds.'

'Were you in the army?' I stop rummaging. I thought people who looked like Evan were typically on the other end of Aussie soldiers' guns.

'Ha! No,' Evan shakes his head. 'Just a product of my misspent youth. Turns out white boys thought the asthmatic, skinny little Asian kid was an easy target. Go figure!'

'Oh.' I turn back to my shelf. Openly talking about race makes me uncomfortable. We don't have a policy about it at the department, but I do always make sure there are enough diverse faces on the annual report cover, including my own if we are running low.

'If we get on each others' nerves we can walk five paces apart.'

'No, no, that's not what I was thinking,' I splutter, except it was exactly what I was thinking. 'Of course, yes. One pm.'

* * *

I hope that Evan does not spend too long mourning me; I want him to move on, have the life he deserves, a normal, happy life. If I believed in God, I would pray that the mum from the park does not cling to the memory of what I did to her just the day before yesterday, although it feels like a century ago. I hope it does not come back to her every night, replaying the terror she must have felt when she could not locate her baby. *Where's the baby then, Kathy? Where?*

My next errand is to pick up a bottle of holy water and a statue of Saint Bernadette to adorn your coffin. I consult a touchscreen, but it appears that Catholic merch is probably the only thing you cannot buy at the Hyperdome. Luckily, I know where there is a church with a gift store.

* * *

The Bradleys have always been regular churchgoers, but after you get sick we ramp up our prayer schedule and the church gets behind us. Every Tuesday of 1984, Dad, our sisters, brother and I gather with our fellow parishioners at the chapel in Kingston and pray a rosary for your salvation while you lie in your hospital bed. Even Mum comes with us from time to time, fidgeting through the decades and smiling and thanking the priest afterwards.

Saint Maximilian Kolbe is the patron saint of our little church, a long, low weatherboard on stilts to keep out the floods and the snakes, surrounded by scrub and sandy ground, which makes it hard for the parish ladies to grow the roses they used to have in Ireland. They have begun to resort to native flowers, planting banksias that we call wah-wahs, because they look like a choir of open-mouthed baby birds, crying silently to be fed.

Saint Maximilian Kolbe is a relatively young saint, like our church. He died in a concentration camp because he offered his life in the place of a Jewish man who he knew had children. You can only be a saint if you *choose* to die. You are not a saint if you just die anyway.

I like all the Mysteries of the rosary, but the Joyful are my favourite. Most people like the third Joyful Mystery – the bit about Jesus being born – but my favourite is the bit that comes before that. As we recite the Hail Mary, I like to imagine

Elizabeth bumping into Mary and telling her the news that she too is pregnant, despite being beyond child-bearing age. Elizabeth is so thrilled! Her baby grows up to be John the Baptist and have his head cut off by King Herod, but in the Joyful Mysteries that is all unknown. Elizabeth and Mary are just two expectant mothers, hearts full of hope for the future.

Our prayers work! Well, sort of. You will never have the use of your left side again. You no longer have the ability to concentrate and your short-term memory is a blur of terrifying blanks. But Christmas 1984 comes and goes and you are alive, defying your one-year-to-live prognosis.

That should be miracle enough for me and I am happy, of course I am. But there is a part of me that can't help thinking: If God could keep you from dying, surely He could be talked into going one step further and help you to really live?

* * *

Our old church has been replaced with a modern, high-ceilinged structure designed to maximise air flow via sliding glass doors. The chapel where we used to kneel every Sunday when we were little kids now functions solely as a St Vincent de Paul gift store. Shelf after shelf groans under the weight of the paraphernalia of a Catholic life. An entire wall is devoted to Confirmation gifts – plaques, holy cards, books of saints. The holy water and a statuette of Saint Bernadette are easy to find – she remains a popular choice. Martyrs never go out of style.

I chose Lucia for my Confirmation name. Technically, she was not yet a saint because she was still alive when I picked her, but the priest deemed her to be holy enough for the purpose. Lucia's two cousins saw Our Lady in Fatima, Portugal. The cousins died young, like Bernadette. But not Lucia: she was destined to grow old and short-sighted and heavy, the toad-like survivor doomed to outlive the cherub-faced martyrs. She was not even given a glimpse of Our Lady, even though the cousins had long, involved, ecstatic conversations with her while Lucia stood by, open-mouthed. Just one time, Our Lady allowed Lucia to glimpse not her beatific face, but her holiest of *silhouettes*, to ensure that Lucia would keep the faith, or keep her mouth shut, which I suppose amounted to the same thing.

As an adult, I read about a nineteenth-century Yugambeh man named Bilin Bilin who had lived and worked the land where St Maximilian Kolbe parish church sits. I wish I had known about Bilin Bilin when I was a kid, and that I could have chosen him for my saint name instead. Apparently Bilin Bilin made a deal with the local missionaries: he would attend Sunday school and distribute bibles in exchange for his family's protection from removal and massacre. Bilin Bilin handed out hundreds of bibles in his lifetime, but, rather ingeniously, he died an unbaptised old man. Conversion was outside the terms of the agreement. That's just the kind of bargain I wish I had thought of myself.

In the gift store there are plenty of dioramas of the Fatima three, but I cannot find a picture of Lucia on her own; she is only ever presented as part of the triumvirate, playing the support role to the other two children's saintly demise.

Back in the car with my Catholic loot, I place the Bernadette statuette on the dashboard for inspiration. I open my laptop. I still have no idea what I am going to say. You were my sister. I loved you. You should never have been sick in the first place, but once you were, you should never have got worse.

I am to blame. I want more than anything else to say it out loud, surrender myself to the mercy of the masses, and be forgiven.

At the same time, I want to point my finger at the gathered. Where were they when you needed to be socialised and engaged? Where were they when you needed to be washed and changed? From my position at the pulpit, I imagine considering Mum's thinning grey hair, her small brown eyes sunk into wrinkles and liver spots. Where was she when you needed to be loved?

Mum always had a bad habit of walking away from us. As kids, whenever we went to the shops, she would march ahead with a speed I have never been able to match. As if Mum felt that in the brightly lit aisles of the supermarket she was free at last, a lioness roaming her savannah. Survival of the fittest, darlings. Catch me if you can.

I know that if Mum had been a different sort of mother, then probably you and I would never have been born – which, considering where we both are now, might have been an efficiency. But this line of reasoning reminds me of carnivores' explanation for eating meat: the cows would not have been bred at all if they weren't destined for the slaughterhouse. I exaggerate of course, but you see the similarities.

And yet. I have a memory from when I was eight. We are in the new single-floor house, 7 Elliot Road, Slacks Creek, which we moved into after you could no longer manage the stairs at 19 Railway Road. You and I share a room. In the middle of the night the door opens and a splinter of light falls across my body. Someone steps inside, and from the speed and bustle I know it's Mum. She pulls your blankets up, then mine.

It turns out our paces are well matched and Evan and I quickly settle into a lunchtime walking routine. He is fit from working on production sets, while my speed comes from all the extraneous nervous energy I carry around with me. The one thing that interferes with our rhythm is the way we each deal with oncoming pedestrians. I dodge and scurry, apologising for being in a walker's way. But Evan does not break stride, then has to wait for me to catch up at the next crossing.

One day Evan draws me to the side of the footpath. He leans toward me, as if about to tell me a secret. 'I don't say sorry. I say thank you.' He smiles into my eyes.

I covertly watch how he moves, how he talks, how he breathes so easily inside his own skin. Evan takes up his allotted space on the footpath, in this city, in this country: no more, but no less, and without apology. I have never done that. I have spent my life apologising for the discomfort I cause to others for being neither one thing nor the other; for being in their way; for being what I am.

But Evan? Evan is just himself. He is nothing like other Chinese Australian men I have met. They tend to look at me with a dog-like yearning: unable to imagine themselves with a white woman, they see me, with my hybrid skin, as within their grasp. The middle-aged white men who leer at me in pubs are not entirely dissimilar, except their looks are of acquisition rather than aspiration. With Evan, I do not feel like an object of migrant ambition, nor a yellow fever trophy. I feel like myself. I feel, for the first time, that might be enough.

One Thursday lunchtime Evan has a mild limp which worsens as we progress down Philip Street towards the harbour.

'What have you done to yourself?' I ask.

'Never let them get back up,' he groans. 'I learned that the hard way.'

I look at him blankly.

'The one time I got into a fight and let the other guy get back up, he came at me from behind. Gave me an ankle that can predict the weather better than the Bureau of Meteorology. Rain should be here in …' he pretends to consult the skies, but winces as he lands heavily on his right foot, 'two to three hours.'

'Let's sit down.' I guide him to a sushi shop and fetch him a cup of miso, seating myself opposite him at a small table.

'Oh, that's what I needed. You're an angel,' he says, swallowing the hot soup.

I glance at him and then quickly down at my menu. I am not used to looking at him front-on. When we walk together,

I don't have to be reminded of what a mismatched pair we are: even though he is more fully Chinese than me, he has an athletic fluency that makes women turn their heads in his direction, no doubt wondering what he is doing next to my squat and unwieldy figure. I know I will never be slim, or blue-eyed, or any of the things that men in this city find beautiful.

'So what happened?' I ask, studying the list of ten-dollar lunch specials.

'I won,' Evan says simply.

'Really? But you got injured.'

'Yeah, but I know kung fu. All Chinese men do.'

I make a face at him.

'All right. But I did learn kung fu eventually, when I was older. Guys kept picking fights with me and I finally realised I was going to have to learn how to defend myself. Luckily when I was a kid, my dad taught me some basics. That got me through quite a few nasty situations.'

'Not this one.' I indicate his outstretched leg.

'Trust me, this one would have been a lot worse if I didn't already know how to fall,' he demonstrates the motion, 'and how to trip.'

I am suddenly looking at a tiger, graceful and dangerous in the swiftness of its shift from cat to predator. I close the menu, sure that my face is red and blotchy from the unforgiving genetic inheritance of my own father.

We walk slowly back to the office, me holding out an arm instinctively in case he needs support, just as I did for you all those years, Annie. When we part ways at the lift, he leans down and kisses me on the cheek. It is just a friendly thing to do, but for some reason I can't stop feeling the burn where his lips touched my face.

* * *

Before I met Evan I would never have considered dating, let alone marrying, an Asian man. I know that sounds racist, Annie. It is. We were raised, we Bradley girls, to consider marrying anyone who was not Anglo as a failure. Which, considering the pickings when our sisters were young, may have been for the best.

Remember the Lin brothers, always slavering after Barb and Bev, coming up with excuses to spend time with them? Richard Lin used to watch the big kids, the only semi-Asian females within the Logan boundaries, like a hungry wolf, while Doctor Lin – our local GP who weaponised the word 'hypochondriac' against you – gazed imperiously down his nose at them, mentally calculating which had the greatest likelihood of supporting his success in life. One time he even asked Barb to marry him. Remember, he gave her that little Holden Gemini, the green car with the newspaper stuffed into the door panels to stop it from rusting. Barb kept the car but turned down the marriage proposal. Classic Barb.

Mum was always warning us against Chinese men, telling us that they drove flashy cars and took advantage of helpless girls. But that is not why I am leaving Evan. If anything, I am the one who took advantage of him, making him think he could have a normal, happy life with me when the whole time I knew, I *knew* that it was only a matter of time until I ruined everything.

After a weeknight special from the fish 'n' chips shop, I drive back to the Logan Hospital carpark. It is a good place to sleep; there are always vehicles coming and going and it is not unusual for people to leave their cars there overnight. But just to be on the safe side, I set my alarm so that I will wake to move the car every two hours.

I am between alarms but only half asleep when a man in uniform with a twelve-hour shift's worth of bristles appears at the nose of the Subaru's bonnet. What at first sight looks like a gun on his hip crackles and burrs. It's a walkie talkie.

I exhale slowly. Carpark security, not police.

The man looks like he wants to tap on the window so I ostentatiously get out of the car, stretch and yawn.

'Yes? What is it?'

'Oh, um. Didn't mean to disturb. Just doing the rounds. You know you're not meant to sleep out here though. Not safe, for starters.' He hitches up his belt.

'I'm just taking a nap out here,' I say, hoping that the tremor in my voice is mistaken for sadness. 'My husband's in the cardiology unit. They told me to go home but I want to be nearby. In case—'

'Oh, I see, well, all good,' the guard nods vigorously, not wanting to have a weeping soon-to-be widow on his hands. Probably not paid enough for that sort of drama.

'Hope he gets better soon.' He waddles away, trying to look purposeful. When the beam of his torch is just a dancing dot of white in the distance, I ease open the glove box. Of course it's still there. I pat the container of powder then slide it back inside. I send up a superstitious prayer that Evan is not suffering from any sort of heart troubles.

According to my car radio it is 1.37 am. Even in Queensland it gets a little cool at night in winter. I pull my jacket tighter over me like a blanket. The air smells like cooking oil and the ever-present moisture of the Logan River flood plain.

Suddenly I am four years old, and you are not sick yet, or at least we don't know that you are sick yet. I am sitting at the top of the staircase at 19 Railway Road, waiting for something, although I have forgotten what. Then the front door opens and Dad walks in, bringing with him the smell of Old Spice and hot chips. I grab hold of his leg and he swings me along as if I am a koala and he the branch of a gum tree, as if I weigh nothing at all. He puts the grease-paper bag on the kitchen table and I run down the hallway to wake you because you and I are still the same person. We sit around the kitchen table, Dad in his nurse's uniform, you and I in our hand-me-down nighties. We don't need to line up the chips in order of size and count them out because the big kids are all asleep. Mum

54

is there too, making Dad a cup of coffee and hovering in the kitchen, hair in rollers. The potato burns my tongue but I say nothing, because I do not want this night to end.

I would, on the other hand, quite like it if *this* night would end. I wonder how Dad did it, the time he went AWOL and drove the same route I just took from Sydney to Queensland, before either you or I were born. How he went back. Imagine if he had stayed away, eluded the military police, changed his name.

When I finally nod off again, all I see are dead people. You are with Dad, coming back to life on the funeral parlour tables. You two are not dead after all! Only crumbling a little, but we can take care of that.

I jerk awake. It is four am, the time of the morning a person can only sleep through if she is happy in her bones. It's as good a time as any to go for a drive. I ease the Subaru past the fancy brick houses built into Loganholme's forested hillsides, automated sprinklers daubing my car with their genteel dew. The overpass delivers me to the other side of the freeway, to the lowlands where we grew up. The houses on this side of the freeway are either kit homes, with castor oil shrubs and rye grass growing in patches in place of a lawn, or weatherboards surrounded by rusting car bodies and lantana-filled bathtubs.

Dad had been dishonourably discharged from the army, but his active service in Vietnam entitled him to a Defence Force discount on loan interest rates. The Bradleys bought a house in Logan, where once the Yuggera and Yugambeh peoples had cultivated some of the richest country in south-east Queensland. Over 150 years, the land and its people were scoured away by would-be farmers and missionaries, leaving cheap lots for sale. Although I know all of this, I cannot stop my body releasing a breath I did not realise I had been holding as I near 19 Railway Road. Home, or at least the closest approximation I have to it.

The houses begin to acquire a tended look. I look for the one-cent lolly-shop, where we once found a cockroach in a bag of jelly babies and got a whole extra bag for free. In its place rears a salmon-pink McMansion with a water feature on the front lawn. When we lived here, Logan was still a shire and the suburb of Loganlea was just a series of grassy lots punctuating the marshy delta of the Logan River, forty-five minutes south of Brisbane in the dry, more than an hour in the wet or even longer if the bridges were under water. Since then, the swamps have been drained; Logan City boasts a university campus and a hospital, where you died less than forty-eight hours ago.

I park in front of a two-storey house which has been rendered in an eggshell white. The lawn full of bindies that we used to wince across with rubbish for the incinerator, our eyes streaming from the smoke, has been replaced with an oval of grass and a tiled courtyard. The concrete verandah where Dad used to stand, hosing us down in the heat, is still there, albeit under a sheath of hardwood cladding. The new owners can tack on as many porticos and vestibules as they like. This house will always be a Bradley in its makeshift bones.

PART 2

ANCESTRY

You might decide to weave into your
narrative some tales of the deceased's
ancestors. This can give mourners a sense
of the continuum of time, love and life, of
which we are all a part.

How to Write a Eulogy

wake to the smell of my own B.O. Our family assumes I am staying in a hotel and I let them assume. I don't want to be a guest in any of their houses, having to explain Evan's whereabouts at this time of marital solidarity. But I also don't see the point in wasting money on accommodation to take care of a body that will be surplus to requirements in a matter of days.

It's barely been four hours since I parked in front of the old house and dozed off, the seat pushed back as far as it will go. Even at the best of times, we Bradleys are terrible sleepers. Our brother Brian still gets up at five every morning to run on the treadmill, and he takes valerian tablets to help him sleep. Val does what I do: lies awake and thinks herself into unconsciousness. Trish works fifteen hours a day then swims two kilometres before falling catatonic into her own version of one-eye-open. Annie, you were the only one of us who could sleep anywhere, any time. I guess all those nights spent in hospital beds made you able to sleep through anything.

I don't have to be at the meeting with Brian and the priest until nine am.

I breathe on the window and squeak off the condensation. A fine dew glitters on the lawns of Railway Road. If I were any other person, I might look at number 19 and think, *what a perfect place to raise a family.*

You know, I have never forgiven our mother for you. For any of us, really – because who has eight children in the twentieth century? – but especially for you. I have not forgiven our mother for keeping you alive after the diagnosis and then proceeding to spend the next twenty-five years sabotaging every chance you had at happiness. I have not forgiven her for ruining my attempts to get you out of her house before you ended up on the floor, being kicked for your failure to get back up. I have not forgiven her for changing your medication dosages from one day to the next, claiming that the neurologist had told her that she could. Whenever I challenged Mum she would reply, 'I am the mother'. Not *her* mother or *your* mother: *the* mother. El Presidente comes to mind.

I acknowledge that I am being hard on Mum. She loved you with the best part of herself. Is it her fault that the best part of herself was not enough? But Annie, come *on.* There are so many things I tried to do for you, and every single one of them our mother ruined. Why? I don't really know. Some were inconvenient for her, I guess; some would have meant depriving her of your pension; some were just about power.

Our mother expressed her love for you in these ways: making sure you were warm, dry, fed, clothed, clean; making sure you had what our mother considered entertainment: TV, radio, a puzzle book always in front of you, even though by the end you were no longer capable of doing puzzles. She sometimes abused you. She sometimes thwarted efforts to make you happy. But here is the clincher: Mum was what you always wanted.

Did you give up the fight in 1983, deciding then and there that remaining with Mum was going to be easier than trying to leave her, internalising the lessons of our sisters' desperate attempts at flight? Or did you do the opposite: did you make the noblest sacrifice of all, enabling us to leave because you stayed behind? Here I go again with my magical thinking, pretending to myself that you had a say in your own cancer. Bad luck can look like poetry from a distance of twenty-five years.

I know that our mother didn't invent violence in 1983. It predates us, this rage; its source is long buried in the unwritten annals of history. At some point in the past I can only hope it was justified: a murder committed, a sucker punch thrown, a fire left to burn the house down.

Let's go back, back; try to figure this whole thing out. The seeds of your death were planted long ago among the abundant mosquitoes of a tropical island and the rancid smells of belacan cooking. I try to picture the Singapore of 1942, right before the island is invaded by the Japanese. The eggs that will one day become her many – too many – children are already safe and snug inside our mother's belly. She is five years old.

* * *

Jia En wishes every day that she was a village kid. Then she wouldn't have to go to the school that her father Li Jie makes her attend. Why does she have to sit in a hot little room next to smelly Jun Kai and Hui Min the nose-picker, when she could be outside catching fighting spiders and winning money?

Everyone calls Jia En 'Sister Baby', even though she is not the baby of the family. But she is the only girl. That is enough of a reason. Jia En's mother is known of in the village as the kind lady who will buy all the remaining buns from the peddling baker at the end of his rounds. Yi Ling is slender with high cheekbones and thin eyebrows she does not even need to pluck. Her mah-jong ga-gee look from Jia En to Yi Ling, shaking their heads and commiserating with Yi Ling on her bad luck.

Even though Li Jie never talks about Shanghai, somehow everyone in the village knows his story. His father and brothers made it through the Purge, only to be executed less than a week later for failure to pay sufficient protection money to the local warlord's son. Li Jie escaped because he had overslept that morning, startling awake to the sound of gunshots. He escaped to Singapore, met Yi Ling, and married as quickly as her parents would allow, wanting to start a new life far from the stench of blood he swore he could still smell during the north-east monsoon. On such days, Li Jie takes to his room like a woman, according to the family's cook.

Hui Jie, Jia En's older brother, has inherited their parents' physique, but Jia En and her little brother Sze Jie must have inherited their stocky frames from a long-dead ancestor. Perhaps, Sze Jie sometimes tells Jia En hopefully, she and Sze Jie resemble the legendary Kublai Khan, founder of the Great Yuan Dynasty that ruled Han China in the thirteenth and fourteenth centuries with the perfect blend of ruthlessness and intolerance. I do not take us that far back except to say, pointedly, *See?*

Some days Jia En's father takes the boys on site visits while Jia En's mother takes advantage of his absence to invite over her mah-jong ga-gee. Jia En spends such days fetching dried, salted plums and tiny glasses of sherry. On one such occasion the sun is already setting when the ladies finally begin to murmur of leave-taking – bags are located, thank yous echo in the reception room. Her mother's friends are going home with purses heavier than when they came. Jia En slides quickly from her place at the window and heads outside. She does not want to be within reach when her mother starts looking for someone to blame for her bad luck.

She could go to the village but the prospect of the muddy walk does not appeal today. She kicks at the earth and jumps back, startled. The dirt is not dirt but the hard shell of a dark, craggy old turtle which begins to amble up the hill behind the bungalow. *Turtle must be going to give thanks to the ancestors,* Jia En thinks, giggling. She follows.

The turtle hobbles slowly: one foot then the other, then the other, then the other. Jia En, normally so twitchy, has to slow herself right down to be able to do the same. She gets down on all fours, trying to replicate the turtle's footsteps. Time passes. When they reach the temple, Jia En is quiet. She bows her head – first to the turtle, and then to the ancestors.

The family has Malay servants to do all the chores, to burn the rubbish and sweep the floors, but Jia En's mother sends her on regular errands to the village after school, which Jia En is happy to do if it means getting away from Sze Jie's whines or Hui Jie's pompous attempts at sternness.

Jia En dashes to the Indian men's stall at the other end of the village to give them her mother's numbers in exchange for ticket stubs. The men always smile at her in a lazy sort of way, and the smoke that comes out of their back room makes Jia En feel swoony, not just from the heat. She likes to weave her way back into the village afterwards, pretending to the other kids that she has had a pipe.

If there is time after her errands, Jia En visits the old lady at the end of the row. Jia En can earn a few cents to thumb her aching back.

'Ahh, not so hard, eh!' The old lady smacks Jia En's hand away, then nods for her to continue. 'You go to school?'

'Yes.' Jia En glances guiltily over her shoulder, but there are just the Malays from the new high-rises and their scrawny dogs playing with a chewed-up ball.

'Good, you're a good girl. You can be like my daughter.'
The old lady spits out a chunk of dark red betel onto the floor
and reaches for something on the table. It is a picture of a
woman, stout and wearing black-rimmed glasses, her hair up
in a bun.

'She lives in Kuala Lumpur.'

Jia En's mother has told her stories of Kuala Lumpur and
Penang, the cities across the Straits. Men in white T-shirts
and fast cars, scars on their cheeks and knives in their back
pockets, roam the streets over there. They catch stupid, bad
girls who have run away from their parents, and sell them at
the harbour.

'My daughter is a doctor,' the old woman announces
proudly. Jia En nods, thinking the daughter must have been
too ugly to be sold. After a few minutes the old woman starts
to snore. Jia En quietly rummages in the old lady's purse,
extracts three coins, then runs to the other end of the dirt
road to visit Alice.

Alice is Jia En's best friend. She is one of the village girls
who doesn't have to go to school; her job is to keep house
and wait to be married. After school (or during), the two
friends do each other's hair and laugh at the boys, the men,
the women – pretty much anyone whose business takes them
past Alice's front door.

On that day in 1942, Jia En did not even need to pretend
to go to school. She, Alice and the other kids hover in front

of Alice's house while the village mothers huddle together nearby, talking in low voices. Even Jia En's mother has come down the hill to stand with the other women. Alice's and Jia En's ears prick at the same time that the dogs start to bark and they run together down the main road. It's Alice's dad with a handful of men straggling after him, just a fraction of those who had left. When it becomes clear that Li Jie is not with them, Yi Ling turns without a word to the women and walks back up the hill.

The girls fuss over Alice's dad, urging the cook to make his favourite things. Alice's dad has a black smudge that reads 'examined' on his arm which he refuses to wash off, even after his wife brings him a cloth and a basin. He pushes aside the wonton soup and motions for Jia En to follow him. Wordless, he starts up the hill. Jia En and Alice follow.

Li Jie seems to have a knack for escaping purges, but this time there is a catch: Alice's dad reports to Yi Ling (the girls crouching outside, eavesdropping) that, upon finding out he worked as a construction engineer for the British, the Japanese overlooked Li Jie's Shanghai accent and put him to work building bomb shelters for the empire's officers. He is alive but must remain at Changi, until when or what, Alice's dad won't or can't say.

The family has to give up its bungalow to the Japanese and move into the kampong, into a village house with three other families. Alice's dad and the other men who have returned are grey-faced and close-lipped about what they saw, but the whole village is awash with rumours of the killings at Punggol Point. Jia En can almost picture the bodies washed up along the beaches of Sentosa as if she had been there, the scent caught in her nose like that of Alice's dad's butcher shop where he can no longer work, not that it matters: there is no meat to buy or sell.

Every week Jia En and her brothers save scraps of dog, sometimes fighting the other kids for it, and wrap them in a gunny which their mother carries down the road in her elegant manner, as if she is merely taking a tray of tow kway to her mah-jong ga-gee. Hours, sometimes a whole day passes, before Yi Ling returns without the parcel. The children know not to ask if she saw him.

When he finally does return three years later, in 1945, after the liberation of Singapore, Li Jie still has the tall frame of the young man who escaped the bloodshed of Shanghai almost twenty years before. But that is all that is left: there is no perceptible scrap of dog meat turned flesh on his skeletal self.

Jia En can still remember what it was like to be rich, or richer than they are now. At least the family still has a Malay woman to come and help with the cooking a few times a week. The family is permitted to return to its bungalow but Jia En does not return to school. She is required to help around the house, look after her stupid little brother or run errands for her bossy big brother. Li Jie works only sporadically now, so the family's hopes are pinned to Hui Jie and just as well he is tall enough for the job, taking after their father in the looks department. But even Hui Jie must be quiet in the house now that Li Jie is back, sitting in his room, alone but for the ghosts they hear him muttering to.

On a rare sunny afternoon during the wet season a few months after the liberation of Singapore, Jia En is crossing the canal that separates the village from the Chinese homes when she glimpses a flash of silver. A flying fish! She has seen the Malay boys catch them with their bare hands. It's all about the timing. She leans over the railing when there it is, sudden and magnificent, twisting its sleek body in the sky. Jia En lunges and falls straight into the water. She hears a whooshing sound in her ears and for the first time in her life she feels thoroughly cold.

Someone grabs her by the back of her dress and hauls her back onto the bridge. The Malay cook tsks and pats Jia En's back. When they reach Jia En's house, the woman gestures for her to stay out of sight while she fetches clean clothes. When she returns, Jia En looks the woman properly in the face.

'If you go near the canal, you learn to *swim*.' The woman smiles at Jia En, then goes back to her chores. Jia En pulls on the dry shift then slips inside. Yi Ling is napping and Li Jie is out on a rare work excursion. No one noticed she was gone.

* * *

I leave Railway Road before any concerned householder can start to wonder why a strange woman has been parked outside their home since the wee hours, and head for the local swimming pool where for $3.50 I have a warm shower and brush my teeth as if I had just emerged from a pre-work morning swim. I haven't actually got my togs with me and I would never voluntarily dive in even if I did. I was always terrified of the water when we were growing up; maybe I inherited Mum's dislike of swimming in my epigenetic code after her brush with the fish.

What did Mum inherit from her own mother? Perhaps all those tricks she used on the big kids: chilli applied to the eyes or to other, less public body parts; forcing them to kneel half-clothed on the front verandah for maximum public humiliation. According to our sisters, Mum had mellowed by the time we came along. For us it was just those bamboo sticks, the kneeling and the crew cuts, scissors snagging our ears while words sliced through something more tender than cartilage.

* * *

It takes almost five years for Jia En's hair to finally grow out from the shaved head her mother used to administer indiscriminately to her and her brothers throughout the war. Now that she is fourteen her curfew is eight pm, but it is so pleasantly cool, sitting in the generous darkness. Jia En and Alice squat in their customary spot on the doorstep of Alice's place. The coolness of the dirt road creates a dream-like mist around their feet. They relax in companionable silence, knees apart, waving at the flies.

Jia En makes a run for it, but Yi Ling is too fast. She grabs a hank of Jia En's bobbed hair.

'You are a bad girl,' Jia En's mother murmurs in a low, mean voice. 'You meeting boys out here?'

'No,' Jia En says in a pleading voice.

'You lie to me! Dirty girl, itchy, itchy!' Jia En tries to wrench herself out of her mother's grasp, but her mother has her pinned against the wall. She had brought her bamboo stick and begins to beat Jia En with the sharpened edge. Alice does nothing. You never come between a mother and her daughter.

At home Yi Ling sends Jia En to fetch her father for dinner. Jia En stands at the door to her father's room, fingering the welts on her arms. She calls softly, trying to keep the tears from her voice. You get more slaps if you cry.

'Pah,' she calls. He is slumped over his desk, perhaps fallen asleep over a calculation. But there is something off about the angle of his neck. Jia En calls more loudly. 'Pah!'

She races past her mother, past her brothers who are already seated at the table, waiting to be served. Jia En does not stop running until she reaches the doctor's house. He is so used to being disturbed that his leather bag is right next to his chair. He follows Jia En back up the hill, not asking her about how she got the scratches across her legs.

According to the doctor, Li Jie must have died several hours previously, probably mid-afternoon. While Jia En was enjoying herself, imagining that Alice's laughing father was her father, that her indulgent mother was Jia En's mother, her real father was taking his last breath. Jia En hoped his ghosts stayed with him to the end. She hoped he did not feel as alone as he actually was.

After the funeral Jia En gets a job in an English bookstore at the newly posh end of Orchard Road. Jia En is not much of a reader, but the owners of the store had known her father and want to help Yi Ling and her three children. Every week, Jia En gives her pay packet to her mother, who uses it for Jia En's brothers' university fees. Every week, before handing the little yellow envelope over, Jia En slips a few coins out and puts them in her pocket.

Jia En loves the cinema more than anything else. Every day en route to work she passes the larger-than-life posters, inserting herself into the romantic scenes, and once a week she goes alone to the Odeon, using her coins to buy a cheap seat for the double feature. She tells her mother she is visiting Alice. Truth is, she has not seen Alice since the day Jia En's father died. They still nod when they see each other in the street, but Jia En is busy with work, and Alice is engaged to a Christian, so she is Alice-all-the-time now and has no time to see movies with her childhood friend.

Jia En emerges into the heavy, humid Singapore night air, her bones still vibrating with the swelling violins of the credits. She has a funny feeling in her stomach, picturing Vittorio Gassman leaning in to kiss her face instead of Elizabeth Taylor's. It is a pleasant kind of nausea, as if she might throw up butterflies.

'Hello, hi hi.'

Jia En snaps back to reality. A large-eyed woman smiles at her. The woman is smoking a cigarette, leaning against a poster of the movie Jia En has just been to see. Jia En has seen her before around the cinema and thought her impossibly chic. Up close Jia En sees that she is probably not much older than herself: maybe eighteen, nineteen at most? It is the languorous cast of the girl's body, the world-weary draw on the cigarette, which Jia En had mistaken, at a distance, for maturity.

Jia En replies, 'Hello, hello,' and giggles involuntarily, a habit of hers whenever anyone says anything to her. Her post-movie mood floats about her, a cloud of anticipation ready to be netted.

'You want to come in, little sister? No one here yet, too early la. So hot la. Come in, come in,' the lady says to Jia En in English, as if she is inviting Jia En into her own home. The lady gestures to a door Jia En has not noticed before, squeezed between two shops. She sees an unlit sign above the lintel which reads 'Starlight Club'.

Jia En hesitates. Her mother has warned her away from such places, telling her they are for bad girls from no-good families.

The girl straightens up and holds out her hand. 'I'm Molly. What's your name ah?'

'Kuan Jia En,' Jia En responds automatically, the full name, last name first, how it goes.

'Ah, no, no, your other name ah,' Molly clucks. 'Kuan Jia En,' she parrots in the accent of a Straits Chinese, making Jia En giggle again. 'The boys won't know how to say that la.'

'Ah, Madge,' she says. The strange monosyllable dangles in the air between them like a talisman. Madge and her brothers all have Christian names for talking to the English, but it is rare for her to hear it outside of work.

'Ah, Madge good name, beautiful name. Come on, Madge, we go inside. You stay for one drink, free, you no pay me ah!' Molly drops her voice conspiratorially so Madge has to step closer to hear what she is saying. 'Men coming later – you know, air force men. They rich, they handsome! You good girl, they know that ah, you no worry, just friend!' Molly adds as if she can read Madge's mind.

She bats Madge on the shoulder. Madge catches a whiff of Molly's perfume, something expensive.

'My girlfriend, she even got beautiful gold necklace! Just friend! Twenty-four-carat,' Molly clarifies, before Madge can even think to ask.

Madge looks down the road towards home, thinks of what awaits: Yi Ling with her hand held out for Madge's envelope; Hui Jie and his permanently disapproving frown; Sze Jie and the superior girl he now courts, looking down her skinny nose at Madge.

'You like dancing?'

Madge follows the click of Molly's high heels against the marble of the stairs that lead down below street level into the concrete-induced coolness of the club.

'I don't know how,' Madge replies. 'But I only stay for one drink la.'

'Aiyayah!' Molly shakes her head. 'Don't worry, I teach you some steps, just one or two la.'

* * *

Was it like this, I wonder? Did my grandmother chase our mother into the arms of the servicemen gathered at the Starlight Club for a drink and some easy companionship? Or did the ancestors, angry at the turtle's ascent, push our mother into the way of her future? I see the hungry ghosts opening their toothless maws wide as she follows Molly down, down into the darkness. Oh, Mum. You should have been paying closer attention.

* * *

Try as she might, Madge cannot attract the attention of the Englishmen. They prefer the skinny girls and, like me, Madge has never been thin.

The Aussies at the club are more familiar. They bump into her, saying sorry, sorry love; then they pull her onto their laps as if they had known her for years. These Aussies make her feel small enough to be cherished, an unfamiliar sensation which she enjoys. How many women's histories can be thus summed up: he made me feel like I wasn't as fat as I thought I was?

The married ones are the first to come up to the girls; they laugh and buy drinks with the greatest display of easy largesse. For Madge they buy gin, the only drink she knows the name of, apart from sherry, which makes her gag; gin makes her cry, but that is not a problem: these men all have pressed handkerchiefs in their pockets. Like the Aussies, she laughs easily despite her tears and, although she is not the prettiest, not by a long shot, she always has a circle of men at the table reserved for her after work, every Friday night.

There is one man in particular who makes sure he is the one standing next to her among the group of smiling, sweaty red faces. Colin. A cook in the army, he tells her. As men drift away over the course of the evening with girls on their arms, the cook remains by Madge's side, rescuing her bolero jacket if it slips from her shoulders, brushing bhaji mix crumbs from her skirt.

'Can I get you another?' he asks, gesturing towards her empty glass. She smiles with her watery eyes and accepts his offer.

On the same day that Britain grants Singapore self-rule, to begin at a date yet to be determined (much like when I turned eighteen), Madge stands at the markets, fingering the fabric of the dress she is trying on. It is cut from a heavy brocade which sits nicely on her hips.

Molly clucks. 'Ooh ah, that one suit you,' she coos. 'You putting on weight though la.'

Molly pinches Madge's waist. Madge smiles but draws her tummy out of her best friend's reach.

Molly is swathed in red, her skinny body transformed into curves via strategic pin tucks. 'I look just like Elizabeth Taylor, uh?' Molly juts out her newly discovered hip.

Madge holds her tongue. Molly is paying for her frock, an early twenty-first birthday present.

After a brief haggle, Molly arranges to pick up the dresses later that day. 'Western style la, no cloth buttons,' she warns the seamstress, who ducks her head and goes straight back to her machine.

The two young women return to the street. Madge buys them each a tall cup of ais kacang. They sip, watching the hawkers, the boys on their bikes, the girls and their ceaselessly waving newspapers – swatting away the heat, the flies, unwanted attention.

The club is full of Colin's mates and Madge's friends from the club. Musicians play Elvis Presley's 'Love Me Tender'. Madge runs up to Colin and giggles. Apart from the dress, Colin is paying for everything at the party: the drinks, the food, the decorations. He is magnanimous in his wealth – the wealth of the Australian Army salary in South-East Asia.

'Are you having a good time?' Colin asks. He likes to look down on her little round head with its curled hair, the sweet upturned face that nods and smiles at everything he says.

She nods now. 'Yes yes, it's good.'

He grabs her around the waist. She squeals and swats his hand away, at the same time letting him pull her closer with the hairy breadth of his arm. He holds his glass aloft and pushes Madge around in what he would call a dance, moving his hips to the whoops of his mates. He sloshes foam onto Madge's dress, but she just smiles. Colin bends down for a kiss. His sweet, beery breath warms her cheek. 'You look beautiful tonight, love,' he whispers in her ear.

Later, in his rooms, they lie together and he tells her more about his family. 'See, here she is. Kerry. My little girl,' he murmurs, one arm around Madge's neck, the other thumbing through photos in his wallet.

'Very pretty,' Madge says, agreeably.

'My wife, here. Leanne. She's OK. Not as pretty as you.' He tickles Madge, who snuggles closer. He has never lied to her about being married. He prides himself on this fact. He is not like the other men, making promises they know that they cannot keep.

Madge curls in his arms, content. She feels warm, taken care of. Her eyes slide over the purple cheongsam that Colin had given her as a birthday present. It is clearly too small, and it is not really the style these days, but that doesn't matter – in fact, it was a compliment that he thought it would fit her. He must really think she is beautiful.

* * *

By the time I enrol at university I still have not had a first kiss.

Partly this is because the only boys who liked me at high school were some brand of Asian. I found it offensive that everyone assumed I was, too. One time I came top of the class in a Japanese test and my Anglo-Aussie teacher grinned and said, 'Good job, although I suppose you have a bit of an unfair advantage.'

I blurted before I could stop myself, 'I'm not Japanese. I'm *smart.*'

You can imagine how *that* went down with the other kids, one of whom parroted my response all the way from the Languages block to Science, her friends falling over themselves laughing.

My hair, I was convinced, was actually dark brown, not full black, and when I opened my eyes wide they were almost hazel. My skin burned easily in summer like Dad's, and I had blond hair until I was five. When I was little I had believed the story Dad told me, that Mum had taken black shoe polish to my golden locks one Sunday, in a fit of pique because I did not look sufficiently like her.

The first time I heard the word 'Eurasian' was in a conversation between Val and Barb. It must have been a few years after you had got sick, because Val was back and preparing for a competition called 'Nurse of the Year', a beauty pageant for nurses.

Val had been restricting calories for weeks already – she and Barb were always on some diet or other, although Barb was the only one who resorted to laxatives and the occasional vomit. It stank up the toilet so I always tried to get in there before she did.

'You should go with Revlon. They have some more Asian skin tones, like yours,' Barb recommended, holding up a tester from a magazine against Val's cheek.

Barb had inherited Dad's tendency to burn lobster red as soon as someone even suggested it was going to be a warm one. This didn't stop her from lying in the backyard next to Val, both in their bikinis, the bindies pricking them through the thin synthetic of their towels, turning over at the sound of the half-hour bell that the radio station played just for this purpose throughout the summer months. Even Val's skin, as brown as a burnt chop, would start to flake if the day had been especially hot. You and I used to gross each other out picking the dead cells from her back and seeing who could peel the longest strip of skin before it broke and we had to start again.

Val paused to review the swatch Barb held up. 'That's too Asian for me,' Val said, turning back to her magazine research.

'Your skin is brown like that,' Barb retorted.

'No it's not. I'm *Eur*asian. So are you. As in "Europe" plus "Asia" equals "Eurasian".'

Eurasian. I had a sudden sensation of homecoming to a word rather than a place.

'I'm going to dye my hair with some auburn highlights,' Val added.

'Good idea,' Barb replied.

It was not only their Asian-ness that put me off my would-be high-school suitors. Mostly I spent my teenage years terrified of our mother's ire if I were to ever show any interest in a member of the other sex. Memories of Mum pulling at our sisters' hair and shoving them into the walls were never too far from my mind. Rationally I knew it was not true that wanting to go out with boys is the filthy desire of an even filthier mind. But the thought of a man's mouth on mine made me feel both exhilarated and absolutely petrified.

I commence my Bachelor of Arts with zero romantic training. And then I meet Peter, a tall man so pale he could almost be anaemic. Peter is descended from mild-mannered English people who live not far from the university, in the comfortably upper-middle-class suburb of Barton. We attend the same psychology tutorial, and, after a failed attempt at romancing another member of my study group, he asks me if I want to go for a drink. We have our first kiss at Mount Coot-tha Lookout, the lights of Brisbane twinkling below us. Peter puts his hand inside my bra, and I feel a rush of electricity from my nipples to my groin. This must be what falling in love feels like.

Later that evening I drive home to 7 Elliot Road, Slacks Creek. The suburb is a step up from the bogan heartland of Loganlea, or perhaps only half a step, being right next to the A1. But at night-time the traffic can be mistaken for the ocean, singing to us of lives touched by a more genteel class of worries than ours.

I creep into the bedroom that you and I share. You sit up suddenly in your bed, a shock of black hair above a ghostly white nightie. I blink; there is nothing there. You are fast asleep. For weeks I dream of an eyeless apparition, pointing an accusing finger at me.

The first time I stay over at Peter's, I get up in the middle of the night and sit on a stool in the deserted living room of his share house.

I have just attempted to lose my virginity to Peter, but he would not take it. It is not a question of hydraulics – Peter got an erection at the sight of me walking through the door, which was a gratifying experience, but not one to give me much actual pleasure. As he pulled my top off over my head, he had murmured in my ear, 'I want to wait for marriage for, you know, *that.*'

I had nodded, just wanting his hands on me. His religious beliefs did not prevent him from asking me to 'kiss him down there', or grinding against my crotch until he had come all over my underwear.

But this is not what has propelled me out of bed and on to the stool in the middle of the night. It is freezing in that way that only Brisbane houses are freezing, built as they are for eternal summer in adamant denial of the annual reversal. I sit shivering, not really knowing why I'm out here or what I want. Sympathy, perhaps, for something I do not have words for. I am not sure I even have words for it now.

Peter emerges from his room.

'What's wrong?' he asks on his way back from the bathroom. On his way *back* from the bathroom – that should have told me right then and there that ours was not an equal affection.

'I can't stop thinking about Annie,' I murmur. That is not true. I am not thinking about you so much as feeling your absence from my body, but not just from my body – from *this*, this experience, this night, this man, however unsatisfying our sexual encounter, however tepid his feelings for me. Flesh of my flesh, blood of my blood.

Peter pats me on the shoulder, possibly unaware that his penis is at my eye level as he does so. After a moment he heads back to his room.

Around three am I again slip out of Peter's uncomfortably small single bed and head home to Elliot Road. I just want to be in my own bed and mull the whole Peter thing over, but you are standing in the doorway, silhouetted by the living room light. I wave hello. You do not wave back. Instead you run, bad leg dragging behind you, away from me, into the house.

'Annie, what are you doing?' I try to open the door but you have locked it.

'Have to lock all the doors, all the doors,' you shout from the laundry.

'They *are* locked.' I take my keys from my pocket and let myself in. Now you are back at the front door, rattling its handle.

'Annie, come on, sit down. Sit down!' I take your good arm, but for the first time since we were kids you are too strong for me. You wrench yourself out of my grip and shake your head, once, twice, thrice, four times, five times until I worry that you are going to dislodge one of your shunts.

'Kathy is an impostor! They've got Kathy too!' you yell.

'I'm not an impostor!' I protest. 'Annie, it's me, Kathy, your sister! Your little sister!'

This makes you stop and look me in the eye. 'That's what they all say,' you tell me, eyes darting away from my face and then back again. 'They want you to believe they're real.'

Mum is too distracted to comment on the lateness of my return. She and Dad are doing something in the kitchen. Mum shouts, 'Annie, Annie! Come here! Annie!'

You push Mum's chair over, stumbling in your haste to check the locks on the windows. Mum's reading glasses, TAB tickets, biros scatter every which way. Dad grabs you by the hand. 'Come on, Annie,' he murmurs in the voice he must use with the patients at the psych hospital. It works; you allow him to lead you to the kitchen table, where Mum has placed a glass of water.

'You have to take your medicine,' Dad says.

You shake your head vigorously. 'You're an impostor too. Dad's an impostor too!'

You attempt to stand but Dad has planted a hand on your shoulder, keeping you in check. He reaches over and for a wild second I think he is going to play 'Who's got your nose?' He pinches your nose and one, two, your mouth drops open. He puts the pill on your tongue and pushes your chin up. You splutter and cough, but there is no more sign of the little white tablet.

You scream and scream and scream.

'A mild sedative and anti-psychotic,' Dad mutters before I even ask. He checks his watch. 'Should take effect in about ten minutes. Keep her away from the stove.'

'Annie, come get in your pyjamas. Annie,' Mum takes your elbow, modulating her voice for the first time in living memory to try to sound enticing rather than commanding. *Poor Mum*, I think, irrelevantly. This whole scene is unnerving on so many levels. Mum *cajoling*. You *ignoring* her. Dad taking *control*.

As Dad predicted, you fall into a deep sleep. Dad sits down heavily in his armchair, a stained old recliner in front of the TV that smells of sweat and mould. 'We kept her out of the psych ward, anyway,' he says, staring at the blank TV screen. Mum silently hands him a mug of Nescafé.

A few hours later we pile into the car, a zippy navy blue Daewoo that has replaced the roomy but fuel guzzler of a Kingswood of our childhood. Although he will always be a

Ford man in his heart, Dad is proud of the little Korean car, the first automobile he has ever been able to afford brand new, not even a demo.

Now Dad drives, his eyes bloodshot from lack of sleep. I try to doze but you keep me up the whole way to Brisbane, laughing to yourself, making complicated gestures with your hands. The air of pre-seven am Brisbane wafts through the open windows, just a hint of the heat of the day to come carried on the scent of frangipanis.

Doctor Blackman has his offices on Wickham Terrace. The Daewoo climbs the long, leafy road that curves behind Roma Street station. Mum has always pronounced 'Wickham Terrace' in a tone that makes me understand, *money*. We drive past the Holy Spirit hospital, a private institution which we have never stepped inside, and again I think, *money*. Not ours.

The office block where Doctor Blackman has his rooms is disappointingly unimpressive. It has a kiosk at the front, which resembles the cafe at the Kingston shopping centre where Mum used to send us to buy potato scallops while she placed her evening trot bets. A woman is just pulling up the shutters and opening for the day, releasing smells of cordial and children into the foyer. I don't know why, because we are the only people here, and you and I are not kids like we were the first time we came here, back in 1984.

The lift is also not as big or modern as it should be. The buttons are round and black and you press them without knowing if it will take you where you need to go, because nothing lights up. You just have to trust the machinery to work.

Then we get to Dr Blackman's floor and enter his offices and I relax, as I always do, because here things start to look appropriately expensive, as befitted the second-best neurosurgeon in Queensland. The waiting room has two sections, one in front of the reception desk and one around the corner, to the right of the desk. There is a big window overlooking the city, and grey cushioned seats lining the walls.

Dad has secured an emergency appointment before usual business hours. Doctor Blackman welcomes us in, smelling like he has just stepped out of a shower of buttercups, which he may well have. Blackman married his secretary between two of your shunt operations and our sister Trish joked that it was because secretaries are the only women who could stand doctors like him, renowned for their poor bedside manner but brilliance with a scalpel. Mum has always been proud that despite his reputation for gruffness, Doctor Blackman is consistently kind to you, as if his warmth is something you had earned by having the biggest, nastiest tumour in contrast with your sweet child's face.

You may not have grown much taller since the steroid treatments, but you are now twenty-one. No more Cancer Council freebies for an adult who is overweight from the meds and mutters to herself about the end of the world. It's dizzying, the speed with which you have transformed from sick child to be pitied, into disabled adult to be avoided.

There are not enough chairs inside the office so I remain standing at the back, leaning against the wall. At my eye level are Doctor Blackman's certificates, arrayed behind him like medals for modern-day heroism.

It takes me a minute to understand what he is saying. 'I didn't know this was a possibility,' I blurt.

'Kathy, shh, it all right,' Mum titters. She always treats doctors as if they are a notch above the rest of us. No wonder Trish became one – not that it has worked in her case.

'Early onset dementia was always one of the potential outcomes of the first biopsy.' Doctor Blackman glances at his watch and then at me. When I was small I loved this man. He has a full head of thick silver hair and wears the metal-framed glasses that I always thought looked like the kind God would wear if God were short-sighted. Now I stare at him with all the contempt I can muster.

There is nothing left for Doctor Blackman to cut out and throw away, apart from, of course, our trust, and this he does with a flick of his practised wrist. He holds open the door and tells his secretary/wife, who has materialised behind her desk sometime while we were in the office, that no further appointment is necessary. We stand waiting for the lift: me, you, Mum, Dad. No one says anything, not even you to the voices in your head, telling you that we are playing you for a fool.

In the week after seeing Doctor Blackman, I make phone calls. I ring the Cancer Council; I dial neurologists who have listings in the phone book. I page Trish and she in turn contacts neurologists she knows personally, which is a rather more effective method. I buzz Val, who has contacts in aged care, and she promises to bring home pamphlets about early onset dementia. I am doing the research. You know I always do my research.

It's not that I expected a cure. Well, all right, maybe I did. But I thought that we had climbed the mountain and reached the plateau, a terrain we could finally navigate without crampons. I have plans for you. I have already got you involved in voluntary work and I want to apply for independent living for you. I might not believe in angels but I still believe in something like divine fairness. I used to wish that God would heal. Now I wish for a more humble miracle – that you won't get any worse.

I can't help thinking that this is my fault. If I hadn't betrayed you by going out with Peter, you would not have got dementia. I am in my first year of psychology, so I can see that this is an attempt to exert control over an uncertain situation, but knowing what I am doing doesn't stop me from doing it.

I leave a number of messages for Peter, and finally get hold of him a week after your new diagnosis. 'I'm sorry I haven't been in touch,' I say. 'I've got a lot of family stuff going on.'

'No worries,' he replies. 'Hey, have you got Sonja's number?'

Maybe I was lucky that Peter held such conveniently inconsistent principles vis-à-vis penetrative intercourse before marriage. If he had wanted to have unprotected sex with me that night, or any night, I would have done it. The feeling he gave me, the sensation of being wanted – I thought that I owed him myself for that, a fair exchange. I would have done anything he asked me to. I guess I inherited my romantic nature from Mum.

* * *

Seven months and three days after her birthday party, Madge lies in a different bed, this one in the Royal Singapore Hospital. The air smothers her like an invisible blanket, the ceiling fans stirring snail trails of humidity against Madge's already damp face. She cries out in pain but Molly refuses to hold her hand. Indeed, Molly draws back from the bed, unable to keep the look of horror from her face.

'She pooed ah,' Molly whispers loudly to the nurse. 'Won't it get on the baby?'

The nurse doesn't answer; pushes her out of the way as she checks between Madge's legs. 'It's crowning,' she confirms. She tells Madge, 'Push now, there's a good girl. Push!'

Madge squeezes hard. She can think of nothing at all. She is fiery red pain, she is blood and shit and guts. She wants them all to get away from her. She hears a mewling sound and wants it to go away too. Who let a cat into a hospital? She wants to complain, but she is in no position to.

'Here he is, a boy.'

Well, at least that is good news. They put the baby on her breast and show her what to do. She cranes her neck down and sees his big black eyes, his red face. She is reminded of his father. He used to suck at her nen-nen in just the same clumsy way, as if its fleshy mass held his salvation.

She feels a rush of something warm, filling the ventricles of her heart and flowing out between her legs. 'Aww,' she murmurs, and even Molly clucks with delight once the baby is wiped clean and swaddled. 'What a cutie.'

'What is his name?' the nurse asks.

'You decide,' Madge sighs.

The nurse shakes her head, but then says, 'Matthew is a good name.' The nurse writes his name on a little tag and attaches it to his ankle. Matthew, son of Madge.

I did not know about the existence of Matthew until I was four years old. It was that year, 1983. Before Val took the pills, before you started complaining of headaches, our half-brother came for a visit.

In some ways, we have Matthew to thank for our existence. Without him, our mother may never have eyed Donald Bradley and thought, *This could be my chance.*

* * *

Mum could not stay hidden from her own mother forever. Singapore is an island. There are only so many places she could go.

'No shame! Itchy! You make me sick!' The slap lands on the top of her curlers as Madge ducks to get away. The baby cries from the bottom of his well-practised lungs and I imagine our mother thinking, *good idea.* She lets loose a scream in bloodcurdling discordance with her child. The men, Madge's brothers and uncles, shuffle their feet and look anywhere but

91

at this embarrassment to the family name. They wish she would take her punishment more like a man – but not being a man was always Madge's principal deficiency.

'Quiet! Shh! No shame? *Ptui*,' her mother's spittle lands on the front of Madge's nylon dress.

Madge covers her head with her arms. 'It's not my fault! I didn't know! You never told me!' she cries.

'Aiyah, you didn't know?' Her mother's voice rises even further, along with the stick. 'You are a dirty girl! Make me *sick!*' Whack, whack.

Yi Ling pauses, panting. Madge waits a moment, then starts to cry harder and louder.

Her mother's voice drops and she yanks Madge's head up by the hair. Madge's nose spews snot. 'I know why you stay here,' her mother hisses, her voice low and mean. 'You are seeing another man ah? You think he will look after you, *and* some other man's baby? You are ugly now, Madge, fat! Only bad ones will look at you now.' Her voice rises again. 'What was he, this man? Nothing! Like you! You are nothing!'

Little Matthew wails from his crib. Madge blurts, 'He was not nothing! He was in the air force! A cook!' she adds for authenticity. If she were lying, surely she would have said he was a lieutenant.

'Not even an officer? I bet he was not even English. He was Aussie!'

'He was English!' She has given them enough truth; now it is time to preserve all possible advantage.

'What was his name?'

Madge's eyes slide sideways. 'Roger! But he has already gone back,' she says, before they can ask any more questions. 'He didn't know' – she gestures to the crib – 'before he left!'

'Why can't you get hold of him ah? Through his company sergeant?' This from Uncle No. 2, who pretends to know all about the English air force because he imports wheaten biscuits from Indonesian factories for them, along with other dry, disgusting things the English seem to like (not quite the real thing, but at only a tenth of the price, who was complaining?).

'Don't know his regiment,' Madge shakes her head. This, again, is true: such information has a habit of slipping into her head and out again, just like the gin he used to buy her, coursing down her cheeks moments afterwards. Those tears had made him touch her face, bend towards her heat-curled head and say, 'I hope I'm not *that* ugly.' At which she had giggled and dried her eyes.

Madge feels a wave of sudden rage at her uncles – what gives them the right to tower over her, these self-righteous old men, with nothing to show for their own virtue but swollen pot bellies? They would fuck her if they could, just to show that they are men and they are right, right, right.

She ducks her head and tries not to think these thoughts too loudly. Her mother has a way of hearing such things.

'Come on, let's go. I want this no-good daughter out of my sight. She makes me sick!'

'Don't you want to hold the baby? Your own grandson!' Now that they are going, Madge doesn't want them to leave. 'Look, look at him! Your only grandson and you come here yelling like this!' She hauls the baby from the crib. He coughs, his face wet with mucus and tears.

'Put him down, Madge!' Hui Jie finally speaks. He points at Matthew's dangerously bouncing head.

Madge has a moment of wild inspiration. She rushes to the small window, which lets in the odours of fried noodles and cat piss from below. 'You make me crazy!' she stomps her foot. 'You want me to throw him out the window? You want me to? I will! I will!'

She holds Matthew over the sill. Her mother says nothing, just watches.

'Acha, stop being so stupid, Sister Baby,' Sze Jie says.

'Don't call me stupid!' Madge's arms are getting tired. She pulls Matthew back inside. He is howling again, limbs windmilling frantically for something to hold on to.

'Quiet, you,' Yi Ling says suddenly to Sze Jie. The put-down of her little brother makes Madge breathe a bit more calmly. Yi Ling addresses her daughter again. '*You* are the crazy one. Make me sick.' But she says it in resignation more than anger, and then she leaves the apartment. Madge's uncles follow after they first make some old-man, desultory threats of further punishment at an unspecified date.

Madge grabs Hui Jie's sleeve. 'Big Brother, wait, Big Brother. I need money. For the baby. Give me two hundred dollars.' She draws Matthew in to her chest, and he instantly stops crying (good baby, clever baby).

Hui Jie puts his hand in his pocket and hands her some notes. He has come prepared for this. 'You have brought shame on this family, Sister Baby,' he mutters.

'Thank you, Big Brother. Thank you, you are a good brother,' she smiles and nods.

Sze Jie now clears his throat. 'You should have thought what you were doing, Sister Baby.' Madge has heard that Sze Jie has secretly become a Christian; his friends now call him Henry-all-of-the-time. She smiles at him and says nothing; she is not yet in a position to bargain. But Matthew whimpers as her nails bite into his soft, untested flesh.

Once the brothers have left, Madge replaces Matthew in the crib and he immediately starts to cry again. 'Ay, quiet, you naughty boy!' Madge smacks Matthew on his dimpled thigh. 'You cry and cry, you bad boy! They left because of you!' She smacks him again, this time on the head where the skin is less padded.

'Ay, what a racket, I heard him from downstairs ah!' Molly bustles in and Madge quickly reaches down so it looks like she is picking up the baby.

'Oh,' Madge straightens, baby still lying in the crib. 'Big Sister, he cries and cries today, and my mother came and beat me, and she did not even look at her own grandson!'

'Oh, poor little fatty la! Your grandma came and got mad at you ah?' Molly picks up the squalling child, who immediately cries harder, seeing his mother standing nearby, arms loose at her sides.

'Don't you worry, Aunty Molly brought you a present la.' She draws a green banana-leaf packet out of her bag with one hand, bouncing Matthew with the other. 'Why haven't you changed him! He's wet!' Molly indicates the nappy, which is sodden and stuck to Matthew's bottom.

'I was about to,' Madge protests, but Molly has already bustled into the tiny bedroom, singing and prattling the whole time. Madge flops back on the couch and peels away the banana leaf to reveal the sticky rice cake inside. She begins to eat.

A month later, Madge asks Alice to meet her at the ferry terminal. Molly is already across the Straits in Penang, where she says there are lots of rich officers and plenty of good jobs for a pretty young girl like Madge.

She knows that Alice, good old Alice from the village, can be relied upon to collect Matthew from the babysitter tonight, take him to Big Brother's apartment, and still not tell anyone where Madge has gone. Alice is good like that. Very loyal.

Alice and her husband are saving up for their own small house in the village. 'You're doing well, Alice. You were always luckier than me.' Madge shakes her head sorrowfully.

Before Alice can make a suggestion, Madge continues, 'What else can I do la? My mother beats me! You've seen her!' Madge knows Alice will remember.

Alice looks down momentarily, but she has to say it. 'A baby needs the mother.'

'No,' Madge responds immediately, ready for this. 'You have not had a baby yet, you'll see. He's fine! He does not even know who I am. He won't notice I'm gone.'

Alice looks dubious. Madge, our future mother, cranes her neck to see how far away the ferry is. Across the water she can see the twinkling lights of Malacca.

'Don't worry. Hui Jie will look after him like a prince. His stuck-up wife can only make girls.'

'You think no one will marry you if they know about the baby, but you're wrong! What about Lee Eng Mo?' Alice's face lights up just as it used to when they were girls and she had come up with a plan for how Madge could stay out longer.

Madge smiles at her friend but shakes her head. 'The one who runs the noodle stall? No way! He smells!'

'You're too picky. You like the air force men too much. See what happens?'

'You worry too much la!'

Madge lets Alice talk, nodding agreeably while letting her eyes drift back across the water. When she was a kid, before Little Brother had come along and Madge was still the primary playmate, Hui Jie used to point to the end of the coastline and tell her, 'That is where the sultan lives, in a palace, with maids and wives and oh, so rich!' Madge remembers the tales her mother told her, about the Malay cities where bad men steal bad girls, girls who had run away from their parents, and sold them to the highest bidder. She prefers the stories of the sultan.

In her letter to Madge from Penang, Molly has written about how rich the men are at the Butterworth base, how tall and handsome. Madge wants to feel a man's arm around her again. She wants to wear nice dresses and laugh and be admired. Is that so wrong? Matthew will be fine. Better even, with her brother and his stern bitch of a wife. They would be lucky to get Matthew. They would be glad Madge had given him to them.

At last the ferry draws in to the jetty, sounding a low, plaintive honk that travels across the night water like the call of a homesick goose. Alice squeezes Madge hard, pressing Madge's arms painfully into her sides. Madge extricates herself from the embrace and looks at Alice's face curiously. Alice is crying. Madge can't help it; whenever she sees someone get upset, she laughs. It just seems so – don't they know how they look la? Even when Matthew screws up his face and screams she can't help but titter, just a little, before picking him up.

'Aw, you're OK, you're OK.' She pats Alice on the back, stifling her giggles. Over Alice's shoulder Madge watches people board the ferry, their identities indistinct, each one just another white moon of a face glowing faintly in the starlight.

'I'm going now, OK?' She smiles and gives Alice one last pat of encouragement. 'You'll get—' Madge pauses over the name, 'the baby, take him to Hui Jie?'

Alice nods through her tears.

'OK. Bye bye. Bye.'

* * *

That is how I imagine our mother leaving her baby behind, propelled forward by a combination of desire and denial, a cocktail familiar to all us Bradleys. If you can't be kind, at least be dangerous.

* * *

The heat of summer has finally subsided and it is almost Easter when I meet our brother for the first time. I have been good all through Lent, even holding my temper when you use my fairy doll as a patient in your pretend hospital. I didn't want Brian's leftover car-model paint daubed all over her perfect plastic limbs. But I took a deep breath and reminded myself of what the nuns had said at Sunday school, that Lent is all about sacrifices. The doll, I thought, is actually a really good thing to give up. I have high hopes of a Humpty Dumpty egg this year, which comes with bonus Smarties on the inside.

It's Holy Week, and we are just back from Palm Sunday mass, me and you still trailing our palm branches from the parade. The Railway Road house smells of something really disgusting, like the ocean just vomited all over our kitchen.

'Ahh, belacan,' Dad says. 'She's cooking all the favourites.'

I am trying to imagine whose favourite food would smell like rotten fish when there is a knock on the door. I race downstairs but Dad gets there before me. A tall Asian man stands on the concrete step. He shakes Dad's hand, and Dad ushers him inside.

Mum stands at the top of the stairs, hands on hips. 'Matthew, Matthew,' she says, as if she has just then been struck with the knowledge of the visitor's name. While we were at church, Mum must have got changed into one of her Chinese suits with matching top and bottom and those hard-to-do buttons. She is wearing all her jewellery and has taken the rollers out of her hair.

'Kathy, Annie, come say hello to your big brother,' Dad says in his jovial voice. I just stare at this tall man who now walks into our house as if his visit was expected.

And, it seems, it was. Everyone else seems excited to see Matthew. I watch him, this new brother. His skin is darker than ours, but he has the same straight black hair as Brian, who is practically falling over himself trying to impress Matthew. Now I know why Brian spent all yesterday cleaning his room, carefully dusting every one of his model cars, extra cranky if I touched one.

The big kids are all on guest-best behaviour. Trish returns from medical school for the weekend, which means I have to move out of the bed I share with you and back in with Mum and Dad like before. Brian will have to share his room for the first time in his life but he doesn't seem to mind.

I gradually realise that I am *the only one who did not know about Matthew.* Even *you* seem to already know about him.

Why didn't you tell me, I want to shout, but all I can do is pinch you when your leg gets too close to my seat.

As my family eats the disgusting food, I wonder, *what else is going on around here that I don't know about?*

Matthew is twenty-six, which is four years older than Trish, who had been the eldest until today. He doesn't talk much, which is like our real brother, Brian. Dad keeps offering Matthew more beer as an excuse to pour himself another glass from the tallies he has bought 'for the occasion', but for once Mum is not rousing on him to stop. The big kids all titter and laugh, as if Matthew is not their brother but a potential suitor, as if they don't know how else to behave around a grown man.

Once my anger has subsided, I realise it is great fun having an extra brother. Matthew comes with us into the living room while Mum, Val, Trish and Barb tidy the kitchen and Dad gets ready for his shift. Matthew lets me play horsey on his leg over and over while Brian sits on the floor, asking him about whether he is Ford or a Holden man (shrug) and which rugby league team he barracks for (Balmain Tigers). Brian doesn't launch into a tirade, just nods as if the Tigers is a valid option.

Brian takes Matthew to his room to show him where he will be sleeping. We follow them down the hallway but Brian shuts the door in our faces. I race downstairs and into the backyard to where Bev is hanging out the washing. Bev, the gentle one, the one big kid most likely to give me some answers.

'The last time I saw him, I was little, probably your age,' she says. She looks past my shoulder, remembering. 'When we lived at Holsworthy, on the army base. Before you or Annie or Brian came along.'

'Where did he go?' I ask.

'He went to stay with a Thai lady off the base, a nice woman who didn't have any kids of her own.'

Panic shoots through me. 'Will that happen to me?'

'No Kathy, don't be silly!' Bev shakes out one of Dad's nurse's tunics. 'It's different with Matthew. He has a different dad.'

'Oh.' I plop onto the ground at her feet and start fiddling with the dropped pegs.

Bev places her hand against my forehead. 'Go and have a drink of water,' she scolds. 'And no more questions. I don't want to get in trouble.'

I put my mouth under the downstairs bathroom tap and then head to the big kids' room. Something about the thickness of the air stops me from wailing as I had planned. Val is pushing herself upright on her bed, red in the face and sweating. Trish sits next to Val, patting her back. They talk in low voices, which means there is something worth listening to. I carefully lower myself to the carpet, hoping no one notices me.

Trish asks something that I can't hear. Val replies. 'I told him, I said, "I'm your sister." He said, "No, you're not."'

'Do you want me to tell Mum?' Trish asks.

'She'd just get mad.' Val glances my way then, and a smile appears on her face like the flick of a light switch. On off, on off. 'Hey, you, what are you doing there?'

I run to find you, upstairs on the verandah, playing doctors with my doll again.

'What's the matter? Aren't you feeling well?' you ask me. I lie down next to the doll, for once not fidgeting as you pretend to take care of me. I want to tell you about what I think Val was talking about, but my stomach eats the words, making me nauseous. Just as you lean over to take my temperature with a plastic stick, I whack you with my pillow.

'What did you do that for?' you ask, more stunned than hurt.

'You were breathing right *on* me.' I give your treasured medical trolley a hard shove and run away before I have to see your face.

* * *

The happy Bradley family show did not last even twenty-four hours. Mum and Matthew got into a fight and he slammed out of 19 Railway Road before dinner time. I wonder if Mum somehow knew what Matthew had done, or tried to do, to Val – if perhaps, for once, her anger was justified?

That was the first and last time I ever met our brother. It wasn't until 2001, eighteen years after his visit, that I could imagine how this all came to pass: the fact, the very existence of Matthew. Based on letters Dad wrote and which were preserved in his army files, I discovered that Dad did not know about Matthew when he met and married our mother. Mum's brothers took care of Matthew until he was nine years old, when Uncle Sze Jie and his wife decided to have a third child despite the Singapore government penalties for having more than two children. And lo! Our aunt gave birth to a boy, the true scion of the Kuan family name. Poor Matthew. Never the real thing.

They tracked Mum down and sent her son to Australia, where he lived with the Bradleys for about a year before being shipped off into foster care.

Would you want us to try to find Matthew, tell him about your funeral? Bev made an attempt after Dad died, but he was never found (unlike Bev herself, whom Val found as easily as locating an alcoholic at a Christmas party).

This is going to sound selfish, or ungrateful, or at least not very nice. If I had been an only child, or perhaps one of two, or maybe three, then I might have tried to find Matthew. But I already have a brother and five sisters – or four, now that you have gone and left me. I already know what a disappointment a prodigal sibling can be. Look at Bev; look at what a let-down that was. Naturally I am glad she seems healthy and has made a life for herself and her four children. But after the initial excitement of finding her again, the fact is that she is still Bev. She is still a bogan from Logan, the exact type of Bradley I have spent my life trying not to become. I have enough Bradleys in my life without looking for more.

The Gold Coast presbytery is nothing like the little old weatherboard where the priest had his mortal abode in the Logan parish of our childhood. This place is built in neatly laid brick, with a decoratively angled cover soaring above the driveway as if awaiting the arrival of angels in finned cars. Brian is already here: his Nissan SUV gleams darkly in the Queensland sunshine. I ease my Subaru into a spot on the other side of the carpark and quickly shove the various belongings strewn across the back seat into a bag. I don't want him peering in and getting the right idea. The glove box is firmly shut. I smooth my still-damp hair and step out.

A man answers the door and for an instant the world spins. It's Evan, here to rescue me from myself. I can hear the words from one of the voicemails I half listened to before deleting them all. He doesn't care about the attempted kidnapping, the protection order, the baby. He wants to try again. He—

As the earth settles to its customary place under my feet, I realise that I have made the common Anglo-Aussie mistake of assuming that all Asian men look the same. After the initial shock of meeting an Asian man in a presbytery, I see that the priest actually looks nothing like Evan, although his name is irritatingly similar.

'Father Kevin Leong,' he says. 'Call me Kevin.'

Call-Me-Kevin is younger than Evan, probably only in his late twenties. He is not bad looking, with symmetrical features, a full head of hair, and a body kept fit through regular squash, which is how he knows Brian. Our brother was never one for talking, preferring to manage the Bradley angst by running himself to the point of exhaustion and pounding tiny balls against concrete walls.

The priest ushers me into a cross between a meeting room and a waiting room. Brian is already seated at a round pine table, dressed in a smart button-down shirt that his wife no doubt chose for him. The walls are painted a dentist-office pastel blue and there is nothing homey about the single portrait of the blue-eyed Christ looking at me from the frame with His usual blend of beseeching and reproach.

It quickly becomes apparent that times have changed since Dad's funeral. Instead of accepting a donation in an envelope after the service, Call-Me-Kevin tells us matter-of-factly that the fee for his services is $340 and the church hire can be arranged directly with a venue manager. Brian and I nod, both keen to be agreeable.

'This is the typical order of the mass,' he explains, handing each of us a print-out. 'You just need to fill in the blanks.'

There are empty lines next to readings 1 and 2, prayers of the faithful, hymns, and speeches. The rote nature of this exercise feels both like a relief and a cheat, as if your death was nothing special, just another day at the office.

Despite his good looks, the priest lacks a spark, not so much of sexual orientation, but of sexuality itself. It's uncanny to be in the same room as an ostensibly single male and scent not an iota of pheromonal presence, a body's way of stating, 'I am here.' Maybe Call-Me-Kevin had to make himself small to survive the scorched earth of an Australian primary school, in the process unintentionally re-wiring his very biochemistry. Which I suppose would have made the Catholic Church an attractive career option.

Evan once described to me how this happened to Chinese men in Australia. 'We have three choices,' he explained. 'We can either fly under the radar, become the funny guy, or fight back. Guess which one I did?' He grinned at me over his miso soup and I am embarrassed to say that I blushed.

Brian, typically, asks another question about the payment. He was always a stingy bugger, our brother, always moaning about mortgage stress whenever I called him to arrange money for Mum's bills. I used to guilt him into contributing, which succeeded until he had the support of an equally aspirational, suburban wife to back up his self-righteous refusal.

To be fair to Brian, it's not as if I contributed to Mum's upkeep out of a sense of family duty. I did it for the purely selfish reason that I wanted a quiet life. I did not want her phoning me at all hours of the day, wheedling or demanding payment for giving birth to me. And Brian was always happy to pitch in for things to support you – the chair lift for the stairs, a new bed at the group home to make you more comfortable. And here he is now, trying to do the right thing by you.

Remember when we were little, we used to play 'In the Future', role playing the careers we each would have when we were all grown up? Brian was the only one in the family for whom our parents paid to have tennis lessons, and he used to stand above us, his arm raised in a serve, pretending to be the future John McEnroe. You always chose to role play a teacher or some other worthy profession, and I would pretend I was an ice-cream lady, tootling about in an imaginary van bringing joy to all the children of Railway Road. We stopped playing that game after you got sick.

Call-Me-Kevin has moved on to the songs.

'Annie would have liked "Star of the Sea", "Here I Am, Lord" and "Suffer Little Children Who Come Unto Me",' I say confidently, pushing away the hymnal. These were the songs from your Confirmation mass, the ones the nuns let you choose because you were so holy.

'And maybe "Ave Maria"?' Brian suggests. 'You know, like from Dad's service?'

'Oh, yes,' I say, surprised I had not thought of it. '"Ave Maria", that would be perfect.'

* * *

108

You have already been a living, breathing miracle for four years by the time you limp up the aisle at your Confirmation mass in 1987. Annoyingly, God has still not seen fit to completely heal you, leaving you with hemiplegia and such poor concentration and attention span that our parents have decided that this, your final year of primary school, will also be your last year of schooling. You have started crying yourself to sleep, thinking I can't hear you.

You are taking Saint Bernadette as your Confirmation name: the martyr of Lourdes, France, who died of consumption when she was nineteen, but not before she had shaken Christendom to its core with her claims of seeing Our Lady; not before she had been tortured and refused to recant; not before miracles began to occur at the grotto where Our Lady first appeared to her. I shiver in my pew. Just the word 'grotto' sounds like miracles could happen.

As I watch you bow your head for the bishop's blessing, the idea hits me like a ray of Queensland sunlight, like a semi-trailer on the Hume Highway, like the voice of God, speaking directly to me.

After the ceremony we head back home. You and I still share a room, because Trish now lives with doctor friends near the Royal Brisbane Hospital, where she works a hundred hours a week. Val has also moved out, qualifying as a nurse after she came back from her Cairns 'holiday' and living in the quarters next door to the Mater Misericordiae Hospital.

The Mater Misery, as Val and the other nurses jokingly call it, is also your hospital. It's actually a nice hospital, run by nuns who sometimes come and sit with you and stroke holiness into your hands. I appreciate that, because every bit counts.

Over the years I have worked out that there is a special geography to hospitals. People who consider themselves good with directions get lost within seconds; there are no landmarks, and every corridor looks the same to the untrained eye. Instead of trying to use your sense of direction, you have to use your sense of observation. I notice scuffs, the shapes of reception desks, which floor has the brighter overhead lights, which corridor smells like it has not been aired in ten years, which ward has the white curtains and which the slightly greying ones. The hospital is a warren and I am a rabbit.

Since 1983 we have been to this hospital eleven times. First there was Val's visit, but then it has all been you, starting with the biopsy and an operation to insert a shunt which drains the extra fluid in your skull to your bladder. Doctor Blackman inserted another when that shunt wasn't enough. In 1985 Doctor Blackman added a reservoir. Dad explained that it is like a pond inside your head. The excess fluid gathers there and once it is full, you come back in for a drainage. Every three or four months, as soon as you start complaining of headaches, you are admitted to hospital. Doctor Blackman sticks a needle into your head and draws the fluid right out of the pond.

You always have the busiest bedside on the ward. If an operation is during term I come and visit on weekends and evenings. If it is scheduled during summer holidays Mum and I spend every day with you, Brian sometimes coming with us, but mostly allowed to be by himself at home. Dad has switched to all night shifts so he can ferry you to appointments and bring us in to see you. The big kids come to visit after work. All these beautiful sisters, Doctor Blackman says, smiling from one Bradley to the next.

I have my hospital routine down pat. First I go downstairs to level four to get water from the bubbler. I make four trips, one for each cup. Then I make a tour of your floor, checking that Dad's reclining chair is still seventh from the left, where I place it every morning. Dad sleeps next to you as often as he can before a night shift. It's the most comfortable chair on the floor – I know, because I tested all eighteen of them.

Then I do the scratchings for Mum at 9.50 am. This means she doesn't waste time and tickets choosing horses that will not be running today. During the day, Mum goes to the TAB and I read out loud to you because you get headaches if you concentrate on the print for too long. When you sleep, or are busy working on one of your poems, I go to the playroom next door to your ward. I am really too big for the plastic ring toys and stuffed animals, but it is somewhere to go.

Once a week, on Thursdays, a warden wheels you down to radiation. While your tumour is being blasted, Mum and

I walk to the hospital cafe because they have a nice lunch special, savoury mince and peas. Occasionally, for a change, we go across the street to the take-away and buy Aussie burgers which are so big that Mum brings a loaf of bread and divides one of them between her, Dad and me. We eat in the corridor outside the ward when you are classified nil-by-mouth, preparing for your draining.

Each operation keeps you alive for a few more months until the next operation, and maybe I should just be grateful for that. *But there should be more,* I think. There could be more, if we just tried harder somehow.

The night after your Confirmation I wait until you are asleep before I sneak to the toilet. I lean a school exercise book on my knees and write in my best handwriting, *Dear Make-A-Wish Foundation, my sister has a malignant brain tumour called an astrocytoma.* I am pretty sure of the spelling: I saw it on one of the doctor's letters that Dad keeps in the bill drawer. *Her wish is to pray for world peace at the grotto of Our Lady in Lourdes.* Then I slip into the living room and steal a stamp from Mum's purse.

A month passes. It's getting hot enough to run under the sprinkler, giggling and wincing from the bindies. But I don't even suggest it, knowing your leg couldn't stand the effort and I couldn't stand your attempts to keep your tears secret from me. Another month passes. In between his three jobs, Dad starts preparing for summer like a man getting ready for a siege, clearing the gutters, burning the leaves in the incinerator, checking the garden hose for kinks and leaks. All

112

the Logan men are doing the same: summer in the suburbs on the floodplains of the Logan River means bushfires in December, followed by floods in January. One summer a tree went up in flames across the road from our house at the same time as the creek broke its banks, gushing muddy water down our street.

I am preparing for a different battle. You and I used to kneel to say our nightly prayers, but since you got sick we have recited them lying down. Now I return to my knees, folding my hands and keeping my back straight, not leaning on the bed. I won't have this fail because I didn't follow procedure.

My strategy pays off. It's November, three months since I posted my letter, when Mum answers the phone. 'Oh, wait, I get my daughter,' she says and hands the phone to me: although she is happy to yell at the top of her lungs at her family, Mum doesn't like to talk to strangers on the phone, afraid they won't understand her accent.

It's a woman from the Make-A-Wish Foundation, telling me that my prayers have been answered. Millions of Catholics travel to Lourdes each year to drink from and bathe in the miraculous waters. This year the Bradleys are going to join them.

Our whole family comes to see us off at the airport, Trish ceremoniously fastening a gold chain with a crucifix around your neck. We travel for thirty-six hours non-stop to get from Loganlea, Australia, to Lourdes, France. We collapse into the beds of our hotel room and the next day you, who have been in good spirits for the whole trip, laugh and tell me, 'You sleepwalked last night!'

'Did not!'

'You did! She did, didn't she Dad?'

Dad confirms it: apparently I got up and scrabbled at the door, trying to get out. Before I can protest further, Mum returns: she has ventured into the outside world and comes back with rock-hard bread rolls, which is apparently what they eat here in France. I gnaw at mine, imagining a race of people with teeth as sharp as dinosaur incisors, baring them at foreigners with ulterior motives.

After 'breakfast', we leave the hotel and, unsure which direction to go, follow the small groups of people who appear to know the way. No one looks at us: the white dad, the Asian mum, the cancer girl and the sleepwalker. In this land of pilgrims, we fit right in.

I have to force myself to walk as slowly as the rest of the growing crowd. My mind is an abacus, and I count off the reasons that my sister should be up for a miracle. Based on my reading of the lives of saints, I have deduced that answered prayers are about being the right person, at the right place, at the right time.

Right place: that's easy. Here we are, at Lourdes, where Our Lady turned ordinary water into a balm of healing for thousands of believers.

Right person: unfortunately we only have me, and I am pretty far from being the right person for the job. The history of the saints suggests that skinny sick children are at the top of the pyramid, closest to God; then skinny sick grown-ups; then fat sick children; then fat sick grown-ups; and then the rest of us. I can't tell you why skinny and fat matters, but if you read the stories of the saints, which I have done, assiduously making notes, it is obvious that it does. Bernadette: skinny child; Angela and Francisco of Fatima: skinny children; Thérèse 'The Little Flower', Teresa of Seville: skinny girls; Maximilian Kolbe (by the time he died): skinny adult.

Anyway, despite being fat from the steroid treatments, you are much closer to the top of the pyramid than me. Which makes the fact that you won't pray for yourself infuriating: I have never once heard you do so. Whenever it's your turn to lead our nightly prayers, you always ask God, in the same sing-song voice the priest uses, for 'peace in our world, peace in our family, peace in our hearts'. But I am hoping that being in the right place will give my prayers the boost that they need to be heard. I am also hoping that God will ignore my recent dabbling with the idea that He might not actually exist. I don't want Him to think I am asking for this miracle as proof. That always backfires.

Right time: this is the hardest part because I cannot know when the right time is. Jesus said that he will come like a thief in the night so all I can do is be ready. After the sleepwalking debacle, I decide to set my alarm to wake every hour and say a prayer for you throughout the hours of slumber so He won't catch me unprepared. During the day I have a prayer for you on repeat in the back of my mind: Please God, may your will be done. It's important to put it in the hands of God: see, for example, Teresa of Ávila. Occasionally I add a little hint: Please God, may your will be to heal my sister now.

There are thousands of people in the cathedral and piazza, but the grotto itself is far less busy than I thought it would be. After a wait of only ten minutes, we proceed through a cave that is big enough for an altar, some flowers and about five people at a time. In one nook there is a statue of the Virgin, and water trickles from a crevice in the dark rock, which is slick with moisture.

Mum takes some photos of us in the grotto. Afterwards, you rest in your hired wheelchair, but I can't sit down anywhere – too young, too healthy – so I shift my weight from left to right, easing one sore footpad and then the other. Mum normally hates seeing you in a wheelchair, but in Lourdes she quickly recognised its utility: in this place, if a person isn't in a wheelchair – or better still, a hospital bed – she goes to the back of the line.

The days pass. We meander at the pace of pilgrims, resting in the shade of trees, going to mass, watching for the coming of Christ and praying. Mum buys dozens of plastic bottles with an image of the Virgin printed on the side and gets me to queue at the wall of taps where people can fill up with holy water. The lines are dense and people shove and heave their way forwards. I want to yell, *You're all supposed to be holy!* but I am too terrified to open my mouth. At one point the mob lifts me off my feet and I stumble, grasping for a handhold because I know with dreadful certainty that if I fall, I will die. The woman next to me is old and squat, and she does not look at me as I pull myself up by her black skirts.

Then it is our last day, the day that we are scheduled to bathe in the water. The day I have been waiting for.

We head to the women's rooms which are housed in cold, grey concrete bunkers. You and Mum are directed to the section reserved for the sick and dying. I had not expected to go in alone and I want to run after you, but a small nun in a grey veil holds my elbow and gestures for me to follow. Inside the bunker stand a row of large, grey concrete baths filled with holy water pumped direct from the source.

The nun doesn't speak English but it is clear what she wants me to do as she points to my dress and then makes a sweeping motion with both her hands. I strip off and shiver, trying to cover my private parts, but the nun is completely indifferent, intent only on grasping my arm and leading me to the tub. This is an industrial-scale operation, shuttling thousands of pilgrims through the icy water every day. I had imagined lying back, letting the water cleanse me. Instead I wade through it as fast as I can, the water so cold that it knocks the breath out of me and I cannot, for love, money or even my sister, actually submerge my body in it. The nun holding my elbow titters, but not unkindly.

I meet you and Mum outside. You are still limping. I try to believe that miracles are not always instantaneous but, in that moment, I feel my faith crumble into motes of dust, because God should be capable of magic in the service of reason.

Dad emerges from the men's bathing rooms. The church bells toll, and a choir singing 'Ave, ave, ave, Maria' disperses the clouds above our heads, blowing our petty selves away like so much unnecessary debris.

'This is my favourite hymn,' Dad says.

We all listen, even Mum, who is not a baptised Catholic, who is typically incapable of sitting still without a pen and a racing guide in her hands. The music washes all the fears and dislikes out of me. Mum doles out pieces of ham and baguette for lunch. Dad stands before us, looking somehow taller and lighter than normal. You sit in the rented wheelchair, accept the proffered sandwich with your good hand, and eat.

By the time we get back to Australia I am an atheist. You smile at everyone like nothing is wrong, but how can you not know that this was our last chance? I want to scream at you for not praying for the right things. Then I remember it is not your fault: it is God's. Then I remember that God doesn't exist. I start to look for someone else to blame, and there I am, waiting for myself.

* * *

Brian is trying to get my attention. 'Kathy? Are we good to go?'

'Oh, sorry yes, thanks Call-M— sorry, Kevin.' I stand.

'No worries,' Call-Me-Kevin shakes my and Brian's hands again. 'I'll see you on Saturday.'

Back out in the sunshine I feel momentarily faint. Brian is saying something. I try to attend. 'Wanna get something to eat before you head off?'

My stomach growls in response and we both giggle like two kids relieved to be on the other side of the principal's office door.

'I'll take that as a yes,' he says.

Brian's Nissan still has the new-car smell even though he explains that he bought it second-hand from the dealership. 'They have that smell in a can,' he says as he reverses, left arm behind the head of my seat as Dad taught us.

'Really?' I had never considered this. I relax back into the woolly seat cover, enjoying not being the one behind the wheel for the first time in days.

'Yep,' he nods. 'They spray it all over everything. Works, doesn't it? Had you fooled.'

'Yep,' I murmur. I feel drowsy: the gentle warmth of the sun through the tinted window, the softness of the fluffy chair, the fact that I have not slept well in ages. I wonder if the developers had that scent-in-a-can, if they sprayed it around generously in the ex-display house that our parents bought after our return from Lourdes. Fooling us into believing in new beginnings.

7 Elliot Road, Slacks Creek, was low-set, three-bedroom brick veneer, and, importantly for you, no stairs. I remember

being excited that we could hook up a stereo in the hallway closet and listen to it play through speakers in the living room. Presumably this was a display home thing, allowing the developers to pipe subliminal messages into the ears of prospective buyers. I imagined our family listening to soothing music, maybe even something classical, definitely something classy to match the downlights and cork tiles of our new lives, our new, more refined selves. The same day we moved in, Mum plugged in her radio so she could hear the races wherever she went.

* * *

There is no more media attention for you after our trip. No one wants to hear about a sick girl who went to Lourdes and came back sick.

In the new house you and I share a bedroom but now we have our own beds. Barb has her own room, and Mum and Dad are in the other. Brian gets the carport, which Dad turns into a room for him, and which almost immediately stinks of boy. Bev has moved into a rental in Loganlea with her new husband, expecting her first baby. There wasn't really a wedding, just a barbecue in the backyard. None of us like the bloke, but Dad says that at least he did the right thing.

Over the years since we've got back from Lourdes, I may have given up on miracles, but I still believe that you can have a life of meaning. I arrange all manner of activities for you, so I don't have to think about you sitting at home, waiting for me to come back from the high school you could not attend. I organise for Dad to drop you off as a volunteer at a local childcare centre on Tuesdays, and take you for volunteer hospital visits once a month. I also arrange for you to volunteer at my school library. The librarian has a son with Down Syndrome who comes in once or twice a week, and she is happy for you to come in and sort books, laminating their corners to protect them from the grubby hands of my peers.

I visit you there each Wednesday, but I can't spend all lunch time with you because then you would know I have nowhere else to go. Every other day of the week, I roam the school, walking the paths, concentrating on a sensation of freedom that comes with feeling the air currents on my face from my own movement.

One by one the big kids move on with their lives. They don't really go to church anymore, once they leave the Bradley home. Trish gets married on a boat. We have to wear disgusting apricot silk dresses with puff sleeves and a drop waist. Flowers in our hair. *Wreaths.* A year later, Barb marries a businessman who gives her lots of presents. I don't know how he can stand her. We have to wear blue satin to her wedding. More puff sleeves. Val, who makes all the dresses, just grins and adds rosettes to the waistline despite my protests. Then it is Val's turn. Mum is in one of her rages when we meet Val's fiancé for the first time, and does her best to derail the engagement, storming around and threatening that she could tell him a thing or two about Val's past. But he just looks Mum in the eye and says, 'You can tell me whatever you want Madge, I'm still marrying your daughter.' Mum huffs and puffs while Val gazes lovingly at this very average man, and soon enough we are clothed in aquamarine silk with the works: puff sleeves, rosettes, even sashes.

At Brian's wedding we are not required as bridesmaids. I am not a huge fan of the bride – she brings back bad memories of the self-satisfied white girls I used to avoid at high school – but she seems to take care of Brian, which is maybe what he needs. I am in university by this time and we now know about your dementia, but the wedding triggers a wave of greater-than-normal confusion for you. You keep getting the bride's name wrong, and talk to yourself loudly, making rude gestures while I grab at your hands and whisper, 'Shh, shh.' Thankfully, the act of walking up to the pulpit snaps you back into the ritual mode of church, and you stay focused all through the reading our brother has asked us to deliver.

I worry what you will be like by the time I get married, and then laugh a little myself, causing our mother to cast a sharp look in my direction. But I wasn't laughing at you, Annie, just at the idea that I would ever find someone who would want to marry me.

* * *

Evan and I agree to meet for an extra walk on the weekend to make up for the one we missed because of his sore leg. Evan needs to vent, he says. The department executives will not agree to his anti-bullying strategy.

'At the moment, the message is this,' he explains. We are leaning against a railing, having just climbed the stairs that rise up the sheer cliff face from Woolloomooloo to Potts Point. Below us sits HMAS *Anzac* at anchor. It's easy to forget that Sydney's harbour is still a working naval base, fortified for defence.

'One: bullying is not OK. Two: if you are bullied, confront the bully with your words. Three: if that doesn't work, tell your teacher. All good, all fine, I totally agree. But there needs to be a fourth step.'

'And what's that?' I ask.

'Four,' he counts on his fingers, 'fight back. You cannot let bullies win. They will not stop. That is the nature of a bully. And you have to decide,' Evan says, looking me in the eye. 'Are you going to run, or are you going to fight?'

'That makes sense. Sometimes you have to take a stand.'

'Exactly.' Then Evan leans down and kisses me on the lips. I brace myself to be repulsed by garlicky Asian desperation, but all I feel is his arms around me. All I feel is safe.

We go back to his apartment and awkwardly undress each other, Evan laughing each time I struggle with a zip or a button. Every foible and fumble is all just part of the hilarious sweetness of the human condition to him. He manages to get the second condom he rips opens to stay on, until he is not laughing but panting, pushing and moaning my name. I try to pant along, but all I can feel is tightness and something pressing against it. From this vantage point he looks how they all look: completely contained, using me as an empty place to chafe his need. Once he is done he will roll off and that will be the end of that.

It only takes about two minutes. 'Sorry!' he laughs. 'It's been a while.'

Instead of conveniently falling asleep while I slip my clothes on and get a taxi home, he looks at me. He kisses me slowly, eyes open. Then he takes my hand and puts it on my clitoris, and he puts his fingers inside me and begins to rub.

'You're beautiful,' he murmurs in my ear, and I can't stop myself; my back bucks and my legs twitch. It's the first time I have ever orgasmed in the company of another human being. I don't know what this means but I know it means something.

I tell Evan about you over dinner. 'One day I plan to move back to Queensland,' I say. 'To look after her.' I watch him closely.

'I like Queensland,' he says, mouth full of pasta. 'Or we could have a room for her in our house.' He pauses. 'We could get a low-set, no steps,' he says, reaching for his wine glass.

Then he starts telling me how one day he would like to move up north, away from Sydney. As he talks I see a beach uncluttered by Sydneysiders, a house with a view of the sea. I see a dog and a swing and kids' bikes out front.

I see handsome young newlyweds, laughing over whose job it is to trim the rosebushes. She is working on a PhD and he is founding an anti-bullying charity. The woman is blonde and the man has blue eyes so I paint over their faces to make them look more like Evan and me, and I add a ramp and a granny flat to the backyard. Then I laugh at myself, because whose dream of a dream home has wheelchair access? Even so, I cannot shake the image of a vast blue sky with not a single cloud in it.

* * *

'Kathy? We're here.'

Four years since I met Evan and here I am, in an SUV that smells of fake new beginnings, in front of a strip of non-descript take-away food shops. I could be anywhere, but Evan would still be too far away to change my mind. When it came to my marriage, I didn't make a choice between running and fighting. I did both.

'They do a good lunch bento box at the sushi place.' Brian hops out.

He gets the teriyaki chicken and I order the salmon. It's a meal deal so he gets a Coke Zero and I follow suit. Caffeine will be required to get through the rest of this day.

'So you and Trish are sorting out the cremation,' Brian says. I nod. The salmon tastes like nothing to me, but my stomach is circumventing the usual communications loop and

I shovel the food in, my body demanding its due if it is to sustain me for the rest of this week.

'Thanks for doing that.'

'Do you want to come?'

'Oh, no, that's all good,' he says, but I can tell from the way he sits up a little straighter that he is happy to have been asked. There are bits of seaweed stuck in Brian's front teeth. I pick at my own with one end of a chopstick, hoping that will send a message.

'Have you invited her Carpe Diem friends to the funeral?' he asks. Strings of emerald green flash at me as he talks.

'They're all dead,' I say flatly.

'All of them?'

'All the ones she was close to. By the way,' I add, 'you have food stuck in your teeth. Quite a lot.'

Brian extracts a toothpick from the holder on the table and picks at his teeth. 'All gone?'

I gesture and he picks some more.

'What about that boy?' Brian asks as he works his way along his top row of teeth.

'I can't understand you.'

'I said, what about that boy?'

'What boy?' I ask. If Brian thinks he knows more about your life than I do, he can bloody well prove it without my help.

'I always wondered.' He returns his attention to the meal, the used toothpicks lying between us on the table. 'Do you think they had a bit of a thing? Like, I don't know. Poor Annie.' He shakes his head into his Coke Zero as if it were a beer and he and I were better friends than we are.

'She never had a thing with Jeremy,' I reply. 'That was all in her head.' I cover the toothpicks with a serviette.

'Well, was it though?'

'I was always there. I would have known.'

'Not always,' Brian says quickly, so quickly I wonder if this is where he was headed all along. 'There was that camp, remember, the one she went to on her own? They went to the Snowys?'

'I went to all the camps,' I reply, poking viciously at the remnants of my salmon.

'No, there was that one, remember?' Brian insists. 'You had exams or something, so there was the camp she went to without you. I dropped her off at the bus.'

Anger pulses through me like an electric current of energy; soy sauce–drenched rice grains resurrect themselves to burn my throat. Brian would never go with you to a single event, but he knows more about you than I, who accompanied you to every stupid activity, who gave you the illusion of a social life despite the toll it took on my own.

We drive in silence back to the presbytery carpark. Brian looks like he wants to say something else, but then shakes his head and rubs a finger under his Ray-Bans. I catch a brief glimpse of his eyes, the wrinkles around them, the bags below. I step down from the SUV. Brian wipes his nose with the back of his fist and then leans over. For a second I think he is going to try to give me a hug but before I can move out of reach he has grabbed the handle of my door and swung it shut.

* * *

Just like the saints, there is a hierarchy to cancer. I learn it at our first Carpe Diem event when you are fifteen and I am twelve. Carpe Diem is a support group for adolescents with cancer and their siblings, run by the Queensland Cancer Council. At the top of the pecking order are the boys who have lost limbs to the cancer but are still good-looking in a private-school way and get around with extremely cool prosthetics. Hodgkin's lymphoma.

Then there are the boys and girls who have had leukaemia but have reached that nirvana of cancer patients: remission. Before we started coming to Carpe Diem meetings, I didn't even know there was such a thing as remission. I thought everyone with cancer just went on and on and on, like you, stumbling towards death. The remission kids seem normal, except that they tend to be uber mature, already thinking about their career options at the ripe old age of fourteen because they know in their bone (marrow) that life is short.

And then at the bottom of the pyramid are the brain tumour kids. These kids can be distinguished by their moon faces (steroid treatment), their thinning hair (radiation therapy), their languid eyes (papilloedema) and their stunted growth (steroids plus radiation at a young age). Some are in wheelchairs or walk with a hemiplegic leg and arm, like you.

Within the brain tumour kids there is a mini-hierarchy. The location and operability of the tumour determine how much you are changed by it. For example: Becky, at eighteen, in a wheelchair but still cognitively sharp. Tumour was malignant but operable. Other kids have tumours that change their personality; bring on epilepsy; destroy attention spans, concentration and memory.

And then there is you. My Annie. The jackpot girl. Your tumour is inoperable. Your tumour is right in the middle of your head. Your tumour sits in the hypothalamus, squatting atop the thyroid gland like a malevolent guard of an unwanted and forgotten pot, long since emptied of gold. As a result, you have never had a period and some of your behaviour is 'socially inappropriate'. Luckily no vagina flashing or rude gestures. Your inappropriate behaviour is restricted to delight. You make completely unrelated comments during conversations, laugh at things that are not jokes, and cannot pick up on social cues. Your tumour makes you think that everyone loves you with the same amount of love as you have for everyone, boundless and grating in its generosity. Mum thinks I take care of your physical needs at these events, and yes, I make sure you go to the toilet before the fluid that is shunted from your brain to your bladder can leak out through the usual exit; but more importantly I protect your soft, sweet heart.

I stick to the fringes of our first Carpe Diem pizza and movie night, too nervous to talk to the cool kids, too scared of potential over-familiarity from the brain tumour kids. I have taken on all the inhibitions your tumour has stripped away from you and am unable to make eye contact with any of these people, while you breeze about, hugging and chatting even though you might not remember anyone's name for the length of a greeting.

But at least you are happy. I watch you go from one group of kids to the other, distributing hugs indiscriminately. Most of the kids smile back, some glancing at one another before silently deciding that this is the correct response. One thing I have to say for these cancer kids: they are preternaturally understanding of difference. Of course they have their cliques, but the cancer seems to have injected them with a sense of propriety beyond their years. They know how to be kind.

Now you are chatting with a boy who stands with the support of a cane. He has an air of polite attentiveness which I realise is the result of a hump on his back, forcing his head forward into a permanent tilt. You point to me and the boy looks over and smiles, bright blue eyes under a mess of black hair. I nod at you both but avert my gaze, not wanting a brain tumour boy to take an interest in me. I scold myself inwardly for my vanity: it's not as if my health will make me an instant object of desire. But I already have you, Annie, cloying me with your eager questions about school, your demands for attention, for me to appear happy. I cannot bear the threat of another person requiring me to smile.

I try to make myself helpful, handing out the food, fetching drinks. I wouldn't mind if Soft Tissue Sarcoma Boy looked at me, or Handsome Hodgkins. They lean on the table where the leukaemia kids have their paper and pens spread out, planning the annual camp. They chat with Bossy Baldie, the quasi-leader of Carpe Diem (her hair grew back thin after chemo, so you can see the scalp) and Earnest Girl, whose eyes roam the room, inventorying everyone's enjoyment. Soft Tissue Sarcoma Boy holds court, private-school hair flopping playfully in his eyes, while Handsome Hodgkins grins good-naturedly, his face dotted with the freckles of an ancestry not best suited to the Australian sun and therefore all the more coveted. I edge closer to them with my plate of food and handful of serviettes. I picture myself standing next to Handsome Hodgkins at camp later this year, offering him my tube of sunscreen. He nods at me gratefully and asks—

'Thanks Cassie,' Soft Tissue Sarcoma Boy says, grabbing two slices from the proffered plate.

Earnest Girl nudges him. 'Thanks *Kathy*,' she says, but Soft Tissue Sarcoma Boy is delivering a hilarious anecdote about private-school shenanigans over on the north side of Brisbane, where they don't even know that Logan is its own city and not just the endless stretch of suburbs they must drive through to reach their Gold Coast holiday houses. I hurry back to the kitchen, even though the plate is still half-full.

You are still with the boy with the hump, now sitting on a low couch, watching the movie. I groan inwardly – it is going to be hard to lever you out. You seem blissfully unaware of the future annoyance you are going to cause me.

'Annie,' I say, blocking the movie. 'Do you need to go to the toilet?'

'No,' you respond. The boy doesn't ask me to move, just politely tries to crane his neck around me at the screen.

'Annie, come on, you better go to the toilet.' I hoist you up before you can protest. The boy uses his cane to stand and offers you his hand even though he is unstable on his feet. You hold his hand a moment longer than you need to before I usher you away to the bathroom.

* * *

I get back into my car and sit there for a minute before I start the ignition.

Rather infuriatingly, Brian could be right. It's hard to remember – the camps all blur in my mind in one long, sunny, cringeworthy summer of abseiling and other adventure activities meant to compensate for shortened lives.

That was definitely the downside to Carpe Diem. Every few months for the duration of our membership, we would receive a phone call from the latest bubbly social worker who had taken on the entry-level job of coordinating the cancer kids. 'I am so sorry to have to tell you,' she (it was normally a she) would murmur, and then the names would slide from her mouth, down the telephone line, to sear themselves across our memories of the living, breathing, laughing humans we had so recently envied (me) or hugged (you). 1993: Soft Tissue Sarcoma Boy, three more rounds of chemo meant no floppy hair left when it came to the end. 1994: Earnest Girl, relapse, remission, relapse. No more remission.

The only camp I remember with crystal clarity is our last one. I would be willing to bet that despite all your memory loss, all the dementia, that you remembered that one too, until the day you died.

* * *

It is 1995 and you just turned nineteen which means you will be out on your ear next year – no more Carpe Diem for you once you are no longer a teenager. Technically I could remain a member for another three years but there is zero chance of that happening. Once you can no longer attend, I am out.

This year's camp is on Stradbroke Island, an expanse of sand just off the coast of Queensland. Part of me is looking forward to seeing it. Apparently there are dolphins and beautiful beaches. If I can get some time away from you, perhaps during one of the interminable workshops on how to deal with cancer (using, you know, crayons), I might be able to take a walk. Breathe deep. Smell the salt air and all the other things I have heard people do while enjoying their holidays. I once read that introversion is natural but shyness is just bad manners. So there you have it: I am a bad-mannered sixteen-year-old. Will wonders never cease.

Jeremy is here for his final camp too. The cane has been replaced by a wheelchair. The hump on his back has worsened and tilts his head down towards his chest so he can only view the outside world with his right eye. Despite this, Jeremy still has impeccable manners. He always asks how I am, even though obviously I am completely fine with my two legs and two arms and a head that works.

In the hierarchy of cancer I'd place Jeremy on about equal footing with you, Annie. His physical disabilities are greater than yours but his attention and memory are better, which makes him more adept at following conversations. You two chatter away happily: that is, you do most of the talking and Jeremy laughs politely at your jokes. When I see you sit next to him and engage in conversation, I feel my heart swell with a mixture of embarrassment and envy.

'Annie,' I say, but you are so engrossed in your conversation that I have to repeat myself. 'Annie. I'm going for a walk. Do you need anything?'

'No, no, I'm fine, you go.' You wave me away.

After dinner you and Jeremy are working on a picture together so I head down to the dock. A pod of dolphins flashes and surfaces through the sparkling, rippling water. The sun sets in a haze of red and gold over a clear expanse of ocean. Even I have to admit that this isn't too bad.

Day two dawns and I am feeling uncharacteristically optimistic. I always look forward to the breakfasts at camp. They really know how to put on a spread. I fetch you a plate of food and cut up the bacon, then I pile my plate high with eggs and mushrooms and find a place to eat. Jeremy mustn't be up yet but you have saved him a spot at your table.

One of the camp facilitators asks for our attention for the morning announcements.

I am on my feet instantly and almost at your side when I find myself veering out of the hall. All I can think about is how the last time I saw him I had not talked to him – but I had smiled over my baked potatoes. *Thank goodness*, I think, over and over again. Thank goodness, thank goodness.

The camp facilitators said he looked peaceful. They said, *what a beautiful place to go.* When someone dies, people seem to say the first thing that comes into their heads. They should really give themselves a minute.

The camp is cut short and the funeral will be on Thursday. Mum won't let you go. Once we are home you calm down a bit, which is to say that you alternate between hysterical tears and staring into space. It is mean-spirited, but your behaviour grates on me. *Settle down*, I want to tell you. *It's not like you're the only one affected by this.* But when you are upset you demand all the available air. I take shallow breaths and wait for you to forget Jeremy, wait for the tumour to do its goddamn job.

* * *

Unwanted memories assail me as I drive along the freeway towards the Mount Cotton Memorial Gardens. That ridiculous birthday party of Jeremy's at an ice rink of all places. I think it was sponsored by a local radio station – honestly, the freebies you cancer kids attracted. I suppose the guilty burden of health was not unique to me. The radio station even organised a loan of a Paralympian's specially made wheelchair with blades attached to the base. I remember you leaning on the handlebars, chatting and laughing with Jeremy as he glided across the rink like an ice king. At the time I assumed you were sticking close to him for the balance his chair offered. Otherwise you might not have been able to go out on the ice at all, because I refused to move from my seat on the sidelines, drinking one watery hot chocolate after another and churlishly wondering how much electricity it took to power an ice rink in Queensland.

My phone buzzes just as I pull into the memorial gardens. No caller ID. Probably Evan. I hit the red button. My husband may believe that calling me every five minutes will wear me down but the opposite is true. It only hardens my resolve.

You don't have to try and make me feel guilty about Evan. I can assure you that he will be better off without me. It's a statistical fact that we Bradleys are not cut out for love. Look at the evidence. It's a small sample, but the intervals are significant enough to be persuasively descriptive:

1. Bev, with her recently deceased ex-husband.

2. Barb and her divorce, which was both messy and predictable. I know blood should be thicker than water, but it is absolutely not thicker than Barb.

3. Val, happily married to a man who thinks he is far funnier than he actually is.

4. Brian and his wife, mortgaged to the eyeballs to live the suburban dream.

5. Trish, whose husband is so painfully kind that she has to rein in her contempt every time she sees his sympathetic smile.

6. Me and, until a week ago, Evan.

7. The catastrophe that was our parents' marriage.

Our parents married on Valentine's Day, 1961. As we were growing up, I always deferred to that fact as the ultimate proof that they must have loved each other; that perhaps on some level they still did. But when I asked, Mum explained that they married on Valentine's Day because it coincided with Dad's weekend leave.

PART 3

FAMILY LIFE

Include stories of the deceased's immediate
family – parents, spouses, children
and siblings. This helps to make family
members feel as though they are part
of the story of the deceased.

How to Write a Eulogy

The Mount Cotton Memorial Gardens are situated on several hundred acres of rezoned farming and industrial land, out past the tip on Mount Cotton Road. I am not sure how they have managed it, but I can neither smell the rubbish from the nearby landfill, nor the smoke from the crematorium, which is a handsome, low brick building with several non-denominational chapels of various seating capacities out front.

When we were kids accompanying Dad on a tip run for anything that wouldn't fit in the incinerator, Mount Cotton Road was still unsealed and this land crouched under scraggly scrub similar to that across the road from our house in Loganlea. You and I used to play spotto, counting how many old tyres and clapped-out washing machines we could see along the verge, dumped by people who didn't want to shell out the fee for the tip.

Trish has texted that she is running late because she was called in to the hospital. She was probably saving someone's life while Brian and I were picking seaweed from between our teeth. I get out of the car and cross the little arched bridge to the spot where Dad's ashes are interred. We paid a premium eight years ago to bury his cremains near one of the artificial creeks, imagining the sound of water soothing his country boy sensibilities.

To understand, we have to go back again, this time to the heart of sheep country. What drove our father out of the New South Wales granite belt into the arms of our mother, seven thousand kilometres away on the humid island of Penang, when none of his family had ever travelled farther than Gunning to sell mutton?

The answer I always return to: Dad was a good man.

It sounds trite, but I don't know of any better way to describe him. In 1983, when I was four, our father sat me on the bed and plaited my hair for me after my bath, and when I was five Mum cut it all off. Dad was the one who we turned to if we needed love. Dad was the one we trusted.

* * *

Donald and his brothers and sisters (six, or seven, or sometimes eight, depending – as with our family – on who is counting) call home a rocky, unyielding smallholding about three miles outside of Crookwell (it's 1958, so we are using imperial measures).

Let's just call a spade a spade: unlike his dashing father, Donald at twenty-one years of age is not that great around girls. At the same age, Gordon Bradley had stepped off the boat from England and by the third sheep property he offered his services to, he had got himself sixty acres. The property was the dowry of his new wife and her four-year-old daughter (father unrecorded, hence the acreage).

Donald is a bit awkward, and a bit clumsy. He laughs too much. He smiles too much. He stands too close, or not close enough, and never at the right time. His oldest brother, Warren, tries to help him. 'Stand up straight,' Warren tells Donald, who obliges by pushing his chest out, but that just emphasises his weak chin. His black-framed glasses fog with the effort. The girls who know him from schooldays take pity and dance with him at the local church dos, but they never linger afterwards, giggling with their friends once his too-clammy hands release them.

But Donald is their mother's favourite – or at least he is between her 'rests' in the women's asylum in Goulburn, which she has been taking for as long as Donald can remember. Esme, the eldest, steps into the role of mother when Rose is away, but when their mother is at home Rose likes nothing better than to place her feet against the grate and talk dreamily about Donald becoming a priest.

In the end, the cancer takes Rose before the madness can, and that puts paid to visions of Donald in Sunday vestments, living at the presbytery and enjoying the best cuts from the Irish butcher in town. His dad has a quiet word, and Donald is glad of a job working as a nurse at his mum's old asylum.

Changing bedpans is not much chop, but Donald enjoys chatting to the saner inmates, and it turns out he has a special flair at cajoling patients back to their wards. The difference between him and the other male nurses is that Donald actually likes the patients. He can see what they are really like, beneath the messianic muttering of the schizos, inside the folds of skin hanging off the frames of the anorexics.

The other male nurses throw their weight around, resorting to the straps to get the residents to settle. But Donald talks to them as he did to his mother when he found her holding Donald's five-month-old brother Ronnie. She had sounded so calm, asking to see her husband or her daughter Esme so they could give her an explanation for the baby's existence, as she held the screaming infant at arm's length over a full drum of water. Esme had given birth to Ronnie while Rose was last in the asylum. Donald had known not to ask questions, but it was clear that his eldest sister had stepped into Rose's place in more than just the household duties.

Donald had gentled their mother as he might a sheep stuck in the mud. 'It's all right,' he had murmured. 'Give me the baby. Everything's going to be all right.'

Soon after that, Esme married and moved to Goulburn, leaving Ronnie at home as if he were really Rose's son. Donald and the others did their best for the boy, raising him by the scruff of his hand-me-down shirts. Rose tolerated Ronnie but refused to see Esme ever again. It was Donald who wiped the sweat from Rose's forehead and changed her sheets as the cancer killed her, who waited outside the door as Father Doherty intoned the last rites, the smell of the blessed oils briefly masking the reek of Rose's last bowel movements.

Things are good for Donald at the asylum, until there is a stupid thing – not even a *thing*, just a friendship – with one of the female patients. All right, she is a bit unstable, but when she takes her meds she is as normal as anything. It isn't as if the others don't have their favourites.

He's staying with Esme while he looks for a new job. She sits him down in the kitchen of her marital home one night, over a plate of his favourite bread and butter pudding, and tells him that she has an idea.

'You're already a reserve, aren't you, Don?' Donald nods. He and his brothers joined the reserves almost two years ago. It means a uniform, which goes down well at the church socials, and a bit of extra cash for what amounts to going bush with his brothers and mates.

'If you join up properly,' says Esme, 'they'll teach you a trade.' She stares at him with that look she gets when she has already decided what you are going to do but is giving you the opportunity to say it for yourself and save her the effort.

Donald has toyed with the idea before, of course: some of the boys he went to school with have enlisted and send home a decent army pay cheque every month. But until now, he has preferred the idea of staying at home, thinking that he might even go to night school and really become a priest. He spoons more of the pudding into his mouth. 'I dunno, Esme.'

'Good conditions in the army,' Esme adds. 'Think about it, all right?'

'All right, Esme. Got any more pudding?'

Esme starts mentioning it every time she sees him, and it isn't a big house. Finally, two Fridays after she first brought it up, Donald heads to the Goulburn enlistment office. They say he should lose some weight. They mark him SG4 on the general aptitude test, meaning that Donald demonstrated 'no outstanding qualities either as a soldier or a leader' in the intake assessment tasks. In a period of history that needed fewer bodies in uniforms, he would not have been permitted to join the army at all.

But Donald was in luck. There was a war on.

At the end of the day, the NCO prods his gut and tells him to report for training next Monday. Rifleman medic, thanks to his asylum experience: Medical Assistant Class III. In a roundabout way, Donald owes his army job and everything that comes with it to his mum.

* * *

I want to shout down the decades to young Donald, wave my arms, stop him in his tracks. 'Stay in Goulburn!' I would say. 'Get a job cleaning toilets at the local jail like your brother Warren. Marry a country girl, a white girl, one who has no baggage but what is in her glory box. Whatever you do, *don't join up.*'

* * *

'Acting as a deterrent to the Communist threat by maintaining a strong show of force' translates into shift after shift of picquet duty for Donald and the other soldiers stationed at Butterworth, Malaya. By 1958 the conflict is largely over, but they are occasionally sent on patrol to look for insurgents foolish enough to still be lurking along the Thai–Malay border.

Out in the jungle as platoon medic, Donald spends much of his time soaking the men's reeking feet in vinegar. More than once it has rained so hard that the trenches have overflowed, Donald waking in water up to his stomach. There are so many reports of jungle rot that Donald practically dusts the rainforest in snow in his hurry to hand out baby talc. The men laugh when he gives it to them and nickname him 'Softie' after someone jokes that the powder made them 'soft as a baby's bum'.

Although he joins in the men's wistful conversations about Yorkshire puddings and roast beef on Sundays, Donald is glad he joined up. Here he is, twenty-one years old, and already a man of the world.

Donald spends his weekends no longer changing bed pans or mucking out pens reeking of sheep shit, instead in Penang, the town across the bridge from the base. He browses markets where you can get anything tailor-made for less than the cost of a counter meal back home in Crookwell. He and his tent mate Kez get safari suits made, with short sleeves suited to the local weather. Donald gets his made in khaki; like his mates, nowadays he is only really comfortable in camouflage. This is the first item of clothing, apart from his uniforms, that was not made for him by his mother or his sister, or that he has not inherited from one of his brothers.

Imagine his brother Warren's face if he could see the China-girls in their clinging cheongsams and their glossy black up-dos! It's as if they aren't real girls – not the way the girls back in Crookwell are real girls, with their broad white faces and steady hips; the girls who'd known you when you were in short pants and were not impressed with what had developed since. They are exotic fantasies, the girls in the dance halls in Penang, created as part of the whole fantastic set-up, existing purely in the dream-state of R&R. In Penang, Donald has no problem whatsoever looking a girl in the eye.

Donald daubs himself liberally with Old Spice. He and Kez have just returned from patrol, and Donald revels in the scent of freshly laundered clothes after thirty days of the cheesy smell of ration-infused sweat and farts.

The hostess of the Moon Club greets Donald and his mates like old friends and shows them to a high round table near the bar. She perches on a stool and chats as if they are the only men worth knowing in the room. They order drinks and she moves on, but so graciously that they feel like invited guests rather than paying customers.

Kez has spotted someone across the room and heads off, soon returning with a whippet of a thing – curled hair, knowing eyes, a body as slender as a reed. Donald is not so much attracted to women like this as in awe of them, as if they are a local danger he has yet to learn to defend himself against. But she comes holding the hand of one of the plumper girls, if you could call any of these China-girls 'plump'; this one has curves where curves should be, and a softness to her cheeks and hips.

'Softie, this is Molly,' Kez says, his arm draped around the slim looker's waist.

'Who's your friend, Molly?' asks Donald, smiling at the girl with the rounded edges.

Molly glances from Kez to Donald. 'This Madge. She good friend of mine, good girl ah? Madge, you say hello to Softie.'

'Hello, Softie!' Madge titters.

'The name's Donald,' Donald corrects, making Kez snigger. Ignoring him, Donald continues, 'You like a drink?'

To which Madge nods, 'Yes.'

Two weeks later Donald Bradley rolls over in bed in a hotel room in downtown Penang, Malaya. He lets the girl's voice ripple over him like the tiny pricks of the feet of sugar ants: slightly ticklish but with a bite to them. She is a talker. She could talk under wet cement. But Donald likes the sound of her chatter, filling the background with a nice patter of inconsequentialities as he lies in bed playing with her titties.

Madge is so soft. He loves the way her flesh gives way to him and then springs back, ever pliable under her slippery nylon dresses. Her plumpness reminds him a little of his mum, before the cancer and the madness. He would never say it out loud, but there is something about the forgiving heft of Madge's hips that makes him feel like he is a boy, sitting before the fire in his Crookwell home, seeing himself through the loving eyes of his mother.

The others make fun of him about her plumpness, but he doesn't mind. 'I like to have something to hold on to,' he tells them, rounding his hands, and they snort. They say she has him wrapped around her little finger, making him stand to if she so much as raises her voice. 'That's not the only thing that stands to attention,' he tells them, and they snigger.

'Donald!' Madge shakes his shoulder.

'Mm hmm, yeah, right,' he murmurs.

'Are you listening?'

He opens one eye, then closes it again. 'Yeah, yeah, of course,' he protests, nuzzling the bare space between her neck and shoulder.

She clears her throat. Perhaps she has a bit of inflammation of the lungs. Donald is forever doling out Irish Moss to the men, his cure-all for coughs, the air too soaked with humidity to allow people's gurgling chests to really clear. Perhaps he could get some for her. He imagines giving her the bottle of cough mixture; her upturned face, her grateful smile.

'I saw a girl, other day, she come into work,' Madge begins.

Bugger, Donald thinks, the image fading from his mind. He had forgotten. Madge works at a chemist. She probably unpacks boxes full of Irish Moss every day.

'Her boyfriend, he rich, English. He give her a necklace, gold, twenty-four carat,' she says.

'The air force men make a lot more than the grunts, and they don't do anything more for it,' Donald responds. This is a topic that he and Kez often discuss. Some days there's not much else to do but compare their conditions to those of the Australian Air Force members with whom 1RAR shares the Butterworth base.

'He not even married to her, he give her the necklace.' Madge clears her throat again and turns on to her side. Now he is too close to her face to see her properly; he sees just a single eye and a mop of black around the periphery.

'Do you want a necklace?' he asks, stroking her skin.

'No, no,' she protests. Then, after a moment, 'Well … He spend his whole pay cheque on it, you know.'

'Where do you get gold like that?'

'You get good price, with the Chinese.' Madge sits up, animated. Her boobs dangle above the sheet, their big brown areoles brushing lightly against his face, making him blink. 'Don't go to the Sikhs, they rip you off. You go to Chinese. You go there, they sell you real thing, twenty-four carat.'

Donald pictures himself, arm around a girl (this girl), walking through the market stalls. Stopping to haggle at a gold stand, the items shining in the sun; the other men passing by, nodding; Donald nodding back.

'We'll go later,' Donald agrees.

'Oh. All right,' she replies, as if the whole thing had been his idea. *Women*, he thinks fondly, rolling on top of her.

Madge has picked up all sorts of slang from the Aussies, and it makes Donald chuckle when they reach the stalls later that day to hear her shout at the vendor, 'You slow as a wet wig!' He pats her on the bum, looking around for someone to share the joke with. His little Aussie haggler.

She turns abruptly to leave the shop and he follows, recognising the universal language of bargaining. Madge reminds him, 'Walk, walk. Don't look back.'

When they are almost out of earshot, they hear the vendor call, 'Wait!'

Madge turns and Donald again follows her, smiling at her bottom as it jiggles up and down in triumph.

'You want this one?' the vendor asks, indicating a thinner chain than the one they had been negotiating over.

'No. That one,' Madge says firmly, and the vendor sighs, as if they are taking the meat from his only son's plate.

After they leave the store Donald stops Madge and turns her around. She holds her hair up and he places the chain against the sweaty skin of her neck. She practically skips down the street.

'What do you say?' he calls after her playfully.

'Thank you, thank you,' floats back to him, as Donald laughs and tries to keep up.

Donald and Madge see each other every leave pass Donald gets. Often Donald will meet Madge at the hawkers for a meal then go on to a bar or one of the back room 'casinos', which are really just fluorescent-lit rooms with a craps table and a card game. Madge sits behind him and giggles every time the dice is rolled. Other times they go straight to the hotel where Donald now rents a room for Madge on a week-to-week arrangement with the owner.

On a Saturday three months since Donald and Madge first met at the Moon Club, Donald is shopping for souvenirs in the markets. He has plans to catch up with Madge later. *What might Esme like?* he wonders, pausing at a table laden with jade pendants and trying to picture one nestling below his older sister's freckled white neck. This is the problem with souvenirs – they seem perfectly fine when you buy them but once you get them back home they are completely out of place.

It is muggy as always and he is already sporting sweat stains under his arms and on his back. He decides to have a break and get an ais kacang. He can already taste the sweet shaved ice sliding down his throat, cooling him from the inside out.

Sitting at one of the plastic folding tables outside the drink stall is Molly, the one who first introduced him to Madge, having a drink with a woman who is cradling a baby on her lap. Donald is standing right at their table before he realises that the woman holding the child is Madge, *his* Madge. She looks up and half stands, simultaneously handing the baby to Molly.

'How are you, Donald? Not see you for long time,' Molly exclaims. This is because Molly has dumped Kez for a warrant officer, but Donald smiles genially enough.

'Can't complain, Molly. And who is the little one?' He smiles at the baby, who blows a raspberry in his general direction and frowns.

Molly replies, 'Her name Trish.'

'That's a lovely name,' Donald says affably. He pulls up a chair. 'How old is she?' he asks Molly.

'Madge? How old she now?' Molly looks at Madge.

'Oh,' Madge giggles nervously. 'Nine month?'

'Is she—' Donald is confused. He gestures from the baby to Molly.

'Ah, she Madge's, not mine!' Molly waggles her head. 'She good girl though la. Aren't you little one?' Molly vigorously tickles Trish's third chin and Trish wails. Donald instinctively reaches out to soothe the baby with a few pats. She stops crying and turns two big black eyes on him.

'You not meet her before?' Molly asks Donald. 'Madge, you should have bring her before la. She beautiful girl!'

Donald looks at Madge, waiting for an explanation, but Madge avoids his eye.

'Baby father, he bad man.' Molly leans over the table and drops her voice. 'He tell Madge, I *marry* you, I take you *home* with me. But what he do? He leave her here. He already got wife in Sydney! Aiyah.' Molly shakes her head.

'Why didn't you tell me?' Donald turns to Madge.

'You all the same.' Madge stands up abruptly, startling Donald. She grabs Trish from Molly's lap. The people at the surrounding tables turn from their conversations to see what the fuss is about.

Donald glances at the onlookers. 'Shh, shh, Madge. We'll talk about it later.'

'Why I care what they think? Chee! You *Aussie*,' she spits. 'You think you're so good, but you all just want one thing. Disgusting, Donald. You *disgusting*.' She pronounces it 'diss-*kuss*-ding', making the very word sound soaked in filth. Trish begins to cry. 'Shh!' Madge hoists Trish onto her hip, causing the baby's head to wobble dangerously from side to side.

'Here, give me the baby,' Donald says before he can stop himself. For a second Trish is not Trish but Donald's little brother Ronnie, and Madge is not Madge but Donald's mother Rose, who has started shaking Ronnie over the water drum when no answers are forthcoming. Donald can practically hear the soft, pliable neck cracking until Rose finally drops the baby, letting him fall into Donald's arms.

Donald holds out his hands but Madge lets go of Trish quicker than he expects, making him stumble forward to catch her. For the briefest second he wonders, *What am I doing?* But then he bounces Trish up and down, gradually reducing her cries to a whiny hiccupping. Avoiding Madge's eyes, he reaches one hand into his pocket for a clean hanky to wipe away the white baby spew that now decorates the shoulder of

155

his shirt. 'There, there,' he soothes. 'It's all right, it's all right. Mummy not mad at you, she mad at me, see?'

Molly laughs at his joke and looks meaningfully at Madge. Madge clears her throat but says nothing. Molly shakes her head. 'Chee, Madge, you crazy!' she laughs.

'Chee, Donald,' Madge says, trying to regain the high ground. She looks Donald in the eye. 'You not come this afternoon now la,' she states rather than asks.

'Of course I still come!' Donald feels indignant. He has just been thinking the same thing, but hearing Madge say it out loud is what changes his mind. He will go out with her tonight as planned, show her he isn't the type of bloke to run at the sight of a bit of baby spew. Then he can break it off at his next weekend leave. He will even get her a parting-of-the-ways present, just to show no hard feelings. He pictures himself quietly pressing a gift into Madge's hand, plus a little something in a red packet to help out with the baby. She will bow her head in gratitude, and Molly will look on, impressed, and offer him food and drinks, but he will hold up his hands, palms outward, and say, *Now ladies, no need to make a fuss.* Then he will kiss Madge on the cheek (or perhaps the forehead? The forehead) and say goodbye. If he bumps into Madge he will always make sure to ask after the baby's health. *One of the good ones*, the women will murmur to each other as they watch him walk by.

'I see you at eight, all right, Madge?' And before Madge can say anything else, Donald jerks Trish's hands up and down in a comical baby dance, making Madge and Molly giggle.

* * *

It's five past three and Trish is yet to arrive. I stand up from the bench and walk back along one of the Zimmer-frame-accessible paths towards the carpark to wait. Perhaps it is being at a memorial garden, listening to the voices of the dead, that makes me do it. On an impulse I get back in my car and open the glove box, my fingers gripping the plastic container of powder before my frontal lobe has had a chance to intervene. The lid is half off before I can remind myself, *Not yet.* I remove my hands from the lid slowly as if it were a ticking bomb or a sleeping baby. *Just a few more days.*

Trish pulls up next to me and I pretend I am just emerging from the car myself. We hug awkwardly, Trish holding herself in a muscular position ready to move on.

Evan taught me how to hug. He used to laugh at me in the early days of our courtship, the way I would hold him in my arms but not allow any other part of my body to touch his. 'Kathy come here, you don't have to time it.'

I had not even realised that at the back of my head there was a counter, ticking to ten, the amount of time required to fulfil the rudiments of an embrace. With Evan I gradually learned how to relax my muscles and allow my body to meet his. I began to enjoy the sensation of being held.

I blame you of course: your hugs always seemed to demand something of me, so I developed my at-a-distance technique. But after I met Evan, and after you lost the ability to speak and move, I began to throw my arms around you, rest my face against your softness. Perhaps because you could no longer ask anything of me, I was finally ready to give.

Trish pulls out of the hug (two seconds – she is busier than me). 'Sorry I'm late,' she says. 'Had to check on a patient. Surgery can wait until tomorrow though.'

'If you need to go,' I start, but she shakes her head briskly.

'All good, my registrar will keep me posted.' She marches towards the reception building.

So here we are, come to organise your cremation, Annie. Your ashes will be interred next to our father with an empty space on your other side for our mother. Annie, the perennial child, buried between your parents like a babe who has passed before her time.

The Mount Cotton Memorial Gardens reception has in pride of place an accent-lit cabinet of urns of various sizes and finishes. We are met by a middle-aged woman wearing a suitably solemn expression.

'Hel-lo, I'm Di-aaana.' I think her sing-song voice is meant to put us at ease. 'I'm so-ooo sorry for your lo-osssss.' She pauses to look each of us in the eye for a moment. We stare back, giving nothing away.

We follow Di-aaana into a meeting room. A small round table holds a suite of brochures fanned out artfully on its gleaming pine surface. *What is it with these small round tables?* I wonder. Perhaps there was a funeral industry special at Officeworks. I have yet to see a computer or even an actual desk, as if the sight of such workaday objects might suddenly give away the business nature of these people's sympathy for our 'loss'.

Di-aaana is flipping through the pamphlets, glancing from us to the pages and back again, attempting to gather from our unmoving faces some clue about our price sensitivity. We do not make it easy for her: there is Trish, who introduced herself as Doctor Bradley and is wearing a smart silk trouser suit, a chunky necklace and designer glasses. And then there is me, looking like I slept in my clothes (which I did) and have not met a hairbrush in several days because, unsurprisingly, a hairbrush was not in the self-led death kit that was all I had with me when Val called and told me you were dying for real this time.

Even at the best of times, Trish and I don't look very alike. She is the only one of the Bradley girls with an athletic physique, the only one who escaped the curse of the Bradley butt, the genetic inheritance of Dad's mild scoliosis and Mum's Mongol peasant thighs. Trish was always your favourite of the big kids, and I am pretty sure that you were her favourite out of the two of us. If you knew the truth about her, you never told me. You had your secrets, Annie, just like everyone else in this family.

It took me a while to work it out, but once I got hold of Dad's army records after his death back in 2001, it all began to make sense. The Australian Army had kept a record of everything. Those files answered more questions than I had ever wanted to ask.

* * *

By the time Donald gets his next weekend leave, the wet season is in full swing and it is too rainy to be outdoors for long. He and Madge spend the weekend cooped up in the hotel room, and by Sunday evening he has not had a chance to buy her that gift. Another two leave passes; another two rained-in weekends. Still, Donald feels all right about it. He isn't the kind of bloke to just stop showing up. He is going to do the thing properly.

At last, the sun breaks through the heavy clouds. Madge is wearing a green dress; he feels her nipples press against his chest when they kiss hello. They can go out a bit later to the night markets, he thinks, leading her upstairs.

The windows are beginning to darken with the coming afternoon thunderstorm when Madge rolls out from under him. Donald throws an arm over her soft body and dozes, murmuring the occasional 'Mm-hmm' in response to her words.

'You take me back to Australia,' she states suddenly. 'Donald? You got to take me there.'

He struggles against the waves of sleep. 'What?'

'I due in March.'

'What? You're pregnant?'

'Donald, I *say* that!'

'No, you didn't!' he protests but doubt slithers into his mind. Did she just tell him that? He can't remember. She

160

talks so much, especially straight afterwards when he is only half awake.

'How do you know?' he asks.

'I tell you! I miss my, you know,' she says. 'When you get leave for registee? When we go back to Australia?' She stares straight at him.

'Wait on, wait on,' Donald replies, combing his fingers through his thinning hair – he is only twenty-two but has already lost more than a third of the hair he is entitled to.

'You go get the form? Donald, I told you, chee wiz! You got to fill out forms from the registee.'

Registry, Donald translates mentally. 'We— are you sure?'

At this, Madge explodes. 'What you mean, am I sure? Of course I sure. Chee wiz! What you think?'

'All right, don't get your knickers in a knot. We just have to think this through.' Donald's mind races. Can he give her some money, let her 'deal' with it? But … he contemplates a thousand years of purgatory accompanied by an unbaptised foetus.

He could keep giving her money once he went home. He isn't a shirker.

'You no good! Donald, I know you! I know what you like!' She sneers at his wilted penis as if she can read his mind and starts slapping him all over his bare, unprotected skin. He covers himself, grabbing at the sheets as he stumbles out of bed. She screams, 'You make me *sick*!'

'Stop it, Madge, stop it!' Madge has also got up, stark naked, and continues to rain her open palms down on him. 'Madge, settle down! We have to get dressed and go!'

'Why? Where you go?'

'I have to get you a ring!' he shouts. In the silence that follows his words he straightens and assumes a look that he hopes conveys injured nobility.

'I come and choose with you?' She watches him closely.

'No, you can't do that, silly woman,' he shakes his head. 'Bad luck.' *There is nothing these chinks hate more than bad luck,* he thinks.

Her eyes are black abacus beads clicking from side to side. 'You meet me after?'

'Yes,' Donald laughs. 'Of course!'

'Mate, there are no medic transfers within the theatre,' Kez repeats. 'Not for the next six months.'

Donald flops onto his pillow. After extricating himself from Madge he came straight back to base to find Kez.

'Come on, Softie! You'll never get one as good-looking back home, no offence mate. And these China-girls, they do everything for you.' Kez has a new girl to whom he is already engaged and she isn't even in a family way. 'I don't just mean cooking and cleaning, though that too, yeah, and the food, it's so much better than the stuff back home.'

Donald agrees with that: Malayan food had been like a spiritual awakening for his stomach and, despite frequent bouts of the runs, he would miss it. But Madge could not cook. She had grown up with servants, she had told him in the early days of their courting, and he had boasted, 'Everyone is rich in Australia.' He squeezes his eyes shut at his own stupidity.

'But aren't you worried about your mum and dad?' Donald asks Kez, eyes still shut as if he could block out the sight of his own looming life. He pictures Madge in her green dress, hobbling across the Bradleys' sorry excuse for a farm, where they harvest more stones than potatoes; meeting Donald's father, skin as corrugated as the tin roof of the family's cottage from years of thankless labour; Donald saying, 'Dad, this is your new daughter-in-law.'

'Mate, they'll be all right! You'll be the only bloke at Holsworthy without a Chinese wife if you don't look out! Better off getting yourself one now, before the good ones are all gone.'

'She already has a baby,' Donald admits.

Kez whistles. They both lie back on their stretchers. 'Well. Is this one yours?'

'Yeah, of course,' Donald replies. 'Kez, what if—' Donald tries to make his next question seem a joke. 'What if I can't, you know, *love* the baby?'

It is possibly the first time Donald has ever said the word 'love' out loud. When he left Crookwell, his father had muttered, 'You know, son, I, your, your mother always loved you,' and Donald had ducked his head and replied, 'Yeah.'

'It won't look like a real baby. I mean, you know, a normal baby, like you or me,' he says. Even Esme's baby, his little brother Ronnie, had the blue eyes and ruddy cheeks of their father.

'Ohh, come off it, Softie!' Kez pushes him off his stretcher. Donald clambers back up. 'Look, what do you expect?' Kez speaks reasonably. 'She's Chinese, and when you have babies, they're going to look Chinese. It'll be fine. You're going to be a good dad, and a bloody better husband than I ever would be.' He grabs Donald by the hair and wrestles him into a pretend chokehold. 'All I can say is you better pray to bloody Christ he doesn't look like you!' he laughs.

'Yeah, you too, you ugly bastard,' Donald replies, shoving his heavy gut against Kez's head until Kez finally breaks his hold, shouting, 'I can't breathe, you cunt! Gerroff!'

'So? You're going to do it?' Kez asks once he gets his breath back.

'Yeah.'

Kez yanks Donald off the bunk and drags him into the common room. 'Softie's getting married! Someone get the beers!'

Kez holds a bottle aloft. 'There's a girl who has found the hard man we never believed you had in you, Softie, although *clearly* you have had it in her,' Kez crows. The other men cheer.

'Careful, Kez, you're talking about my future wife,' Donald admonishes. Kez ruffles Donald's quiff and Donald grins. Someone takes his empty and hands him a fresh one, which he gulps down in two.

* * *

I can understand why Mum married Dad: a woman with a baby in 1959 Penang was a woman who needed a man. But what was it that got Dad down the aisle in a black suit, with a studio photo afterwards, incontrovertible proof that he entered into the state of matrimony with our mother with consent on both sides? He could have walked away, back to Crookwell, straight through the swinging doors of the Grand Hotel. The publican would have pulled him a schooner, on the house for his service to the nation, and he could have regaled his brothers about the Penang girls.

I suppose it was his Catholic upbringing, forcing him to do the 'right thing'. But was it also, could it have been, love?

* * *

The next day, Donald asks Madge to sit at the hotel room's small round coffee table.

'I'll take care of you and the little one,' he says. 'There'll be plenty of other Chinese wives on base, so you won't be lonely.'

Madge remains silent.

The ring! Donald had almost forgotten. He reaches into his top pocket and withdraws a small velvet box.

'Here you are. I hope you like it.' The ring is shaped like a flower with diamonds in the petals. Kez helped him choose it at the night markets, after an afternoon of celebratory boozing. The ring is small enough to be inexpensive but set so cunningly that the whole thing sparkles in the light.

Madge's face opens. 'OK,' she replies.

'OK?' Donald laughs. 'Does that mean yes, you'll marry me?'

'Yes, yes, Donald,' she giggles. 'We get it resize? It too big for me.'

Donald feels like he might burst; his grin stretches from ear to ear. He has made the right decision. He swings her hand, making the ring jiggle loosely on her finger on their way to the jeweller, but he doesn't care – he wants to hold her hand as high as it will go so everyone will know that he asked and she said yes.

Madge interrupts his thoughts. 'The ring, it bit too big for my finger ah? Maybe something else fit better? I see a girlfriend, she have diamond this big,' she makes a circle with her fingers. 'Her boyfriend spend six month wages on it. He in army too.'

Donald's smile narrows. 'Madge, you can't swap your engagement ring. It's a gift. It's not like' – he searches for something she might understand – 'a dress, or a pair of shoes. I gave it to you. It's from *me*.' He places a palm against his heart.

'Oh, OK, OK,' she giggles. 'Donald softie,' she adds, taking her hand out of his to adjust her dress.

* * *

I always thought that Mum's engagement ring was very pretty, and she wore it for more than thirty years, until she sold it, along with all her other jewellery, to a loan shark at the TAB. Mum without her bracelets and rings was one of the saddest things I have ever seen.

Not that she needed the money. Trish, Val, Brian and I paid for Dad's funeral expenses and all Mum's bills after Dad died. Dad's army records for Malaya included a letter of claim from a Penang hotelier, sent to my father's commanding officer a year after his return to Australia. It seems that taking care of Mum was always an expensive business.

To be honest, all of us Bradleys are terrible with money. We just don't understand how it works. Val readily admits that she learned about fiscal management from her unfunny but prudent husband. Barb married someone as materialistic as herself, and since her divorce she has rotated her calls to each of us for loans. Brian's money anxiety expresses itself in a confusing combination of stinginess and materialism, while Bev – well, I've already told you how I feel about the golden car.

Dad's files told the extent to which Dad was in and out of (mostly in) debt throughout his life, providing a bit of context to the credit card bills I had found in his shoeboxes after he died. But after you got sick, Dad gave up all his vices: the gambling, the drinking. Mum went the opposite way, doubling down on her gambling; I do not have a single memory of her without a race guide or TAB tickets close to hand. When we were kids Dad made sure that bills were paid and there was always food on the table. He did his best. That might not have been great by some people's standards, but for me, it was enough.

* * *

Donald has been married for four years when he seeks, and secures, a tour to Vietnam. Which is just as well. Donald needs the Vietnam allowances. Madge miscarried the baby that got them to the 'registee', and Donald, in his darker moments, wonders if there had ever been one to begin with. But even if there wasn't a baby then, there are more than enough now. Since their marriage, he and Madge have had two children, plus they have Trish and another on the way, so Donald needs all the extra loading that active duty can offer.

He wonders for the hundredth time why Madge is not like the other wives. They seem in awe of their husbands, and he is sure they do not expect their men to hand over their pay cheques, no questions asked. The other men certainly aren't about to have four screaming children under the age of four; although that, he knows, is not really Madge's fault. He is not very good at timing it, that's all; and then before he knows it, she is throwing up into the toilet bowl and he is looking for another posting, the next training camp – anything to earn a few extra quid. And get some days of quiet into the bargain.

Even so, ten wakeys into his year-long tour, he is already fantasising about leaving Vietnam right here, right now, and going back to his army-owned house at the Holsworthy base in western Sydney. Things were always good after he returned, even if just from a practice bivouac. The kids were so happy to see him that they behaved well, clamouring to sit on his lap. Madge would stand in the kitchen doorway, smiling and asking him if he felt hungry. His shoulders would dip; he would rest his head back against his chair and begin to think, *It will always be like this*; until, of course, it was not.

Sometimes he got a week, although more often just two or three days, before she would start getting on his case again, nagging about the bills or complaining about his going out for a drink ('Just a drink! With a mate!'), until it would all come to a head in a shouting match, her screaming, him protesting and falling over the furniture to get away from her slapping hands and that bloody rolling pin. Donald is not a violent man and would never raise a hand against his wife or children. But Madge does not have the same qualms about him or the kids.

When it came it was almost a relief, like the start of the wet season here in Vietnam. Madge would slap one of the girls and the girl would cry. Madge would shout, 'Stop crying! Chee!' and the child would gulp, but be unable to check the tears, making Madge scream louder. She would turn to another child, striking her if the girl were stupid enough to still be within arm's length. Madge would scream, 'You just as bad! You no good, make me sick!'

Donald might say something like, 'Stop it, Madge, just stop it.' Then she would round on him and it would really get going. 'You worse than the lot of them. You no good, always drinking, thinking you Christian, you so good, better than other people, but you not, you make me sick!'

Donald would shout over his shoulder, 'You crazy, woman,' and then stomp down to the rec club, not thinking of what she might do to the children in his absence; not thinking at all until the third cold beer in his hand relaxed him enough to turn around from the bar and see who might be up for a flutter.

That's a positive about being in Vietnam: there is always a little Vietnamese man, only a little lame, who will run your bets into town for you, limping across miles of mud and jungle for a few cents.

Finally, after a five-hour march that felt like ten, Donald sees the Nui Dat camp rise out of the fields ahead of them, with camouflage mesh strung around the perimeter like a ragged welcome home banner. Donald thinks he can hear something deep and bass-y, more like a vibration in the ground than an actual sound.

'That'll be Little Pattie, getting ready for the concert tomorrow,' the signalman says, ear tilted upwards. Donald's own ears ring to the note of C these days – a gift from the relentless mating call of the helicopters.

The next afternoon, Donald joins the others at the dustbowl – the dirt amphitheatre at one end of the camp where the troops have set up a makeshift stage for the entertainment.

Donald doesn't even know who these entertainers are, but he has heard that they play a bit of country music, which sounds good to him. He has his field glasses with him, and some of the other men look at them enviously.

Little Pattie is a blonde in a short skirt and looks no older than a teenager. For a moment Donald has to do a double-take: a girl like this against the backdrop of the jungle, the sound of mortars in the distance – it just isn't the way nature had ordered things. But the moment passes, and he turns his attention briefly to Col Joye, who plays the guitar and croons with a rockabilly lilt to his voice. The music is good, even over the tinny loudspeakers.

Just as the musicians finish their set, choppers fly overhead and the siren sounds. Donald, who has been lingering to see if he can get an autograph, turns and races to the field ambulance dust-off pad. Casualties are arriving from a plantation called Long Tan, where D Company patrolled today, looking for the VC that the radios had been picking up over the last few days but so far no one had sighted. Donald is put to work, carrying men from the helicopters, inserting drips, bandaging, suturing, cleaning wounds, checking temperatures and pulses, closing eyelids. He is relieved at ten pm, but only because he is detailed to accompany D Company the next day on what his superior officer ominously calls 'the clean-up'. That night they have a stand-to, so by the time five am roll call comes around, Donald is asleep on his feet. He and the company set off to Long Tan.

It's a battlefield, if you can call a swamp covered with dead bodies that. The smell is unbearable. Donald ties a handkerchief over his face, his glasses fogging up with the sweat and damp. He puts on a pair of surgical gloves and offers some to the others nearby, but pretty soon they are slippery with blood and mud and he strips them off, favouring his bare hands for the job. Donald is to search and identify dead bodies, as well as treat any living he finds, including VC (who might, after all, have useful information). So far he has found seven VC bodies which he has searched gingerly, in case they died holding grenades at the ready, or are not actually dead.

In some parts of the sodden field, the slide marks of bodies being dragged through the mud are unmistakable. The VC have been busy during the night, reclaiming their own, but even to Donald it is obvious that there are a lot more enemy corpses here than Aussies. The sheer volume of the dead is staggering: before today, Donald had only ever seen VCs in small groups: two, maybe three, in sight. He has treated VCs at the base, bandaging their wounds while guards pointed guns at their heads, and this is what he pictures when he thinks of the VC: handfuls of men, roaming the jungles in an almost accidental semblance of order. Now, looking across the field, he is reminded of what the VC really are: an enemy army. The thought is almost more sobering than the job at hand.

It is five minutes to smoko when he finds his first Aussie. Donald identifies him as a D Company man and calls for a stretcher. Leaning down, he covers the eyes with a muddy handkerchief (they are too stiff to close) and fingers a packet out of the dead man's pocket. The tobacco is mostly sodden from the rain, but one or two that the man must have pre-rolled are dry enough to attempt. Donald nods at the corpse, beginning to wonder if he should put the packet back; if perhaps his mother or best friend should receive the soggy leaves along with the other effects.

He casts his eyes down and mumbles, 'Our Father, who art in heaven, hallowed be thy name ...' When he is finished his prayer, he keeps his eyes closed for a moment before lighting up, shielding the flame with his hand. Faint messages of smoke curl towards the sky from other men scattered across the field who, like him, are resting for a moment among the dead.

Dad was sixty-four years old when he died in his sleep. The attending doctor wrote 'ischemic heart attack' on the death certificate after our sisters told him he was a veteran. I took Mum and that death certificate to the RSL where a big, beefy fellow with a red nose organised the paperwork for Mum to get a war widow's pension, worth $30 more than the old age pension per fortnight.

Do you remember the rosary ladies from church telling us what an auspicious date Christmas Eve was to die; that only someone truly holy could have died on such a date? As if that could somehow make up for the way I found him that morning, just hours after he and I had fought. The first Bradley death to be my fault. Not the last.

* * *

It is Christmas Eve, 2001, and I nurse secret hopes for a conflict-free Christmas. Barb and Val each have toddlers and husbands, which encourages both sisters to reduce their usual animosity to a gentle simmer for the sake of the children. Brian just finished his second year as a maths teacher at a Gold Coast Catholic school and is bringing his new girlfriend to lunch, which means it's serious. Even Bev and her family are sorting themselves out, living in a caravan park north of Brisbane on the Sunshine Coast while they pay off the debts from her husband's failed bobcat business. Trish has loaned them enough to get the more insistent creditors off their backs. You are responding pretty well to your meds, sleeping a lot but not having psychotic episodes.

Dad is the only one to worry about. He has had heart troubles off and on and was diagnosed with prostate cancer at the start of the year. He is receiving excellent medical treatment: his application for Total and Permanently Impaired Veteran status was approved, and I can tell that he secretly enjoys being chauffeured to his appointments in government cars. But since he retired at the end of 2000, Dad says his 'nerves' have been playing up. We encourage him to seek treatment, and I cite studies about the high incidence of post-traumatic stress disorder among Vietnam veterans. He now counts a psychiatrist among his specialists, but he complains of all the pills he is required to take and has started drinking, even though he thinks we don't notice. I found a cask of moselle in the laundry basket last week – it had leaked all over the whites. I threw it straight into the wheelie bin before Mum saw it.

I have just completed my Honours year in psychology and am working through the summer as a checkout chick at Coles with a doctoral scholarship starting next year, studying the variable of temperament in the life outcomes of siblings.

Unlike many of my peers, I really enjoy the statistical side of research. I like the idea that woolly concepts like love, hate, sorrow and joy can be broken down into measurable effects. I especially like the puzzle of designing the methodology for a research project. How do you control for all the variables when you are trying to measure the impact of one particular life event on a person's future outcomes? Say, for example, a woman ends her own life. Of her two children, one becomes a drug addict and ends up in jail, while the other trains as a mental health worker, marries and has a family. How do two people who have experienced the same event experience such different life trajectories?

My feet are aching from standing all day, scanning people's Christmas puddings and fruit mince pies. I am looking forward to a shower to get the smell of plastic packaging off me before we go to Christmas Eve mass. But when I get home, Dad is slumped in his armchair, a half-empty glass of rosé in his hand.

Anger unexpectedly roils inside me like a power surge in a faulty circuit. It's Christmas Eve, for crying out loud. He is rostered on as a Eucharistic minister.

'Dad,' I say, trying to keep my voice even, 'You shouldn't be mixing alcohol with your meds.'

'Argh, those meds.' Dad sets his mouth like an obstinate boy and gets up to fill his cup from the boxed wine which he has left openly next to the fridge, at least while Mum is out with Barb. He pours a plastic cup of wine for me.

'Come on, 'ave a drink with me.'

'Go on, Kathy. Have a drink with Dad,' you say. He won't pour one for you because of *your* meds, but here he is, blithely swigging away.

I twist my entire body away from the cup. Dad doesn't seem to notice or care about my silent protest. He plops back heavily into his armchair and starts talking. It's a long, meandering diatribe about his various illnesses. Soon enough he returns to his favourite anthem of late: how the big kids don't treat him right.

'After all I did for them,' he shakes his head. 'I painted Trish's house for her, you know. And does she ever call? Does she ever visit?'

'She's a doctor,' I remind him. 'She's busy.'

'Bah, doctor. She just doesn't appreciate me. Doesn't care. None of them care.'

He gets up to refill his glass before sliding unceremoniously to the dining room floor. You reach down and pluck ineffectually at his clothes.

'All I want is a little affection,' he slurs. He waves the glass, making the drink slop from side to side. 'I can't even get it up anymore.'

'Come on, Kathy!' You have given up pulling at him but you are still bending over, trying to give him a hug. I absolutely will not touch him. Everything inside me curdles at the thought of my body being anywhere near that sweet-smelling skin.

I grab my car keys. 'I'm taking Annie to Christmas mass.'

'Lemme get dressed,' he says, trying to stand. He stumbles, then puts his head back down on the ground, giggling and weeping. Dad has always been a soppy drunk, leaking sentiment all over the carpet.

'I'm disappointed, Dad.'

That's not completely true. What I am, though I can't say it, is afraid. It's not that Dad usually makes me feel safe – he has never been able to protect us or himself from Mum. But when he is like this he threatens something more basic than safety from harm. It's a constancy, a steady there-ness: Dad in his armchair, Dad complaining about traffic, Dad arguing with Mum. It might seem a rather shaky base in the world but it is mine.

'If you aren't in bed by the time we get back, I will be very … *cross*,' I finish lamely.

'Bah,' he says again, and waves me away.

At mass, the Christmas carols and festive candles cheer me up. I don't believe in God any more, but I do believe in Christmas: families coming together, drivers waving each other ahead at roundabouts. On the way home from mass, we meet Mum and Barb at the TAB, say goodbye to Barb, and return home to find Dad already snoring in bed. You, Mum and I watch the Christmas carols on Channel Nine as we do every year, eating scorched almonds and singing along to the old favourites.

I wonder, as I do every year, how Rhonda Burchmore makes a living on the other 364 days: the only time I ever see her is gussied up, singing 'Joy to the World', hands bouncing the sky. If Dad were awake, we would all be forced into a rendition of 'The Little Drummer Boy'. *I am a poor boy too, pa-rum-pa-pum-pum.* His favourite.

After the last carol, I help you into your pyjamas and put toothpaste on your toothbrush. I have been yawning since the traditional visit from Santa Claus to the stage of the Myer Music Bowl. I should sleep well tonight.

Only a few hours later, I jolt awake. I tiptoe quietly down the hallway to the loo so as not to wake anyone. I hear snoring from Mum and Dad's room. It is louder than normal, and has a crackle and rattle to it, like someone is half-choking, trying to breathe phlegm out through their ribcage.

I keep walking down the hallway; part of me will always be walking down that dark hallway. I remember what I said to him before going to mass, and I think, *If he dies, it will be his own fault.*

In the morning, Mum says not to wake Dad as he has been having such trouble sleeping in the last few months, but something impels me back down the hallway. I open the door. He is not breathing. Something black oozes out the corner of his mouth and nose.

In what seems like mere seconds, the house is full of Bradleys. I hear a keening noise and turn around, and the sound is coming from *Mum.* It is the first time in my life that I have seen her cry. Barb puts an arm around her. You are prostrate on the couch, and Trish is checking your blood pressure.

I pull Val aside. I have to tell someone.

'I had a fight with him before he went to bed,' I say. 'And then later, I heard him snoring so loudly, and I thought – but I didn't *mean* it. I never thought death was a real possibility!'

I burst into tears. Trish and Val exchange glances, and Val heads down the hallway to take her turn with Dad's body while Trish pats me on the back.

'Listen to me, Kathy,' she says in her authoritative doctor's voice. 'What you heard was the death rattle.'

Trish looks at Mum, who stutters, 'I was next to him all night, I should have known.'

'Once a person makes that noise, it's the end. *Neither* of you,' she nods towards Mum and me, 'could have done anything for him. I am a doctor. I have heard that rattle hundreds of times. Do you understand? By the time you heard that sound, he was already gone.'

In the days between the death and the funeral, I go through the paperwork Dad kept stored in a number of shoeboxes. I know it's busy work – my sisters just want to keep me occupied – but I will do it properly. It is the last thing I can do for Dad.

I sit on the carpet in our parents' bedroom and rummage under the bed. There are two boxes, one labelled 'Bills', the other 'Receipts'. I methodically sort through dozens of papers about pharmaceuticals, paid bills, income tax assessments. I come across a credit card bill, then another, and another. It takes me a few minutes to understand what I am seeing. Here are bills for, I shuffle some papers – five maxed-out cards, each from a different bank.

There may be a logical explanation, I tell myself. *Just be systematic.* Under the bills, I find the explanation, but it is not logical. It does not make any sense at all. There is a letter on yellow stationery. Then another. And another.

When I show Val the credit card bills, the yellow letters, she just says, 'Oh, Dad,' as if she has been waiting for something like this. When I ask her why she is not more surprised, she just sighs and says, 'Dad was into that sort of thing before you two were born.' *What was he into exactly?* I want to shout. *Debt? Extramarital affairs with girls who draw love hearts over their i's?*

Later that day there is a knock on the front door. I get there before Val can, and standing with her fist raised to knock again is a young woman who cannot be older than me. She has long, straggly brown hair, a skinny frame, desperate eyes.

'I'm looking for Donny?' she says, eyes darting.

'He's dead,' I reply, and slam the door in her face.

For Dad's funeral, my sister Barb gives the undertakers the most ridiculous clothes I have ever seen. A completely mismatched summer shirt and shorts from Lowes which she claims she had been about to give Dad for Christmas. At the church his body rests in a polished wooden coffin, his head dignified despite the lurid red hibiscus flowers of the jolly holiday fabric covering his chest. I look at him and wonder if the body has released the soul entire. Or has the soul been frozen too, suspended in the ice that preserves him so that I have a chance to say goodbye? I lean down to Dad. To an observer it would appear as though I am kissing his cheek. I whisper, 'I don't feel anything. I don't feel anything at all.'

I deliver the eulogy. When I return to my pew afterwards, I hear an animal howl as if the moon has set for the last time. Mum hands me a tissue, her own eyes red, and you, Annie, you put your arm around me. 'Shh, Kathy,' you say. 'Shh, now.'

A week after Dad's funeral, our sisters, brother and I have a family meeting about you. Mum has always taken care of your physical needs – bathing, eating – but Dad and I have been your conduits to a social life: I would take you to see movies and live music, and Dad and I would schedule one night a week for board games and card games to keep you mentally alert. Dad used to take you to mass and you would go along with him on volunteer catechism lessons, although recently he had been leaving you at home, which I now realised was so he could visit his yellow letter friend.

I had imagined Dad's retirement as a halcyon age for you, Annie, and a reduction of the burden on me. But now that Dad has died, you will be home alone with Mum, and it's implicitly understood by everyone at the table that is not a good option.

The waiter has just delivered our cups of coffee when Trish and Barb look at Val, who nods and turns to me. 'It's just an idea, but – do you think you could stay at home? Just for a while? We think, well,' she laughs, trying to lighten her words, 'Annie might need a chaperone.'

Barb nods thoughtfully, as if this is the first time she has heard this proposal. Trish shifts in her chair, and Brian stares into his latte. Bev is not here – we find out later that she was halfway to Bundaberg by the time I got my peppermint tea.

I see the years stretch ahead of me: Mum demanding lifts to the TAB, you relying on me more and more. 'I can't,' I say without thinking. 'I'm moving.'

'Yes, I know you are, but this way you could save on rent, and—'

'No, I'm *moving* moving. To Sydney.' I name the first place that comes into my head.

'Oh. I didn't know.' Barb tries to stare me down. I maintain eye contact.

'It's your turn to take care of her,' I shrug at the Bradleys, four sets of brown eyes all now turned towards me, the first time in my life I have ever had their undivided attention. *It's my turn,* I think, almost hysterical, my heart beating a tattoo in my chest, the blood pumping so loudly in my ears that I can barely hear the scratch of aluminium on concrete as I push my chair back.

'I have to go. I have a lot to organise. I leave next week.'

Val's mouth is still open as I walk out. When I am well out of view, I double back to an internet cafe. I type 'psychology graduate positions, Sydney' into the search bar, and settle in for a long night.

It turns out that a first-class Honours degree in psychology qualifies me to work in exactly one field: human resources. I secure a graduate job in the HR section of the New South Wales Department of Education. I load up my rattly old Subaru Leone with books and clothes and drive down the New England Highway, stopping only for fuel and pee breaks. I can't stop crying. I can't stop picturing your face as I drive away.

It doesn't take me long to decide that I do not like Sydney. I do not like the way Sydney people look at me as if they are sizing up my square footage and finding it wanting. I do not like the smug excess of the place, the way its residents take credit for its golden beaches, its sea-salt air, its crystal harbour. I cannot understand directions; people use street names rather than motorway exit numbers. Brisbane is interlaced with freeways and toll roads, a heart encircled by arteries.

My boss is not much older than me but is far more put together, adorned by a husband and asymmetrical, local designer jewellery. She invites me to Friday afternoon drinks. I don't want to go – I have the enzymes of our mother's side of the family and flush whenever I so much as smell a glass of house red. The only alcoholic beverage I can drink without flaring up in hives is very expensive French champagne, which I doubt is on the wine list at Blood on the Tracks, the encouragingly named bar where work drinks invariably are held thanks to proximity rather than atmosphere. But, *You moved to Sydney!* I tell myself. *You can reinvent yourself as someone who goes to drinks!*

I sit at the table, nervously twiddling a champagne glass in my hand and smiling in case anyone looks my way, my neck turning red with every tiny sip. Next to me is someone's friend, or the friend of a friend. He is tall, thin, and for the first hour he completely ignores me. Six beers later, he turns to me with a grin.

I go home with him that night. He does not call me the next day, or the day after that. When I call him, he does not recognise my voice.

'Lachie, hi.'

'Who is this?'

'Kathy? From the other night?'

Pause. Sound of a liquid sliding down his throat. 'Oh Kathy, right. What are you doing later? Want to swing by?'

I think of my half-unpacked studio flat in the dodgy part of Surry Hills, and the cockroaches that I surprised in my bathroom the previous night at two am. I tell him I will be there in an hour.

Lachie lets me sleep on the carpet next to the bed, which suits me, because I have never been able to sleep in a bed with another person since I used to share with you – I just lie awake, hyper alert to any move the other person might make. In the mornings, he makes me leave before his housemates wake up, and that's fine because I need to get to work anyhow. A small part of me knows that this is not how a boyfriend is supposed to treat a girlfriend, but the larger me shouts that part down. When I go home to my empty flat – Lachie doesn't like to have sex when I have my period, so I have to go home every few weeks – the sound of silence is deafening. When I wake up alone, I realise all over again that Dad is dead, and the knowledge pins me to the bed with the full weight of grief. I lie in my bed, saturated with the pain of what I have lost. I never knew that Dad's love had knitted together calcium and carbon to create my bones. But I know it now as I feel it ebb away. I try, but I can't stay mad at Dad for the yellow letters or the debt.

When I am with Lachie I don't feel at peace but at least I can breathe. Things are going well for me. I have a relationship that has lasted longer than the Peter debacle. I have been losing weight since I met Lachie, and managed to rid myself of my virginity without letting Lachie know – he likes things a little rough anyway. I have a job and the people I work with seem to like me, enough to invite me to work drinks and sometimes even their own personal events.

On the three-month anniversary of our relationship, I buy a nice bottle of wine. I consider cheese and crackers but decide against them – last time I saw Lachie, he said something about love handles being a euphemism for fat, and pinched my hips, leaving a red mark.

When I arrive at his house he opens the door and smiles broadly. 'I've managed to get the housemates away so we have the place all to ourselves,' he says.

My heart leaps. *He has remembered.* I knew I just had to be patient. I hand him the bottle, which he cracks open and necks, and I head towards the kitchen, thinking we might order some dinner if his housemates are out, but he grabs my hand and leads me upstairs, two at a time, like a kid on Christmas Day, making me laugh. When we get to his room, I do not see rose petals or candles. There is a black cloth and a pair of handcuffs in the middle of his unwashed doona.

'Lie on your stomach,' he murmurs in my ear, making me shiver.

He grabs my hands and clinks the metal over them. I bite my lip, trying to keep an unreasonable panic from welling up and over, but when he puts the bandana over my eyes, I start screaming and screaming.

'Quiet!' he shouts, pulling the black cloth from my eyes and turning me over to face him. 'Do you want the neighbours to think I am fucking *raping* you?'

'I'm sorry, Lachie, I'm sorry.' I am sobbing. I don't know what is wrong with me. Everything has gone red, and I am four years old and I am on the bed, and someone is saying, 'Quiet,' and it is not Lachie. A memory has been ripped out of my viscera. The light of this memory has an orange cast to it, like the inside of a stomach, or a womb. There is someone touching me in a way an adult should never, ever touch a child. Although I am only four, I think, clear as a bell, *This is my fault.* Although I am only four, I think, *I must want this, because I want to be loved, and this is what you do for love.*

I murmur broken words. 'Shh, shh,' Lachie says, more gently now, holding me as I weep. He fetches me a tissue, and after I have run out of tears, he pulls the covers over both of us, letting me lie next to him. My heart might break open with the love I feel for him in that moment.

In my half sleep, I am hazily aware of a sensation of tugging. I try to move but someone has tied my arms to the bed frame. I want to shout *No!* but nothing comes out. The calm voice in my brain says, *This may seem bad, but look at it this way: it is the first time he has kept his eyes open during sex.* Afterwards, he whispers into the back of my head that he hoped he was helping with my healing. The calm voice continues in my head. *See? I told you it's all OK.*

While Lachie takes a shower I get out of bed, my whole body aching, and see bloodstains on his bed linen. I panic and tear the sheets from the mattress. I open my legs gingerly, the muscles spasming in my thighs. The source of the blood is not early menstruation, but a series of abrasions on the inside of my legs. I sigh with relief.

Over the next two weeks Lachie becomes more and more creative. Sometimes he uses the bandana, sometimes rope, handcuffs, sometimes belts. When I get my period he tells me to come back when it is done. I am surprised and even a little hurt. I thought we had grown beyond that.

At my apartment there is a notice in the mail from the National Archives in my letter box. My application to access Donald Bradley's military file has been approved. The letter was badly addressed and must have been sitting in a neighbour's mailbox until they shoved it into mine. It says that the file will be held in the Canberra Reading Room for one month before being sent back to the Archives. Standing at the kitchen bench, I scarf down toast with one hand and brush my hair with the other, my eyes resting on the letter. The final date for viewing is tomorrow.

The following day I am in the Subaru Leone. My boss told me to take as many days as I need, but I only need this specific one.

On the way to the national capital I take a pee break in a rest area named for a Victoria Cross holder. According to the sign, the Australian government dubbed this stretch of the A1 as 'Remembrance Highway', a 'living memorial' to those who served in World War II, the Korean War, the Malayan Emergency and the Vietnam War. It is about three hundred kilometres of smooth, four-lane road connecting Sydney and Canberra, making its way through the New South Wales granite belt where Dad grew up. Rows of hay bales lining the tops of hills appear deceptively bucolic; the languid, undernourished cattle and the skinny sheep waiting for rain to green the sides of these stony hills tell the real story. One match is all it would take to burn the whole country to the ground.

The National Archives Reading Room is open once a week on a Wednesday afternoon, so I time my arrival to alight into the blistering midday sun of the nation's capital. At the top of the street a man-made hill raises Parliament House aloft, the national flag hanging limp in the dry stillness. To the left of the Archives, national institutions line up like old men at a pub urinal, their fountains pissing into Lake Burley Griffin.

The lobby is small and stuffy, and I feel sorry for the receptionist until she tells me unsmilingly to place all my belongings in a locker and carefully examines my notebook, pencil and camera as if they might have Tardis-like qualities for smuggling out state secrets. The Reading Room itself is high-ceilinged and airy, and people are sitting at long desks, poring over folios like medieval limners illuminating the lives of the saints.

After about twenty minutes, an archivist bustles over to me, apologising for the delay – the file had been placed in someone's out-tray, ready to be returned to the off-site warehouse. She places a file as thick as the Bradley family Bible in front of me, and I am about to tell her she must have made a mistake – why would Dad, a mere lance corporal, have a file as long as my Honours dissertation? But there is our father's name on the cover, and, even more conclusively, there is his dog tag number.

The Reading Room is only open for another two hours, but still I hesitate. It feels wrong, almost sacrilegious, to simply open up the file and peer inside. I wonder if your neurosurgeon felt like this before he drilled a hole through your skull to reveal the sacred human within. I glance at the other readers, trying to work out what the etiquette is for shoving my hands into the guts of a man's life, but they offer no clue apart from the tradition of silence while reading. I whisper a wordless prayer, similar to grace before a meal, and open the file.

* * *

It's 1971 and Donald is thirty-five years old. He lives at Ingleburn, near the Holsworthy base, with his wife and five children. He is a private in the Australian Army, and he is broke.

The thing is, he was going to put it back. He had planned to get a part-time job and replace the money before anyone knew anything about it. It was just his luck that the army auditors would do a check two days before Christmas, only two weeks after he had borrowed the $500 from the regimental kitty.

They court martialled him, found him guilty of the lesser charge of negligence, and reduced him to the ranks. His army lawyer told him to be grateful. Private Donald Bradley. Thirteen years of service, two wars, five children (four of his own begetting). And here he is, back where he started, but far, far worse for wear.

Donald writes a note to Madge, seals it and leaves it on his desk so someone will see it and give it to her. He takes three canisters of sleeping pills from the store and pockets them, then grabs two more.

At the junction with New Illawarra Road, Donald turns left and heads north. He would like one more trip to the sea. After thirteen hours of driving, he crosses the state border and arrives at Surfers Paradise. Donald finds a carpark fronting on to sand dunes at Broadbeach. He is numb from driving, except for his arse, which aches from sitting for all those hours. He gets out, creaks forwards and backwards, trying to get some feeling into his arms and legs. His stomach churns disagreeably with the meat pies he ate at his last petrol stop in Murwillumbah. The taste of fatty mince is still in his mouth. He wishes he had brought his toothbrush.

Donald gets back into the car and lowers the seat back. It stinks like stale chips in here, but the sea breeze is getting chilly so he doesn't crack a window. He tries to make himself comfortable, but the seat back is unforgiving. Eventually he rolls over and puts his slouch hat over his eyes.

The last time the army had reduced him to the ranks was for something so trivial Donald still couldn't believe they had gone through with the whole court martial song and dance. Over a drink! It had been 1965, and Donald had still been young, only twenty-nine, but already he had Trish, Barb and Val at home – what man wouldn't need a drink? All he had done was fake a doctor's signature on a medical certificate so his mate Kez, Private John Kerry, could go with him to the pub. It should have been a fine and a clip over the ear, except that earlier in 1965, Donald had already been charged. Apparently he had walked off shift without cleaning the needles and been AWOL for three days. Conduct to the prejudice. Neglect to the prejudice. Conduct to the prejudice. Neglect to the prejudice.

For a moment the face peering through the window has slanted eyes and the angry mouth of the dispossessed. Instinctively Donald reaches for a weapon. His hand grazes the dials on the radio instead of the metal of a trigger.

'You can't sleep here, mate.' The man's features gradually settle into their actual lines: blue eyes squinting through the fogged glass of the Ford's window; perspiration starting under the copper's hat although it can't be later than 0600 hours.

'Sorry, officer,' he says. 'Just taking a nap.'

'Well, you can't nap here, mate. Move it along.'

Donald puts his seat back up and starts the engine before the copper can think twice about giving him a ticket. He heads back out on the Gold Coast Highway and stops at the nearest greasy spoon.

The pubs open at noon up here in Queensland. It is now 0915 hours. It's not true that he has a drinking problem. It's just that sometimes, in the beatific buzz between the third beer and the fourth, he can practically see his other self walk past, smiling and holding his hand up in a benign blessing of all the drunks in 1RAR, leaving him to sit at the bar and wonder who let in the draught.

Donald buys a newspaper. He has a good feeling about Mercy's Love, a roughie in Race 2 at Rosehill. Mercy's Love has gradually moved up from last place to eight then sixth at the last three meetings. It was time for it to peak.

Donald returns to his car and switches the radio to AM 1008.

'Aaaaand theeeeey're racing,' the caller announces. Donald grips the sides of the steering wheel. 'And Beauty's Loss coming up on the outside and Mercy's Love, it's Mercy's Love that has the lead, it's Mercy's Love a leg in front and Beauty's Loss coming up but Mercy's Love is across the line. It's Mercy's Love first place, then Beauty's Loss and Remember Martha in third place. Now to Doomben Race 3.'

'Yes!' Donald punches the ceiling of the car, making a light dust shower down on his head. He knew it! He should have put $1 on a win/place. At those odds, he would have won $20.

By the end of the week, Donald has used up all of his money, but instead of taking the pills, he drives to a used car lot and trades in the Ford Falcon for a slim wad of cash. He buys a train ticket and two sandwiches for the journey. He gets as far as Hornsby when two coppers board the train and place him under closed arrest. They have the photo of Donald from 1958, the one that the army took to use in news reports in case he was killed in action. In the picture, Donald is in full dress uniform and stands in front of an Australian flag.

'Let me see that?' he asks the copper, who shrugs at his partner and then hands it to him. Those old horn-rimmed glasses! The policeman doesn't ask for the photo back so after Donald is finished looking at it, it dangles between his cuffed hands, growing damp from the sweat on his fingers. The canisters he had taken from the RAP are in his back trouser pocket and make Donald shift around from butt cheek to butt cheek, trying to get some surreptitious relief from their constant pressure against his arse.

When they arrive at Central Station the coppers hand Donald over to two military policemen from Eastern Command. The MPs drive him home and place him under open arrest, telling him to report to HQ tomorrow at 0800 hours. 'Take me to the cells,' Donald almost says, but Madge is opening the door.

* * *

'Character: Weak' says one report in Dad's files. 'Friendly but lazy and needs to develop a sense of responsibility' says another. There is also 'Cannot be trusted to do his tasks without supervision,' 'This member has reached his zenith as an NCO and in light of the charges, should be reduced to private,' and my personal favourite, 'This NCO is apparently dominated by his wife. If a posting is not to her liking then the NCO becomes an administrative liability.'

From 1969 onwards the charges accumulate. I sort through page after page of demotions, more absences, more conduct to the prejudice. The records tell the story: before 1969, when he was still in his twenties and early thirties, the commanding officers saw our father as a harmless buffoon and treated his misconduct (drinking, clocking up bills) with a paternalistic eye. Boys, after all, will be boys. But as he gets older, the reports sound increasingly exasperated, ever curter, until the words stain the page with genuine dislike of Donald Bradley. The COs have no more patience for his complaints about not being made sergeant, or not getting a reposting. They don't want to hear about how sorely done by he is by his wife. *Be a man, Private Bradley*, seems to be the implied message in their disciplinary reports. *Take your hardening-up pills.* Poor old Dad. No one likes a man who stops at ninety yards in a hundred-yard race.

* * *

Donald gulps down a handful of tablets. *That'll show her I mean it*, he thinks furiously, shaking his head. Droplets of sweat land on the basin. Next to him is a mixed bag of tablets that he has pilfered from various lockers on his ward, a couple of wallets and a cheque book.

It is this last item that has him in here, holding a razor against the skin of his left wrist. Donald had found the cheque book in a patient's bedside table. He had looked at the blank pages and his heart had risen, unbidden, with wild hope. In that instant Donald could see his entire life rise and fall, like shaking a snow dome and watching his victory and ultimate demise play out in an Alpine village showered in plastic snowflakes. He could see a car free and clear, straight off the lot; an arm around Madge; them sweeping across the vista of New South Wales. *All this really is mine,* he would say, *just like I told you, only you wouldn't listen.* Madge would have to nod and agree that he was right. 'I'm sorry, Donald,' she would say. Yet as Donald saw this, he also saw the bleak holding cell; the contempt in the prosecutor's eyes. 'Guilty,' 'Guilty,' 'Guilty.' That was Donald all right. Guilty of hope.

That was when he had turned and walked into the staff toilet on level two of 1 Military Hospital.

Do it, he tells himself. He takes another slug of wine from the flagon. He turns his head and shuts his eyes, then lets himself fall against the razor while bracing himself against the sink's S-bend.

'Bloody hell!' he says out loud. His eyes swim. He takes another gulp of wine and repositions the razor against his right wrist. He stares at his outstretched arm and butts his body forward once, twice, trying and failing to push himself against the blade. As if he is being held back by invisible ropes, each one a child calling for him.

* * *

Di-aaana is pointing at the shelves of urns lining the walls of the room. They are tiered by price, the most expensive and elaborate at the top. I shake my head. You will not be any less dead if we pay $2000 for an oversized vase.

Trish shares my opinion. 'We do not actually need an urn. The standard receptacle that you place the ashes in will be fine.'

'Oh,' Di-aaana begins. 'We-eell, no-ooo, technically you don't *need* an urn, but most people do take comfort from placing the ashes of their loved ones in something a bit more personal. I think I read your sister was not even forty years of age? We have some lovely pink feathered urns here, perfect for a young woman?'

And just like that, I feel myself wavering. Annie, you did love pink.

'Last time I was here I was conned into buying an urn for our father, because I did not realise an urn is not compulsory.' Trish's voice is trembling with what even Di-aaana cannot mistake for sorrow. She stands and I scramble to follow suit. 'Send me an email confirming that we are booked in for a cremation this Saturday.'

'Tha-aannk you,' I say to Di-aaana as we leave the room. 'Remember to wear pi-iink on Saturday.'

I have to hurry to catch up with Trish who is heading towards Dad's plot. Instead of sitting on the bench, she remains standing, looking down at Dad's memorial plaque.

'Nice work back there,' I say. Trish shrugs.

Dad's plaque is bronze and has the Australian Army crest in the corner. Veterans Affairs stumped up a subsidy for it. Lest we forget, I suppose.

Trish wants to deliver a short speech at your funeral. At Dad's funeral she did not want to deliver the eulogy even though she was the eldest. Which I now understand but at the time I thought it was odd, because she normally always stood on her rights as the eldest, particularly over Barb. Trish refused even to do a reading at Dad's service, finally agreeing to deliver one of the prayers of the faithful. She stood at the lectern to read out her two lines, *May the Lord bless the sick, the sad and the lonely, Lord hear us,* and Doctor Trish's melodious, enunciated voice, which had for years overridden the cadences of our shared bogan youth, broke. Her husband, who had been standing right behind her, opened his arms and she stepped back into them without even needing to see if he was there.

Their relationship had always been a mystery to me: Trish her brusque and busy self, keeping words to a minimum to conserve all her available energy for working hundred-hour weeks; her husband the homemaker, cooking her dinner, packing her lunch, getting her a hot chocolate after she collapses on the couch to check her work emails after another fifteen-hour day on her feet in surgery. But there at the pulpit: a split second of surrender, Trish allowing herself to be supported, knowing he would be there. *Oh,* I had thought. *I get it now.*

* * *

A few days after I return from my Canberra trip, my period is finally over and I get the bus over to Lachie's place. When I knock, he calls out that he is in the kitchen. Tears well up in my eyes: it is the first time he has prepared a meal for us – well, he has ordered in pizza, and although pizza gives me heartburn, I munch through two pieces, not wanting him to think I don't appreciate the effort.

After dinner, we go upstairs and he tells me to bend over. I can feel the acid of tomato paste inflaming my chest. Bile rises up my throat, my body trying to restore balance. *This will only take a few minutes*, I tell myself. *When it's over, everything will be fine.*

'Is this how your daddy did it?' He cries as he shoves his bony hips against me.

'What are you saying?' I ask, but my voice is muffled by the doona.

Lachie climaxes and rolls off, panting hard.

I get up, wincing slightly from the pain his love-making always causes. The bile refuses to settle; I think I am going to throw up right there, all over Lachie's skinny white arse.

'I never said it was my dad,' I say slowly.

He sniggers with his eyes shut. 'It's always the dad.'

I wait until Lachie is snoring on his side before I pull my clothes on. I am shaking, so it takes longer than normal. I stand over my boyfriend, watching his face slack and at rest. I can almost picture what he might have looked like to his adoring mother, watching him sleep in his cot as a baby. Like a dog pissing on its territory, I spit on my finger and smear saliva across his forehead. *Forever mine.* He won't know it's there, but future girls will smell my mark on him and turn away, and he will rub his unsatisfied cock and wonder where he went wrong.

Lachie and I end things – I never call him again and he never called me at all. I find I don't miss him as much as I thought I would.

I get into the habit of going for long walks. I stay away from the densely forested national parks that surround the city, mindful of the bushfire risk; the dry spell continues unabated. I stick to the coastal paths, listening to the crash of the waves and mulling over the information in Dad's files, trying to match the man in the army documents with the man we knew. My favourite trail is the cliff walk from Bondi to Coogee, where the path hugs a jagged coastline that is alternately caressed and rammed by the ocean, like someone trapped in a violent marriage. I am trying to reconcile the Donald before 1983 and the Donald after. The Dad we knew was a man who worked night shifts so he could drive you to all your appointments. The Dad we knew was a man who did not run.

At work a colleague of mine named Jess asks me if I would like to come to her book club. She had mentioned it before, but I had been on my Lachie schedule. That night I show up at Gertrude and Alice's Bookstore where book club is held. Jess is sitting in a circle of smart-looking women wearing fashionable dresses and hairstyles, laughing over glasses of wine. I am about to back out of the shop when Jess spots me and waves. She is dressed in jeans and a woollen jumper that could have been knitted by a child on their first attempt, her ginger hair spilling in tangled curls down her back. She looks genuinely pleased to see me and gestures to a stool next to hers.

'How's your, um, friend? Lachie?' she asks.

'No longer my friend,' I reply.

'Oh *good!*' She giggles at her own reaction. 'Sorry, but – he is such an arsehole. You deserve way better than that.'

Do I? I wonder. I take the seat she has saved for me.

I diligently go to book club every month, and Jess and I become what I am pretty sure qualifies as friends. I never had many real friends in school and had hoped that would change in university. But after capital D Dementia Day, I decided to focus on you, which suited me anyway, if I am being honest.

At one point during winter, Jess gets sick with a bad cold, so I get the train to Chatswood and drop off some hot lemon and honey in a thermos for her.

'People from Sydney never do things like this!' she says, and I am about to apologise for overstepping when she draws me into a bear hug. I can smell eucalyptus lollies and Vicks Vaporub, and am transported back in time to Railway Road, lying in Mum and Dad's room while Dad applies the strong-smelling lotion to my chest.

Jess pulls back abruptly, and I feel the cold loss of arms around me. 'Shit, sorry, I don't want to give you my germs!' She laughs. But I don't mind. It is the first time someone has touched me since I left Lachie. I offer to go and get some DVDs, and then we sit on her couch with snacks and blankets.

* * *

Even so, I didn't tell Jess. I didn't tell you. Apart from Lachie, I didn't tell anyone.

For a long time I wanted to believe that it was a false memory; I would rather blame myself than have knowledge I cannot control. But I am familiar with the research: false memories of sexual abuse are much rarer than people might think, and when they do occur, it is through repeated prompting from someone external to the survivor. A false memory rarely, if ever, simply springs from a person's mind, fully formed, unless that person has other serious mental health conditions. I check my copy of the DSM-IV, but despite scoring highly on the depression and anxiety scales,

203

unfortunately I do not qualify for any of the delusional disorders.

It had been such a small thing; it was nothing compared to the abuse that thousands of children experience. This is what I used to tell myself.

But I have come to realise that the size and duration of the crime is not always relevant. Touching a child the wrong way, even for just one night, can affect her ability as an adult to date, have sex, even love. Taking a child from its mother, even for a moment, can scar that woman, destroying her trust in the kindness of strangers.

It only takes a few seconds to save a life.

The opposite is also true.

* * *

After I leave Lachie I have more time to myself, so I go about the question in the only way I know how: with a spreadsheet. *Be systematic,* I tell myself. I comb through my memories. Every night after work I come home and click on the file and add names, memories, evidence for, evidence against.

Could it have been 'Uncle', Mum's gambling friend from the Woodridge TAB? Remember him? His roving eye gave us the creeps, but I don't think we were ever left alone with him. What about one of our sisters' boyfriends, who came to pick them up and then hurried out before Mum could have a go at them? Or even our half-brother Matthew, considering how he treated Val? Doctor Lin and his brother Richard were both extremely creepy, but they only had eyes for Barb and Bev, never us.

I would be a poor researcher if I did not also consider Dad.

I call Trish. She is the eldest of the girls. If anything had happened, she would know.

'Yes?' This is how Trish answers the phone, and it always wrong foots me. Perhaps that is the point.

'I— I won't keep you long,' I stutter. I take a deep breath and dive in. 'I just need to ask you a question. As far as you can recall, did you experience any form of sexual misconduct at the hands of our father?'

Trish pauses, and I am thinking that I should have tried for at least some opening banter when she clears her throat and says, 'Why do you ask?'

'Oh, just a feeling I have. I am not sure. I just … wondered.'

There is another pause at the other end of the line. I imagine Trish drumming her fingers against the marble countertop of her kitchen in a house utterly unlike the one we grew up in, all clean lines and leather seating, carefully choosing her words. 'Well, he tried, once. Before you and Annie were born.'

'Oh Trish, I'm sorry.'

'He was drunk. And that's also how I found out. About, other things.'

'I know about that,' I interject, 'about your … who your father was.'

'How do you know?'

'I worked it out. The timing never matched up.'

Silence. Then, 'Yes, well. I don't know if the others know.'

'I haven't mentioned it.'

'Good.' She pauses. 'Thank you.'

I have opened the gates now. I might as well walk through. 'Do you think he could have tried anything with any of us?'

'We kept a pretty close watch,' she says.

'Oh. Thank you.'

We make desultory small talk, perhaps because it feels to her as much as me that the conversation should not end in what feels like the middle of something.

After, I tap out a text message to Trish; reconsider; delete; tap out another. 'Thanks Trish. I am sorry you had to find out that way. About your father.' I add 'xx'. Two x's indicate real consideration; one x is just what people use as a friendly full stop. I hit send. Moments later, Trish texts me back: 'x.'

I add Trish's information to my spreadsheet. Then I try to process it. Dad made a pass at Trish; *but* Trish was sixteen, not exactly a child, and she was also not *his* child. I do a database search about childhood abuse perpetrators. I discover that only a small proportion of abusers are motivated by genuine paedophilia. Most crimes against children of a sexual nature are statistically significantly correlated with access, impulsivity and criminality. Substance abuse also lowers inhibitions. Perpetrators tend to be motivated not by sex but the desire to exert power.

Well, let's be methodical about this. Dad had the proximity, the access. And don't forget, the files describe a man who was a stranger to me: drunkenness, gambling and a dishonourable discharge. There was all that business with the yellow letters I found after he died. But even including that, admittedly *very* poor, behaviour in the reckoning, I simply cannot believe it was him. What about the practicalities? Dad was working night shifts at the hospital and driving buses during the day. When would he have had the time? In the interests of due diligence, I try to insert him into the memory, but it is impossible to imagine him doing such a thing. An affair with a consenting adult is not a predictor of paedophilia; it is, perhaps, consistent with his behaviour towards the teenage Trish, but not with anything untoward with four-year-old me.

With you and I, Annie, he was such a *prudish* man. All our lives, Dad gave goodnight kisses so dry they felt like withered leaves. At least he kissed us – Mum used to hold out her hand like a bishop, not letting us near her face with our puckered lips. Dad loved us in a very uncomplicated way: we were his children, so he took care of us. Whatever his sins, Dad was a good man.

* * *

'We need to decide what wording will go on Annie's plaque,' Trish says. 'I was thinking, "Anne Maria Bradley, beloved daughter, sister and aunty. Rest in peace."'

'That's good,' I agree. 'But can we add her motto at the bottom?'

'What motto?'

'"Smile, God loves you." You know. She wrote it on the inside cover of all of her poetry books.'

Trish inclines her head but doesn't respond, an old tactic for when she doesn't know something but still wants to look like she does.

'She used to write it in the cards she made for birthdays. She always decorated it with clouds and rainbows. Smiling suns. Remember?'

'Yes Annie, I remember,' Trish finally says.

'Kathy,' I correct.

'Oh, Kathy, sorry.' Our sister looks at me. I shrug. The big kids have always mixed up our names, as if we were two halves of a single person.

I sit on the bench. The trickling stream running past your plot really is very peaceful.

'We couldn't, it wasn't really fair on my family,' Trish suddenly says as if taking up an unfinished conversation. 'She had her own room downstairs, right near the bathroom so she could find it in the night. I organised outings with the local respite centre, and the nanny was there for the other times. But she just wasn't – she wasn't the sweet little Annie when she first got sick. She made rude hand gestures, said bad words. She used to fight with my son – only two years old! And the nanny was going to leave.'

Why is she saying all of this now? Does she want absolution? But you are already dead, Annie. Maybe she thinks I can deliver forgiveness by proxy.

I offer the next best thing – my own guilt.

'One time,' I say, 'I lost Annie.'

'She was always getting lost,' Trish says.

'Yeah, but this time it was definitely my fault.'

* * *

It is my first visit after Dad's death and my move to Sydney, and I am determined to give you a proper birthday treat. We are going to the movies at the Hyperdome, and I am not going to employ the usual Bradley method of smuggling in home-brand chips concealed in a handbag. I buy drinks and popcorn from the cinema snack bar with a swipe of my credit card, as if to say, *Only the best for my Annie.*

We have forty-five minutes before the start time, so we browse a nearby bookstore. I go down one aisle, you another. I hear you calling for me, and I call out loudly, 'Here I am.' I turn the corner of the aisle, expecting to see you there. I check each aisle. There is no sign of you.

My heart races. Why did I disappear down a different aisle anyway? Was it some kind of perverse test? If so, I am the one who has failed it. I race to the information desk and ask them to do an announcement. I sit, picking at the cuticles of my nails until they bleed. The movie has started.

I go to a payphone and call the TAB. We are on first-name terms with all the TAB staff between Slacks Creek and Loganlea.

'Is my mum still there?' I ask.

'Yes, darl. Is everything OK?'

'Oh, can I just talk to her for a minute?'

'Ma-adge!'

A rustle as Mum wipes the phone receiver on her clothes. 'Yes? Kathy? What?'

'Mum, I've lost Annie.'

'Oh, poor Kathy. Don't worry,' she giggles when she hears me hiccup with tears. 'I do it all the time.'

She tells me to return the movie tickets and then look again. Part of me thinks that returning the tickets is a low priority, but I don't know what else to do so I go to the cinema. And I see you.

You are sitting on a bench, kicking your legs, talking to yourself. An empty box of popcorn sits next to you. *You must be really thirsty*, I think.

You had remembered that we were going to see a movie and you came straight here after we got split up in the bookstore.

I can't stop hugging you. 'Sorry! I'm so sorry.'

'It's OK, Kathy. It's fine.' You look at me like I am maybe a little crazy. I laugh through my tears. It is too late to see the next session; my flight is leaving in three hours. I cry as I drive all the way back to the airport, away from you.

* * *

'Why didn't you go to the cinema straight away?' Trish asks.

I stare at her until she says, 'Oh, I suppose you thought she wouldn't have remembered.'

'Yes Trish, what with the dementia and all,' I reply.

'Well, you were wrong.' Trish stands. 'It happens.' She checks her phone. 'I'll email the wording to the woman, whatshername.'

'Di-aaana,' I say automatically.

A genuine laugh breaks Trish's face out of its usual set lines of responsibility. 'Yes, Di-aaana,' she repeats. 'By the way,' she adds, jingling her car keys, 'Evan called me. He didn't seem to know that Annie had died.'

'I wanted to process it myself first,' I reply. 'I wanted it to be just me and Annie for a little longer.' I would not be much of a Bradley if I could not lie at a time like this. Trish is too preoccupied with whatever crisis is now unfolding at the hospital to question me any further. It's always been this way with our siblings – surface-level concern, followed by a grateful retreat to the safety of their own vacuum-sealed lives.

'I have to head back to the hospital,' she says, pocketing the phone. 'You take care driving. You look tired.'

PART 4

CAREER

Try to use workplace anecdotes to illustrate
the deceased's career. If the deceased
did not work in the traditional sense, be
sure to still include stories illustrating their
contribution to the family and community.

How to Write a Eulogy

park in the visitor spot outside Mountainview, early again. I spent last night down by the river, swatting at mozzies that had sniffed me through the Subaru chassis and finagled their way through the vents. Now here I am, smelling of dried blood and two- or is it three-day-old clothes? I check the phone calendar. Thursday. Two more sleeps until your funeral.

There are ten group houses in this complex, all shiny new and with well-tended garden beds. The door to your house is extra wide to accommodate motorised wheelchairs.

I like this house. It has a real kitchen even though most of the residents eat through feeding tubes. There is a spacious courtyard and living area, and each bedroom is large and airy.

Val and I will clear out your belongings for the next lucky person to make a home here. I don't mean that sarcastically, Annie, you can stop scowling at me. Mountainview was, is, a great residence for people with high-care needs. The bed we will donate to the Youth At Home charity that runs this complex. We bought it at wholesale cost via Val's medical supplies business, along with the deluxe wheelchair and hoist which we will also leave for another resident.

It was not easy or cheap getting you a place in this publicly funded group home. I can't imagine what it must be like for people who don't have half a dozen highly educated, well-resourced and, on top of all that, *angry* siblings to lobby for them. Well, not impossible actually – they would be in an aged care home like the one you lived in, where you were first taken after the fall that happened three years ago, after my wedding. Another story not suitable for the eulogy.

Val arrives in a van. 'From the work fleet,' she explains. 'I figured I might need something with a big boot.' I am happy for our sister and her success. I can see how having money has filled out her spiritual gauntness, helping her to walk more confidently through the world, laugh at Mum's jibes rather than be laid low by them. No more green hospital sheets for Val. She has made it out.

I help her carry dozens of cardboard boxes, textas and a sticky-tape dispenser to the house and Mary, the primary carer, lets us in. Mary is a broad-shouldered, easygoing woman who moved here from Sudan in her twenties. She clucks when she sees us and offers a round of tea. 'Would you like some help?' she asks, handing us the mugs as we stand in the doorway to your room.

'Oh, that's OK,' Val says. 'This is probably a sister thing to do.'

There are three other residents, all girls – no, young women, I correct myself. Like you they are also in wheelchairs and are non-verbal, although they can and do make sounds that represent the full spectrum of emotions. The housemate in the room across from yours loves company, and would always call excitedly whenever I came in. I would say hello and wave but would make it clear I was here for you. Another housemate was often to be found outside in the courtyard, turning her face up to the sun like a flower and chatting to the house's pet budgerigar. The third was an indoor person – I saw her rarely, but sometimes could hear the sound of explosions and high-speed car chases coming from her room as she watched action movie after action movie.

You would normally be in your chair, and one of the carers would have placed a puzzle book on your stable table like the ones you used to fill in when you could still grip a pen, or old family photos.

'She looks at them, you know,' Mary told me on one visit. 'She gets down close, you know how she does.' I can imagine you short-sightedly peering at the pictures, passing your soft palms across the laminate that Mary has placed over them so they don't get damaged.

I unhook the stable table from the chair and start plucking the photos out. Here is one of you and Dad; must have been taken when you were twelve, so five years after you were already supposed to be dead. You are dancing together, you in your white lace confirmation dress, Dad in his good safari suit. He is holding your bad arm gently. You are both smiling at the camera. There is a picture of you and me on the couch, me in my high school uniform, our heads together, touching; numerous images of you with our nephews and nieces. A whole timeline of family gatherings, our siblings' children getting older, taller, transitioning from guileless to surly to self-possessed, under your fingertips.

'Let's make a memento box and take it to the wake, so everyone can pick something to remember her by,' Val suggests. She picks up a hand-painted wooden egg. 'Oh, I gave her this last Easter. I think I will keep this.'

I find a love-heart-shaped cushion that I gave you for your birthday last year. I wasn't going to take anything, but on impulse I place it next to my handbag. I could use a pillow.

An anthropologist might make something of how Val and I are drawn to the objects in the room that we gave to you. We imbued these items – a toy singing butterfly, a rainbow lampshade, a heart-shaped necklace – with something of our wishes and hopes for you Annie. But we have no real idea of what they meant to you.

Val finds a pile of old notebooks and hands them to me in case there is anything in there useful for the eulogy – a mixed bunch of A5-size hardcover journals with pretty covers, of which I recognise several that I gave to you over the years. When we were in our teens and early twenties you were still well enough to write poetry and so it was easy to know what to buy you for birthdays. Not like later. Decorated wooden eggs and novelty shaped pillows, for crying out loud.

'How's the eulogy going anyhow?' Val asks, packing up your music CDs.

'Fine, thanks.' I have my head in the wardrobe as I box up your clothes, surreptitiously smelling them as I do so. Fresh laundry and talcum powder. Dad was the one who always praised the benefits of talc, liberally applying Johnson's baby powder whenever we complained of rashes or chafes.

'Is Evan coming up for the funeral?'

'Hmm, depends on work.'

'Is everything all right with you two?'

'These are for charity?' I ask, pointing to a pile of fleecy Kmart blankets.

Val passes me a texta. 'Yep. Make sure to mark the box with what is inside and where it is going, charity or Mum's place.'

A few minutes pass when she asks again. 'So, you and Evan?'

'All good!' I say, making my face bright. 'The mortgages in Sydney are a killer though. Do you want the curtains?'

Val had made the curtains for you using a brightly coloured floral print with block-out backing. She was always good at crafts. Remember, she sewed all those bridesmaid dresses for us, blithely ignoring my pleas for no frills, the two of us matching so there was no mistaking us as anything but family.

We stop for a lunch break. Val has brought sandwiches and fruit, which we eat at the outdoor table in your personal courtyard. Afterwards, we finish the packing and then clean the room. This is not strictly necessary, but it feels like the right thing to do: make the place as sparkling new as it was for you when you moved in, a place of hope, a new beginning.

Mary comes to help us carry the boxes out. We stand back, surveying the small pile that your belongings have made in the back of the van.

'I will bring the mementoes box to Brian's and drop the rest off to charity and Mum's place,' Val says. 'Hey, can you come over tomorrow? I might need some help with the coffin decorations.'

'Is the morning OK? I am going to wash and dress Annie in the afternoon.'

'We can do that?' Val asks.

'Yes. You just have to ask them.' I had a terse phone call with the funeral director yesterday, who would have preferred I not insist. But I know my rights.

'Well, let's see how we are going after the coffin session.'

'OK, see you tomorrow.' Val is a kisser rather than a hugger, and she pecks me on the cheek before backing out the van, beeping as she reverses.

It's already getting dark when I pull into a strip mall almost indistinguishable from the place where Brian and I had lunch yesterday, except that it is almost two hours away and in another city. Brisbane has some lovely old Queenslander architecture in the eight-kilometre radius of the city centre, but the rest of it is this: category-killer warehouse stores, inflatable tall men bouncing erratically in carsale yards as far as the eye can see. A city of interlinking motorways, highways, service roads and suburbs. It is depressing that when I feel homesick, this is what I yearn for – the familiar sight of prefab buildings, scrub and mobile billboards on the back of rusted-out cars. When I see grubby children circling the legs of their parents exiting a TAB I can't help it: I feel a tug of nostalgia, not for the TAB, but for that feeling that comes from being together. Family.

* * *

Ten months after that first kiss, when Evan asks me if I will marry him, I cannot believe my ears. He has to repeat himself, which makes him laugh and laugh as he holds out the diamond ring that belonged to his grandmother. I stay awake next to him all night, then in the morning I ask, 'Is it real? Are we engaged?'

'Yes we are.'

'So I can tell my mother?'

'Yes you can.'

I roll out of bed, dress and kiss him goodbye. I have to take the ring for re-sizing before work. On my way I call Jess. 'Guess what? Evan and I got engaged,' I say. My whole body is trembling from fatigue.

'What? That's amazing! Congratulations!' Jess sounds as though I have just woken her up. I look at my watch. 7.35 am. The shops won't even be open yet.

'Is it OK to think of this as my first marriage proposal?' I babble. 'I don't think I can handle it otherwise. It's just, what the fuck? I'm getting married?'

Jess laughs. 'You can think about it however you want, lovely. I am going to be your wingman all the way. I'll keep the car running.'

'Thanks Jess,' I say, my voice shaking. 'I better call my mum.'

Mum takes the news better than I thought she would. 'Oh, congratulations,' she says. 'Oh, that's great news. Evan, what he do for a job again?'

'He works with me, Mum. Head of digital.'

'Oh that's right, yeah. I don't even know his mother.'

'I'll bring you down this weekend,' I say promptly. 'We'll get you a discount flight. You can meet his whole family.'

'Oh, I don't know, I got Annie.'

'Annie can come too!'

'She not well enough for a plane, Kathy,' Mum admonishes. In my sleep-deprived state I had momentarily forgotten. You have been going through a particularly bad spell recently, in and out of hospital with some sort of immune system failure that has caused a blistering rash all over your body.

'Sorry, yeah of course,' I say. 'We can ask Val to go sit with her for the day. Just Saturday, we can get you an evening flight, same day.'

Now that the idea has formed, I really want to see our mother. *Something primal must be going on*, I think, too tired to analyse it closely. Leaving the nest. Starting the next generation. Whatever it is, for the first time since I was a kid, I actually want Mum by my side. I want her, just this once, to choose me.

In the end Mum decides it's better if we come to Queensland, so Val organises a family barbecue at her place so the Bradleys can meet Evan. You are there, sleepy and tucked up with a crocheted blanket over your knees. I park myself next to you.

I am not sure how you are going to take the news of my engagement. It's yet another step I am taking that you can't. I turn my ring inwards, so the diamond is not too obvious as I slice up the meat on your plate. The last thing I want is to compound the confusion you spend most of your time in these days.

'Are you behaving?' I ask you, forcing bonhomie into my voice.

You have been muttering under your breath, smiling at unseen others. I repeat myself a few times until you look at me. With visible effort, as if to humour me, you say, 'Oh, you know, of course, of course!'

I ask you about the day respite centre that you have been attending twice a week, thanks to Val's intervention. 'Oh it's OK, I keep telling them they need to have more whatsits, whatdoyoucallthem, you know—'

'Craft tables?' I guess. 'Scissors? Biscuits? Glue sticks?'

223

'Yeah, glue sticks, to make the costumes, you know, for the play me and Jeremy – I mean, that I am helping with.' For once I do not chastise you for mentioning Jeremy. *Let her have something*, I think. Let her believe that he is alive and she is a helper at the respite centre rather than a client. I am impressed that you have taken your situation and layered it with your own agency.

We all perch on the edge of the plastic-cushioned outdoor seats, balancing paper plates on our laps and politely pretending that the mozzie coils are working. Val moved to the north side of Brisbane when she married to be closer to her husband's family, but the house itself reminds me of 19 Railway Road, with its two storeys of brick veneer. Val can probably afford something nicer now that her business is taking off. Perhaps there is something about this place that reminds her of home, although I have no idea why she would want that. She got out as quick as she could. We all did, except for you.

From where I sit, I have a view of the above-ground pool and the Hills hoist, but instead of an incinerator there is a smoking oven down the back, which Val and her husband brought back with them from a holiday to the USA. As a result, we are eating smoked chicken with our iceberg lettuce instead of the usual burnt chops from the Weber.

Evan comes over from the huddle of brothers-in-law by the smokehouse and smiles at me and you.

'You must be the famous Annie,' he says. When you don't

look up, he squats down on his haunches so he is at your eye-level. 'I'm Evan.'

'I know,' you answer without looking at him.

'Up for a game?' he asks. Now he has your attention.

'Don't be mad when I beat you,' you say and he laughs. We clear a space on the table and he produces a pack of UNO cards I didn't know he had.

Dessert is inevitably one of Barb's inedible trifles. Dad used to make trifle each Christmas, and after he died Barb took over, but now she also makes one for every family gathering. Is it a not-so-subtle reminder that she is carrying the flame? That she is the good daughter, simply because she combines Woolies sponge cakes with ready-made custard, a few packets of Aeroplane jelly and cheap grog that Dad would have happily swigged standing behind the pantry door?

Over lunch, Val asks conversationally if I now know Chinese.

'No,' I laugh, slightly mystified. She knows that Mum never taught us any Chinese. Evan has a smattering of Mandarin from his grandmother, but how would I have learned it? Via osmosis? 'Do you?' I ask, but Val looks at me blankly.

'Are you going to have a baby?' Barb asks.

'Asian babies are so cute!' Val smiles.

'Yes, we *were* quite cute when we were little,' I say pointedly, but my sisters stare at me without comprehension.

Either I have actually become more Chinese because of Evan, or just more attuned to racism because of the way he is treated. More than once, Evan has been mistaken for my brother by casual acquaintances, even though we look nothing alike. Evan says it is because people cannot conceive of Asian men as romantic leads, even in their own lives. I protest, but until recently I had not been able to conceive of it either.

Then there was the time we were walking along the cliff path between Bondi and Coogee beaches. I had spotted a whale in the cove and must have stared at it too long while still moving forward, because I tripped over a crack in the footpath. Sitting on the ground, I shook my head at the local council's lack of risk management. Blood dripped into my eyes. Seemingly out of nowhere, two surf lifeguards materialised with an entire camera crew.

'Can you speak English?' one of the sandy-haired men with skin the colour of leather shouted at me, while the other draped a silver foil blanket over my shoulders.

'Mate, she can speak English better than you,' Evan laughed.

The lifeguards called an ambulance, a little disappointed that I was able to stand and did not need the stretcher. At the hospital I received stitches from a pretty Icelandic intern whose name, she told me, meant 'Little Island'. A week later, I received a $400 bill for her services. Despite our explanations to the lifeguards, the paramedics, the hospital admission staff, I had been processed as a foreigner. I had to present myself, my Medicare card and one hundred points of identification to demonstrate that I was born in Logan, much closer to Bondi Beach than any little Icelandic island.

Of course I had experienced racism before I met Evan: there had been the usual name-calling and one memorable egging from a moving car which had been perversely gratifying because the thrower had missed. But this constant undermining of my identity is new to me, this experience of being regarded as foreign by people who were not even born here. In cafes, British waitresses in breach of their holiday visas focus on my lips, frowning as I talk to them until they eventually realise that I am speaking English with no trace of an accent, apart perhaps from the Queensland drawl that still clings to my tongue.

Evan lets it all wash over him, amused at how I am constantly enraged. But I know on a visceral level that if I was in physical danger, Evan would fight, and he would win. This knowledge makes me feel safe in a way that is also new to me.

You and Evan have been playing round after round, Evan throwing hand after hand and ignoring your mistakes. I lean over and kiss you on the cheek. 'We need to get going,' I say to Evan, although the plane does not leave for another four hours. He nods without a moment's hesitation.

'It's been great to finally meet you all,' he says, smiling at the Bradleys. 'Especially *you*,' he says, leaning down and kissing you with a noisy smackeroo on the cheek.

You laugh and wave him off. 'All right, all right,' you say, grinning at us. This may be the first time I am going to leave you without either of us crying.

Mum proffers her cheek to be kissed, not the hand. Mellowing in her old age, Val reckons. *Losing her power,* I think, but only to myself.

'He drive a Lamborghini?' Mum says suddenly, looking at Evan who does not even own a car. Is she thinking of Chinese gangsters, the ones she heard stories about when she was a child in the kampong, cruising for girls across the Straits of Jahor?

'No Mum, Evan is a good man,' I say gently. Maybe Val is right; maybe Mum is growing old and senile, deserving of more sympathy.

'You need to lose some weight before the wedding,' Mum adds, pinching my hip. *And then again,* I think as I straighten up, smile plastered on, *maybe not.*

After the Bradley family barbecue, Evan and I decide not to bother with a formal engagement party. We save our money and eleven months later we manage to purchase a two-bedroom apartment in Wollstonecraft, one of the inner-north suburbs of Sydney close to the harbour and work. It's not the dream home yet but it's a peg in the market and we can manage the mortgage with our two incomes. I enrol to do my PhD part-time starting next year. We are entering stage one of the dream.

Except that I have not slept deeply or long enough since we moved to dream anything at all. I tell Evan that it is the stress of the move and planning a budget wedding. And it is these things and something more. I feel like I am living someone else's life and am just waiting for the cameras to swarm and for everyone to shout, *Gotcha!*

I phone home every week. Mum reports that your rash has finally cleared, but your incontinence is getting worse. She has begun waking you at two am to get to the loo in time but even with adult pads on it is frequently too late: your bladder retains the fluid from your brain until you relax in bed and then it all eases out and straight through the multiple bed protectors, the layered mattresses that make you sleep like the princess and the pea, no pun intended.

You no longer attend any of the activities that I arranged for you in the days after Dad's death. Mum takes you to the tavern with her instead. While she bets on the races or plays the pokies, she sits you in front of a one-cent machine. This is Mum's idea of meaningful activity and social interaction for her disabled daughter.

Do I sound bitter? I am. Do I sound judgemental? I am. Do I sound arrogantly superior, as if I would have done a better job in her shoes? I am fairly sure I would have. Except that, of course, I didn't, and that's what really matters.

The rare nights my eyes do twitch in REM sleep I wake up minutes later, shaking and sweating. When I was at university I learned that there is another name for REM sleep: 'paradoxical sleep'. When dreaming, the brain acts in a way similar to when a person is awake. The anterior paralimbic REM activation zone includes areas linked with emotion, memory, fear and sex. The key difference between waking and paradoxical sleeping is that the body is paralysed; you cannot run away from your dreams. My night-time mind is a cave of sheer inchoate redness and blackness, the silhouettes of horned beasts emerging from the shadows to leer and sneer and taunt me by almost, but not quite, showing their faces.

One night before the wedding I jerk awake, my pyjamas damp with perspiration although it is a lovely cool night in August.

Evan snuffles and half-wakes. He puts a hand on mine and I think he is going to say, 'Go back to sleep,' but instead he murmurs, 'I'll still love you if you're having second thoughts.'

I say into the darkness, 'There's a difference between doubt and fear. Right now I'm experiencing a lot of fear.'

'Hmm?' He has opened his eyes now and is looking at me.

'Doubt is where you aren't sure. You know, "Is Evan the guy for me? Am I just marrying him because he asked me?"' I stare at the ceiling and giggle in a poor attempt to take the edge off my words.

'And fear?'

'Fear is when you are just. Afraid.'

'Of?'

'Everything.'

I think he's fallen back to sleep and am about to creep out of bed to my insomniac activities (surfing science websites, pacing, stress eating, making lists) when he lays an arm across my abdomen.

'When I feel like that,' he draws me to him and whispers in my ear, 'I think, why not be brave?'

Within minutes he is gently snoring. It takes me almost fifteen minutes of infinitesimally small manoeuvres, but I finally manage to slip out of his grasp.

By the day of the wedding I have not slept through the night in more than four weeks. After the bridal cosmetician leaves, Jess re-does my makeup, smearing off the layers of foundation so I feel less like a performer at my own wedding, but adding concealer over my dark bags and a daub of additional rouge to my cheeks.

We wanted a 'low-key' (inexpensive) wedding, and Jess has outdone herself, organising handmade decorations and wedding favours, managing a skittish bride and overseeing the army of adolescent Bradley nephews and nieces carrying chairs, eskies and crates of food and drink up and down the hill from our apartment to the nearby park. I decide at the last minute that I do want a bouquet, what was I thinking not organising a bouquet, so Jess dashes to the florist and comes back bearing a bunch of white chrysanthemums.

'Oh no, oh no that's not good,' I shake my head. Jess gently rests her hands on either side of my face so I don't loosen any more bobby pins from my elaborate up-do. 'Chrysanthemums mean death! Mum never let us give her them on Mother's Day!'

'Well, luckily for your mum, whose wedding this is not, I bought two back-up bouquets.' Jess whips out one bunch of white tulips and one bunch of wild roses seemingly out of thin air.

I have asked my brother Brian to walk me down the park 'aisle'. 'Kathy, I just want you to know,' he says, looking from his feet to my eyelashes. 'Dad would be so proud of you. I am proud of you, OK?'

'Thanks Brian.' Our brother is taking the man of the family thing seriously, but I am truly touched. Jess must have given Evan's buddy the all clear, because the sound of an electric guitar playing Cyndi Lauper's 'Time After Time' floats up to us on a mild April Sydney breeze. We start walking.

After that, everything is a blur. The one thing I clearly remember from the ceremony is you.

On cue, you limp to the front of the group of guests without once looking at me. Mum has dressed you in a beautiful golden jacket and trouser suit and Trish has done your hair. You have a few grey strands emerging, but your skin is as soft and downy as when we were children playing 'In the Future' with Brian.

You clear your throat. 'If I speak in the tongues of men or of angels,' you begin. I am standing directly behind you but I have to lean forward to hear the words.

You blink, look up. Stand up a little straighter.

'If I speak in the tongues of men or of angels, but do not have love, I am only a resounding gong or a clanging cymbal. If I have the gift of prophecy and fathom – can fathom all mysteries and all knowledge,' you declaim.

A beat passes. Two. Trish walks calmly up the aisle to your side and points to the page.

'—and if I have a faith that can move mountains, but do not have love, I am nothing. If I give all I possess to the poor and give over my body to hardship that I may boast, but have love, I gain nothing.'

You pause. 'Sorry. But do *not* have love, I gain nothing.' The guests release a collectively held breath.

'Love is patient. Love is kind. It does not envy, it does not boast, it is not proud. It does not dishonour others, it is not self-seeking, it is not easily angered, it keeps no record of wrongs. Love does not delight in evil but rejoices with the truth. It always protects, always trusts, always hopes, always perseveres.'

You look up. The guests all applaud. You nod graciously and walk back to your seat.

When the celebrant asks me if I take Evan to be my husband, I watch her lips move and hear the anticipated words but my brain cannot seem to connect the two. The celebrant, an older white woman, looks at me through her glasses, frowning slightly as if I am an errant student. I snap to attention and, looking at the celebrant, I say, 'I do.'

Later, when someone kisses me on the cheek, I smile. When someone tells me I am living the dream, I smile. When someone's toddler drops chocolate cake on my wedding dress, I smile. Not because I have reached a state of Buddha-like serenity, but because I feel nothing. I am in a state beyond feeling. I am in a state of emotional shock.

Jess coordinates the clean-up, shooing Evan and I towards a waiting taxi that will take us to a hotel by the beach, where we will spend a two-day honeymoon. Before we get in the car we make our way down the line of waiting Bradleys and Lees, saying our goodbyes. Finally we come to you.

'You take care of my little sister,' you say to Evan, making two fists. 'Or else you know what I'll do.'

Evan pretends to stagger backwards from your play punches and you smile triumphantly. In that moment I love Evan more than I already thought I did. On my wedding day, he has managed to make you feel as though you were the winner.

* * *

There is a twenty-four-hour discount chemist not far from Val's where I park for the night. The cushion from your room at Mountainview is actually a great improvement on my bundled-up jacket as a pillow. Even so, it is hard to doze off when I know there is a box of powdered sleeping pills within arm's reach which would make it so much easier.

I pull out the laptop and stare at the blank page for a while. The blinking cursor is a heartbeat, pulsing as if it will go on forever. I close the document and insert the thumb drive Val gave me of the photos for the slideshow, looking for inspiration. What am I supposed to say about the 'career' of someone who never had a paid job in her life?

* * *

After a week of married life I decide I need a separate bedroom so I don't keep waking my 'husband' with my insomnia, which has not abated, as I had hoped it would, after the wedding. I remove myself to the spare room where I still have nightmares, but instead of dreaming of faceless monsters I wake up in the morning having witnessed Evan's accidental crushing by a tractor, Evan's accidental death by drowning, Evan's accidental death from a train derailment.

I wonder if this means I really do love him.

I just don't know what love is supposed to feel like. Here is what I mostly feel: morbidly terrified that something is going to happen to him.

When we have sex I ask him to tell me that he loves me.

'I love you,' he mutters into my ear and I feel myself opening, letting him in. I respond to words; I try to believe in words; I cling to words because otherwise I am just a piece of meat. I don't think of this the whole time we make love. But I do think of it.

Six months into married life, we have established a soothing evening routine: after work, we take it in turns to cook dinner and then we sit in the living room, companionably working on our projects. Evan taps away at his laptop, researching governance structures for his anti-bullying charity. I sit on the couch with papers fanned out all around me, reading through the literature for my PhD confirmation review.

Tonight I have a cup of hot chocolate, perched on the side table, which Evan has made for me just the way I like it: three parts soy milk, one part hot water. He senses me looking at him and glances my way. I smile. He smiles back.

I reach for the phone. 'Calling your mum?' he asks, and I nod.

'That time of the week.'

After two rings Mum answers. She sounds out of breath. 'Annie just fell over. I got to go.' She hangs up on me before I have a chance to say a word.

'Everything all right?' Evan asks.

'Not sure. I better call Val.'

'Hello Val speaking,' Val says in her business voice, even though she would have seen my name come up on her screen. I don't have time to make fun of her.

'Hey Val, can you call Mum? I was just talking to her and she said Annie had a fall.'

I flip through the pages of a journal article about twin studies, waiting. Ten minutes pass. Even though I am expecting it, I still jump when the phone rings.

'She forgot to hang up on me,' Val says. 'I could hear her yelling. Kicking her on the ground. "Move, you fat thing, move! Make me sick! Wish you were dead!"' Val can do a fair impersonation of our mother. And we had both heard Mum say these words before. We just never thought we would hear them directed at you.

Val calls the Department of Disability Services the next

morning. Over the years since Dad died, both she and I have tried to get the department to place you in a group home, or a program, anything to give you some social stimulation and at least slow your decline. What we now discover is that if you are a danger, or are in danger, the state moves with the speed of a runaway train with no regard for what stands in its way. Val tells them what we have agreed: we think our mother is no longer fit to care for you. The department calls Mum in for an interview.

When the time comes to put your disabled child in the care of the state, there is a form of words that you have to use. Like when you get married, but the opposite. Wedding words bind. These are meant to sever.

'Relinquish,' Mum says on the phone. 'They say I got to say I "relinquish" her.'

There is a pause. For once I cannot even hear the sound of Mum clearing her throat. There is no one else in the background, no Annie murmuring to her imagined friends. You are staying in emergency respite accommodation. This must be the first time Mum has slept in a house alone, since when exactly? Malaya? Singapore? Ever? 'What does it mean anyway, "relinquish"?'

My turn to pause. 'It means to let go. It means, you let go of Annie.'

'I am not relinquishing!'

I never thought I would feel this relieved to hear anger in my mother's voice.

'Chee wiz, what a word! I am still her mother!'

'Of course you are,' I agree.

'Relinquish. Huh.'

'It's just a word, Mum. Just the word they make you say so we can get the best help for Annie.'

'Chee! You and your sisters, all want to lock her away,' Mum says.

'Mum. You can't get her up any more after a fall,' I say, the same thing I and Val, Trish and Brian have said to Mum since the fall, each of us finding our own way to avoid the word 'abuse'. I can't think about that too much. I can't face the image of you on the floor.

'It's too much for you,' I repeat.

'Yeah yeah An— Kathy. Oh,' she says, as if remembering her manners. 'How Evan? Is Evan OK?'

'Yes Mum, we are fine.'

'OK, good. Bye, bye.'

'Love you Mum.'

'OK. Bye.'

I fly up to Brisbane to help with your move. The department does not have a place in a group home but will put you 'temporarily' in aged care. Val and I argue that it would be better if you stayed at home with Mum until a space frees up, giving Mum more home support to help her manage. We think you will just get more confused if you have to relocate again. But the department writes that they will have to take legal action 'to arrange state custodianship in the best interests of the client', meaning you, Annie, if we do not comply with the order to transfer you to Daisy Hill Aged Care Home within thirty days of receipt. We are now in the Kafka-esque world of the disability bureaucracy. There is no turning back.

Val meets me, Mum, you and Barb at your new room at the aged care home, wielding an allen key. We go inside and immediately I feel happier about our decision to contact the department. Val has transformed a beige, institutional room into a homey place, strung with fairy lights, draped with colourful cloths and furnished with pink IKEA bookshelves and drawers.

We sit around on the bed and armchair and talk loudly about how bright and cheery it is, trying to leave no gaps in the conversation for hearing the screams of the residents of the closed dementia ward down the corridor. You get in the bed and turn your head away from me, but we are everywhere, we Bradley women: Val sits on your other side, Barb at the foot of your bed, Mum bustling around, checking you have enough blankets, a water jug, plenty of pillows. You say nothing. Not even to yourself.

At last it is time to go. Val and Barb leave, taking Mum with them as we discussed. I lean over you to kiss you goodbye.

'Don't leave me here, Kathy,' you say. It is the first time I have heard you speak so clearly since I can't remember when, possibly since before Dad died, five years ago. Since then your speech has become gradually more slurred, our conversations limited to what you had for dinner, peppered with words you make up to fill the growing blanks in your vocabulary. But now you look straight at me. You know exactly what you are saying.

'I'll be back soon to see you,' I lie. You close your eyes.

* * *

Ahead of the funeral, Val has scanned snapshots of Bradley Christmas dinners, bespectacled faces smiling at the camera. There are pictures from Trish's graduation, and Val in her cap and gown after completing nursing school. Here is one of Brian's graduation, back when Brian still had a full head of hair; and finally one of me in cap and gown, with you smiling at my elbow.

At my graduation, you presented me with a beautiful little crucifix on a gold chain, which I still wear even though I am no longer a believer in God. But I have always been a believer in you.

Val has also digitised what I call the 'hospital series': pictures that Mum took when you were in and out of the Mater Hospital from 1983 to 1990. I hated it when she did that, whipping out the camera and making us all stand and smile around your bed. You in your dressing gown. You with half your hair shaved off. Here is one of you with your head bandaged. You are asleep and I am leaning against your bed rail. Not doing anything. Just watching.

If you had a career, it was as a professional patient. Not

everyone knows how hard a job that is – how much hope is in your hands.

* * *

When you finally wake up three days after I leave you in the aged care home, you can no longer swallow or speak. You are moved to Logan Hospital where they implant a PEG tube for feeding. I fly back to Brisbane.

Val is ropable, pacing your hospital room.

'I called them,' she says, trying to keep her voice down because you are sleeping. 'Later that same day, just to see how she was getting on. The nurse on duty said she had given Annie Phenergan for her rash. I told them not to give her that – the rash was all in the notes, they should have *known* about it. I told them Phenergan was not a good idea combined with the anti-seizure meds. *Also* in her notes.'

Val reaches the door to the toilet, turns and paces back to the bed.

'I made them show me the log book, but there is no record of them giving her *anything* in that. They've amended it.'

'This is fucking outrageous,' I say. I try to keep my voice conversational so as not to affect what I hope are your peaceful dreams. 'We need to make a complaint.'

The complaints unit is part of the department it is meant to be independent of. The Ombudsman is funded from the same portfolio. Now we are really in the maze.

After a week you are moved back to the aged care home, despite the considerable combined efforts of the Bradley siblings. You can still walk to the bathroom yourself and write in a shaky hand, but now you are fed through a tube and cannot speak at all, not even the slurred speech that I now miss.

Once I am back in Sydney, Evan and I coordinate the campaign. He uses his digital skills to create an online video to gather grassroots momentum. I tackle the major media outlets, managing to get Val on to *News Today*.

Barb calls me when she finds out. 'I am older than Val. I should be the one to do it.'

'By that logic, Trish should be the one to do it,' I reply. I can't afford to get Barb offside – she is the big kid closest to Mum and could use her influence to mess with my efforts if she thought it worth her while.

But I want Val for TV because she is the friendliest, most likeable of the Bradleys, and since she stopped sunbathing in the backyard at Railway Road, she has become the whitest as well. The studio lighting picks up the red and chestnut accents in her hair as she describes how you developed dysphagia after you were incorrectly prescribed a contra-indicated medication; how you were the subject of a cover-up; how you deteriorated so quickly in aged care, like an estimated six thousand other young people with high-care needs.

The TV appearance leads to a spike in views of the video, and later that month you feature on a front-page article in Queensland's major tabloid newspaper, looking, to my eyes, just as angelic as twenty years ago when your face graced the cover of *The Catholic Leader*. I get Barb to be there with you for the shoot and she appears in one of the secondary images on page six, make-up carefully applied, looking at you adoringly, which allows me to secure, without complaint, a spot for Trish on talkback radio.

Almost twelve months since you entered aged care, the same week that Trish appears on 3AF AM, Mum receives a letter from the department stating that a vacancy had opened up in the new Mountainview complex. We have probably elbowed out some other equally needful human from the top of the waiting list. By the time you move into Mountainview you can no longer walk or hold a pen. You can barely hold your head upright without support.

A Pyrrhic victory, but a victory nonetheless.

Even after your move, I keep up my lobbying activity for young people in aged care; it doesn't feel right to walk away simply because our own family's need had been met. At a fundraiser event, the host, a zealous young marketing director for a non-profit charity, hands me a wireless microphone. 'Tell me Kathy,' she says, 'What is it that you want for your sister?'

I think for a moment.

'Joy,' I finally answer. 'It's that simple. Just, joy. I want Annie to live as though she is living, and not waiting around for the other thing.'

I can't say I ever genuinely liked your poetry. It was all a bit too 'praise Jesus' for me. You wrote about Christ's tender mercy, praying for world peace, the love of Our Lady. I don't remember a single poem of yours that did not mention God.

But God is welcome at a full eucharistic funeral mass. Perhaps there will be a poem in these journals Val and I gathered at Mountainview that I can use in the eulogy.

I switch on the car light, open a book labelled '1989' and laugh out loud. In red marker across each poem you have scrawled notes to yourself, and just like that, after all these years, I can hear you, Annie. I can hear your voice.

Well, the voice of 1989 Annie. Your dementia was still a long way in the future then. You were thirteen years old and I was ten. We had moved to the house at Slacks Creek so you didn't have to drag your semi-paralysed left side up the internal stairs of 19 Railway Road.

'Top poem, I like it!' you have written across one poem. Over the page you have run red lines through another, with a note to yourself: 'Stop remembering the pain – look on the bright side. God's *there*.' Another poem is circled. 'Superb poetry, even if I do say so myself.'

You always had more self-confidence than me, both before and after the tumour. It always annoys me when our siblings go on about who you would have become if not for the tumour. To me, you became simply more like yourself, more concentrated into the key elements that made you, you. More judgemental but also more fiercely loyal. More God-bothering but also more loving. Even after the dementia, you were still *you*.

Mary, the carer at Mountainview, told me about how you would hold up your finger and point to her when she was trying to feed you. 'She wants to make sure I have something to eat first,' the carer explained. 'She's good, this one,' she said, stroking your hand affectionately and I welled up with pride. All the residents were lovely, but you must be her favourite. You were the best.

I flip open another notebook. On the first page you have glued in a family photo and written the year: 1992. On page two you have written in capitals, underlined, 'Why this book?'

For a long time, Kathy has said I ought to write my memories. Never let it be said I don't listen to her advice. I am not kidding myself, I know I shall go on forgetting and confusing myself from time to time, maybe even falling into my quiet depressions. But this is a start!

I take another look at the cover of the book. It's a hardback with glossy blue marbled covers. I bought this one for you for one of your birthdays. I hoped that, if you could record all the things you could remember that happened before the tumour, maybe it would jog your memory for the things that had happened since, like what we did yesterday, or what you had for breakfast.

So where do I start? My brain says, at the start, stupid!

My eyes fill with tears. Your start was me. My start was you.

First memories

Kathy's birth, 1979
Someone in my family, perhaps one of the big kids, perhaps Dad, lifted me, arm on either side, over the huge steps into the hospital. I distinctly remember wearing my little pink dress, my hair put up by Dad. I remember viewing Kathy through a glass window. She was in an incubator. I have a vague memory of Kathy being carried into Mum's room and I could see her more closely. Touch but do not carry!

Kathy's first steps, 1981
Dad or Mum held Kathy, I think I was watching from the side, in or near the arms of Trish or Barb. Anyway, what is most important is Kathy walking. Mum (I think it was her) stood with a packet of Smarties, shaking them in

front of Kathy. Whether Kathy first walked towards Dad, or Mum, or crawled, I don't know. But obviously she did learn to walk and has been running ever since.

I turn the following pages – anecdotes of you, me and Brian playing, fighting, spending time with the big kids. And then it seems you have run out of memories, or got bored of writing things you already knew. The passages morph into diary entries.

28 January 1992

Kathy started high school yesterday, my reaction needless to describe. I know this is an opportunity for her, but Lord, I need your help. I'm falling apart. I tried to be cheerful, I hope Kathy didn't notice the tears in my eyes. Mum, I must say, isn't very helpful. Dad is trying. But they still argue. Lord, I need you … I need Kathy. No. I can do it. Give me strength.

I am starting the computer course next week. Mum is still against it. Please Lord, help her to understand. I need to use the computer so I can work on my poetry which is for you Lord.

I remember you did that course at Logan TAFE near the hospital, just after I started high school and convinced our parents that it would be a good use of your time to learn how to type up your poems, maybe even put them into a book. I always meant to help you do that, perhaps find a small market in the Catholic miracle-child line, but that got harder to imagine the less child-like and less miraculous you were.

1 February 1992

Thank you Lord, just another wonderful day.

5 February 1992

Mum came on heavy today, I survived with your help.

5 March 1992

I spent some time at the hospital today, I do love visiting the babies in the neonatal wards. I brought a cuppa for a tired mum and when she had to go rest I sat and held the baby's hand through the little glass window. That way the little ones are never alone. It's peaceful. This one was almost completely bald and a bit yellow from jaundice, reminded me of Kathy when she was in the incubator.

20 July 1992

Today was not too good, Lord give me strength to get through. Thank you for Kathy. When I get confused she is my angel, helping me out of the fog. I wish the fog weren't so foggy!

30 August 1992

Kathy was in a foul mood today. Wish she wouldn't be. Doesn't she see it just makes Mum worse and then we have to deal with that? Went to see Barb and the kids, thank you Lord for all your blessings.

10 September 1992

Dear Lord, I'm tired of being treated like a little kid. Is that wrong? I feel ignored around the big kids. Tonight was lovely, although I bit back the pain the big kids seem to give rise to in me of late. Did they see? Did they feel? Did they even think of it? I'm still grappling for respect, independence (maybe adulthood).

I extract a perverse amount of pleasure from this entry, the fact that the big kids came off worse than me.

Most of the entries are short, with one notable exception.

16 September 1992

Dear Lord, the past few days up at camp were wonderful. Sharing and creating friendships, enjoying the beauty of the snow-covered mountains. Jeremy and I spent many beautiful moments together, thank you Lord for such a friend.

Brian was right. I had forgotten. I couldn't go with you that one year to the Carpe Diem camp because it clashed with my high school's camp. I never thought I would say this, but I would have preferred the Carpe Diem camp. At least I would have had you.

I must say I was glad Kathy couldn't come on this camp. At first I missed having her with me, but everyone is so friendly and I got swept up in it all. I had that one fit under the strobe lights, but that was the only incident. I wish the organisers hadn't felt the need to tell Mum about it. She gets angry and I know it is just because she is worried, but it hurts. Lord please stay with me when she goes on at me. Sometimes it is hard to feel you there, but I know that is my fault, not yours. You are always with me, I just need to reach out and have faith.

Jeremy and I did the talent show together. We decided to act out a scene from Ghostbusters. I was the Ghost, dressed all in white. Jeremy was the Ghostbuster. We fashioned a pretend machine out of an old ghetto-blaster and taped on some metallic tubing. During the act, I was hiding and popping out in all sorts of places and Jeremy acted confused, as if he could not see me, so the audience had to shout out where I was. They got right into it, which was fun.

At one point I thought I might fall as I was hurrying, but I was all right, Jeremy turned and grinned at me and I sat right on him in the wheelchair. That was not planned but it got a good laugh.

Afterwards when we were resting and basking in the success of our act, he said to me, 'We should do that again some time,' and I nodded and joked, 'Next time we can be on the same side or else I might squash you.' And then he said, 'I liked having you there,' and then he kissed me on the cheek and Lord, I hope you'll forgive me, but I turned and kissed him on the lips.

I know you'll approve Lord. Jeremy is a good guy. In many ways he reminds me of Dad, very gentle, listens more than he talks. I go gadding about, then he is, I don't know Lord, he is present somehow, like he was always there. Is that what you mean by a soulmate, Lord? I feel as though Jeremy and I have known each other in physical form only since we met at Carpe Diem, but like we have known each other throughout all time.

I told Jeremy I would call him when I got home, so I will tell Mum I need to call about camp stuff and that is not a lie.

I switch from the notebooks back to the laptop, looking through the photos that Val has collated, searching for pictures of Carpe Diem. Here is a snapshot of you and the other tumour girls, all round-cheeked from the steroidal treatments and the thyroid problems. Here's one of me scowling with my eyes and smiling with my teeth, as we do yet another interminable aerial rope course designed to make us face our fears. And here is one of you and Jeremy. I flicked through these photos when they were first developed, but now I see something I had not noticed before. You and Jeremy are holding hands.

Annie, you pipped me at the post yet again. Your first kiss, sweet sixteen.

* * *

It's October 1997, towards the end of my first year of university, about six months since the Peter debacle and the first time I found you searching the house for impostors. I am immersed in preparation for exams, and when my stomach rumbles for the third time I grudgingly emerge from Brian's old room (which Mum is letting me use as a study) to find a snack. It is about four pm and the house is already getting dark. I didn't hear Mum and Dad go out, but they are not here as I rummage in the pantry for the vanilla biscuits I know Mum keeps in here somewhere.

I am munching, my mouth covered in crumbs, when I see you.

You are in your underpants, sitting on the couch, smiling at a private joke and muttering. Your clothes are in shreds around you.

I slowly put down my plate. 'Annie,' I say in a singsong, as if you are an endangered animal and I a would-be conservationist. 'Annie, aren't you cold?'

You stop talking and look carefully at me. 'Nothing, it's all right,' you say.

'Annie, it's me, Kathy.' I come closer, slowly, not wanting you to take fright. I have not seen you this bad for months. Where did you find the scissors? And where are they now? I cast an eye around while trying to seem like I am just here for a friendly chat with my half-naked sister.

'You're not Kathy. He said you would do that. *He said you would do that.*' You are not smiling anymore. I have just spotted the scissors. They are sharp, and long, and jut out from under your rolls of thigh fat. You must have tucked them under yourself to keep them hidden. From me.

'Who said? What is it Annie? Remember me? I'm your *sister.*'

I can't tell you how many times we have had this conversation over the last six months. I insist, repeat, insist that I am your sister. You don't believe me. I cite facts from our childhood. I tell you the year, the date, where you live. I ask you what you think is happening. Finally you tell me, as if for the first time, although we must have got to this point a dozen times, that there is a secret war on. You have to stop the baddies from taking over the world.

Meanwhile, I am measuring my progress. I have convinced you that I am really your sister. I have you back in my grasp.

But you waver. You start to weep. If none of this is real, then what is real?

'I am real,' I say.

'But Jeremy,' you say. 'And the babies.' You rub your belly.

'Jeremy is dead,' I say. 'He died years ago.' I point to your stomach. 'You aren't pregnant,' I say. 'That's just fat.'

I deftly swipe the scissors from under you as I help you into clean trousers, talking the entire time about your volunteer work at the local childcare centre. I talk and talk and talk, painting a picture with my words of a world in which you are engaged in purposeful activity.

* * *

You know, I understand your urge to have babies. There used to be a part of me that wanted children too. I was terrified of the idea, and it turned out that I was right to be scared. I should have embraced my fears, my completely rational fears. I won't make the same mistake again.

I didn't know it then, but the childcare centre arrangement will fall through in a matter of weeks. *Insurance,* they will shrug. As the demented episodes become more common, the same happens with the hospital visiting, the school library. Even the church choir is loath to let you sing with them (another reason, I think, not to believe in God). Over the ensuing months, the whole edifice of meaning I have attempted to build around you crumbles at our feet.

Why? I ask myself now. Why couldn't I just nod every time you talked about Jeremy, and say nothing? God knows you had a more meaningful existence inside your own mind than you did in reality.

I try to picture you and Jeremy, leaning your heads together over your drawing project at the last Carpe Diem camp. One soft moon-shaped face lifted to another. The stars above. The flash of recognition and the quickening of blood. In your demented fog, you and dead Jeremy had each other, you had children and a purpose. Just because I couldn't have that, did I have to destroy it for you, too?

I look through the rest of the pile but there are no more diaries. From one of the poetry books a slip of paper floats out. *Doubtless another ode to God,* I think, but there is no mention of the Lord, or Christ, or any of their coterie. It is a poem for Jeremy.

Jeremy, / The greatest Buster of Ghosts / Who starts every day with Vegemite on toast / Let no one come between him and his chess / or they will be check mated under duress / Jeremy, my friend, you I can't do without / Let there never be a shadow of doubt / For your cheeky grin and heart that is true / I have counted my blessings, since the day I met you.

There are no red marker notes on this one. No comments. Nothing but this rather trite poem.

I pack up and try to sleep in the back seat. I push the cushion out from under my head and think, *I didn't know that Jeremy liked chess.*

It's almost midnight when I sit up and drive. Officeworks is open late and I navigate my way to the computer terminals. I select twenty of your poems and several illustrations: the rainbow, the smiling clouds, and a crucifix that you wreathed in roses. I make it back to the car with a receipt to pick up a box of print-outs tomorrow, just in time to give them to everyone when I say goodbye.

In the morning I pull on the pink nylon blouse from Kmart that I bought for your funeral. I simply cannot wear the same shirt I have had on for the last three days. True, it's a good-quality white cotton button-up, which I'd paired with navy blue trousers and my work shoes, the black flats I wear with everything. I wanted to keep all the arrangements simple for Evan, and this, I had judged, was an outfit I could be buried in. But now it reeks of sweat and the cotton is a crumpled liability, telling too much of a true story.

* * *

After Val calls to tell me that you are finally, actually dying, I drive the same route from Sydney to Queensland as Dad did, all those years ago. Like Dad, I am running away; but unlike Dad, I have had the good sense not to park my car in places that could attract the attention of the law. I just need to stay under the radar for long enough to deliver your eulogy. Then the mum from the park, her children and Evan will be safe from me.

By the time I arrive at Logan Hospital the next day it is already dawn, a blush pink spreading across a sky hazed with smoke from winter burn-offs, the nation's annual valiant, vain attempt to keep the summer bushfires at bay. I walk to the medical wing where you usually are, before realising my mistake and retracing my steps until I find the palliative care unit. Trish and Barb are sitting on either side of you.

I knew what to expect but I am still shocked to see your face is already purple.

'Can you please leave the room? I want a minute alone with Annie.'

Barb clearly wants to protest but Trish shushes her and leads her out into the hallway.

Now it is me and you, just like it always used to be.

I sit next to your violet face. 'Annie,' I say. I touch you and hug your soft, still warm self to myself.

I hold your hand and I whisper in your ear, 'You can go now, if you want to, Annie. I'm going to be all right.' I have tried to never lie to you Annie, so I cross my fingers like we did when we were kids, pretending we had not eaten the last of the hot chips.

I let Trish and Barb come back in. Three minutes later, you open your eyes. You look vaguely confused.

'A seizure?' I ask Trish.

'This is not a seizure,' she replies.

'It's OK, honey, it's all right,' I say. I stand on one side of you and Trish stands on the other, your biggest sister and your littlest holding your hands, forming a protective tent over you with our bodies and words.

'We're here Annie. We love you.'

You close your eyes.

Trish looks at me. 'Is she?'

I nod.

Barb is standing although I don't remember her getting up. Trish fetches a nurse to confirm what we know. He puts a stethoscope to your chest, waits a moment, then stares out the door as if something more important has caught his attention. 'Yeah, she's gone,' he says and walks out.

All this time Barb has been saying, 'Oh my God, is she, Kathy? Is she really? Is she gone? Oh my God,' and all I can hear is a woman fifteen years older than me trying to feel something real. I keep saying to her, 'Shh, Barb, her spirit is still in the room. Be quiet, shh,' and then Trish has the much better idea of getting Barb to go outside and call our mother.

'She waited for me,' I say to Trish, who replies, 'Yes, she did,' and then I cry on her shoulder, and I hold your hand, keeping it soft and warm for as long as I can.

Val comes in and whimpers when she sees you, kisses you and puts some make-up on you so Mum isn't too startled when she arrives. Val may have done too good a job; when Mum walks in with Brian and Bev, she pushes her way to the bedside and shouts, 'Annie? Annie! It's Mum.'

When you don't respond, Mum looks accusingly at the six of us aligned on the opposite side of the hospital bed: Trish, Barb, Val, Bev, Brian and me. Six pairs of identical brown eyes staring at her with varying levels of sympathy. Six pairs of glasses glinting at her, reflecting her own stubborn face. Six mouths shut without even being told.

'Mum, she's gone.' Trish, the eldest, speaks first.

Mum sits back, stunned that you have really gone and done it this time. She is so small, this seventy-year-old lady. In her chair next to your head, she looks like a confused old woman. Then she leans forward suddenly and taps your cheek. If we weren't here, she would probably pinch it. The flesh of your face yields, then returns to its former place.

A priest arrives and we say a decade of the rosary, and then, after all these years of waiting and hoping and pacing hospital hallways, there is nothing left to do but leave.

The Bradleys file out one by one. Barb is the first to go, making excuses about needing to turn off the oven even though we all know she only ever cooks food that can be prepared in a microwave. Brian and Bev offer to take Mum home and sit with her until the meeting with the funeral director. This leaves Trish, Val and me to sit with you. We complain quietly about the nurse who announced your death so casually, then we complain about Barb. It is lucky at times like these to have a Barb in the family.

As we talk, I keep my wishes small and relevant to the task at hand. I do not wish you had never got sick. I do not wish you had not died, although of course I wish that. I wish for you to leave us as if you are drifting off to sleep on yet another night in yet another hospital, to the rise and fall of sisterly conversation.

Soon enough, we must leave you behind because the hospital needs your bed for someone else to die in. I remind myself that you spent much of your life in hospitals, so perhaps being left alone in the morgue is not as awful as it would have been otherwise. Perhaps it is a familiar sensation for you: the comedown after the last visitor has left, alone at last among the beeping devices and the shuffle of rubber-soled nurses' shoes. This may not seem like something to draw much comfort from. But as with my wishes, I try to keep my comforts small and relevant to the task at hand.

I am the last of my sisters to leave Logan Hospital. I'm walking down the corridor. An elderly patient hobbles past me, pushing a Zimmer frame. 'There's a fire, a fire is coming! Look out!' he says to me, steaming past in a cloud of Old Spice and urine. A nurse is soon holding him by the elbow. She is cajoling and whispering to him when, instead of the hunched old man, I see our father.

I have this memory in my viscera. The light has an orange cast to it, like the inside of a stomach or a womb or a vagina, or my parents' room with the red lampshade covering the overhead light.

There is Dad, touching me in a way a father should never, ever touch his child.

I do not see him so much as smell him. Old Spice. The smell of safe harbour.

I think, *This is my fault.*

I think, *I want this. Because I want to be loved and this is what you do for love.*

The knowledge sinks seamlessly into my soul like a key fitting an oiled lock. I thought I would feel triumphant or destroyed, but all I feel is a tired sort of disappointment. *Oh Dad,* I think, shaking my head.

I take the Bernadette statuette and the bottle of holy water to give to Val for the decorations and let myself in through the flyscreen door.

'In here,' Val calls from the dining room, which has been turned into a makeshift art studio. The table is draped with a white sheet and your coffin rests on top, a single ship on a paint-dappled sea.

'It's beautiful.' I mean it. Val's daughter is at art school and has clearly earned her place there. The coffin is completely covered in paintings of pink and violet flowers, linked by a swirling pattern reminiscent of a mandala. Atop the lid, right about where your heart will be, Val has placed a cross. I recognise it from your room at Mountainview. It is brightly painted in all the primary colours, more Carnivale than crucifixion. It's perfect.

Val is seated at the table, stitching something. I peck her on the cheek and see a cotton broderie anglaise pillow case in her lap, partially embroidered with your name, date of birth and another date which it takes me a moment to realise is the date of your death.

'I thought it would be nice for her,' Val explains. 'The funeral home gives them each a satin cushion but I just thought—' She puts down the needle and rubs her eyes under her glasses. I nod, my throat too constricted momentarily to speak.

'Want a cuppa?' she asks.

'I can get it.'

'Nah I need a break. Besides you don't know how to make a good coffee.'

In the kitchen Val bustles about with kettle and water. We go out the back and sip from our mugs, observing the chickens peck at their breakfast in the coop Val's husband wired together. It's ostensibly winter and not yet mid-morning but it's warmer than a Sydney spring day. I close my eyes and raise my face to the sun, feeling heat penetrate my skin to the deeper layers.

'I know about Joy.'

The hot coffee sloshes over the side of the mug, scalding my hand as I stand up.

'I called Evan.'

'I didn't know you had his number.' It's the only thing I can think of to say.

'Well, Trish called me. So I called him.' The Bradley telegraph. I should have been more prepared for this. I try to think of something to say, but my voice is stuck somewhere below my chest.

'Let it out, Kathy. Let it out.'

I shake off the hand patting me on the back. *I am not crying*, I want to say, *just trying to breathe*. My hands are on my knees and I am standing by the chicken enclosure, peering through the mesh as if my life depends on finding eggs for breakfast. Val takes my arm and leads me to a garden bench.

'You might not know this, but I had a miscarriage. Before my youngest. That's why there was such a gap between him and the others. Five years. And you remember about the troubles Trish had, having her baby.'

No, I don't, but as Val talks I recall Trish's husband's strained smile each time a Bradley asked when he and Trish were going to start trying for a baby. Trish would say something about cementing her medical practice first, and the conversation would move on, the Bradleys silently wondering how cold Trish could be, how single-minded.

I wonder how many other things I don't know. I think of Bev and her flight from Brisbane. I think of Val and her pills, the green hospital. This family has had enough of not knowing. I will tell at least one Bradley about what happened in that orange light, back in 1983, in case – well, in case anyone else in the family needs the reassurance of knowledge.

I stand and pace the backyard until breath can refill my lungs sufficient for speech and then I begin.

'Oh Dad,' Val says after I have finished, which makes me laugh a little at how exactly she has echoed my own sentiment. She places her mug on the ground next to her and looks as if she has decided something.

'You know how you told me that you argued with him the night before he died?' Val asks. I nod, unsure where this is going.

'Well, when I got there, there was a mess of pills by his bed. I just gathered them up and threw them out. I'm not saying ...' she looks at her hands. 'It wasn't your fault.'

'I have to go. I need to get to the funeral home, to wash and dress Annie.'

Val shudders slightly despite the sun. 'You're a brave one, Kathy. Braver than me.' There is a faint ringing sound which could be a washing machine cycle ending or a doorbell chiming. Val looks towards the house. 'Just one second. I have something for you.'

She hurries inside. My body seems to need to stay in motion so I walk over to the shade of a sprawling Moreton Bay fig growing in the backyard.

I smell him before I see him. His own unique mixture of male-ness and kindness.

'Kathy,' Evan says.

I turn around and walk straight past his open arms, out the gate.

PART 5

LEGACY

Use this section of the eulogy to reflect on
what the deceased leaves behind them, not
just in material goods, but in life lessons.
How has the deceased left the world better
than when they came into it?

How to Write a Eulogy

The funeral director has set up the viewing room very nicely. The walls are painted pigeon-wing pink, making me wonder if they have a blue room for male bodies. Your body lies in the centre of the room on a raised trolley, covered in a satin sheet so only your head, feet and arms show. The mortician must have applied make-up to your face so there is a touch of rosiness in your cheeks.

Sometimes funeral homes have stupid rules about no open flames, which is ridiculous really, considering what is scheduled to happen, so I wait for the funeral director to leave before I bring out the candle and oil I bought from the Hyperdome. This time last year I would not have thought to do this. Now I have all the experience a person needs to treat you well.

The candle casts a warm glow over your face. I am prepared for the iciness of your skin, which is hard yet rubbery, as if I might simultaneously leave a thumbprint and shatter your cheek into myriad pieces.

I got here a little late, after all that happened at Val's. I had to pull the car over a few kilometres from her house, far enough so that Evan couldn't try and follow me. That was when the howl came. I rested my head on the steering wheel and wept. I ached from the absence of his arms around me, from the absence of my baby in my arms.

By comparison, being in this room with you is a relief. I am sad, but I have been sad for you for so long that grieving for you is like coming home. I begin to rub frangipani-scented oil into your hands, reminding me of the countless times I rubbed warmth back into your feet and arms when we were kids, then teenagers, then twenty-somethings, then after. The tumour affected your blood circulation so that even during a Brisbane heatwave your extremities could be freezing.

Your hands are getting warm with the heat of the oil and my own flesh on yours, and soon we both smell like the happiest of Queensland summers. As I move around your body I find myself talking to you out loud.

'There we go Annie, just going to rub your right hand now. The ladies have done a lovely job, your cheeks are really pink.'

As if in response to an unspoken question, I say, 'Mum is not here right now but she will be there tomorrow. I am going to stay with her tonight and Bev has been there all week so she is not alone. Don't you worry. We'll take care of her.'

I am not going to tell you about what Val told me, about Dad and the pills. As I knead your feet and calves, I think, *I should feel guilty about that*. But I don't. It's hard to explain, but I know that he did not do that because of me. The knowledge is cellular, like the fact of flesh. The only time I have felt a similar certainty was when Evan asked me to marry him and I did not feel love, or what I thought love would feel like. I didn't see fairy lights or hear angels singing. I simply felt, yes.

'Trish and me and Brian are going to say something, and Bev and Barb will do the prayers of the faithful. I haven't written my bit but not to worry, I'll do it tonight at Mum's. I put a notice in the paper so people will know to make donations instead of flowers. You should see what Val and her kids have done with the casket, it's really lovely, you'd love it I reckon.' I always lapsed into my original bogan accent around you, instinctively speaking the language of our youth in the hope that it would help you understand it was me talking to you, for real, your little sister Kathy.

If heaven is a place where we are all restored, will it be as if this cancerous timeline of our lives together had never happened? In which case, I wonder, will you remember what I told you on that last visit?

I lean in close and whisper in your ear, 'If you see her, tell her, you know, everything good.'

You're the only Bradley I told. I didn't want my baby to become family property, the thing our siblings talked to me about at gatherings because we had nothing else in common but our ability to procreate. In the end I made the right decision, because I failed at even that most basic Bradley skill. A month after I visited you at Mountainview for the last time,

I wasn't pregnant any more. I can just picture you looking around as if you had misplaced your glasses. *Where's the baby then, Kathy? Where?*

* * *

It's not that I don't want a child but I am shit-scared – I believe that is the technical term – of making one out of my body. Flesh of my flesh. Wound of my wound. I start making lists. I convince Evan that we need to exchange my car for a Subaru wagon, because it has the highest star rating on the National Child Safety Register. I import an Infant First Choice capsule from Italy because it is the safest one to be had for love or money – quite a bit of money. I order a sensor monitor for the crib so I will know if the baby stops breathing. I buy a double breast pump in case I have trouble getting my milk to come down. I order a one-hundred per cent merino wool blanket, six one-hundred per cent organic cotton muslin wraps, five one-hundred per cent soft cotton onesies in 0000 as well as five in 00000, in case the baby is premmie. I buy a Baby Björn carrier so I can hold my baby against my heartbeat, which the research says will send it to sleep, dreaming of the womb.

At the twelve-week ultrasound, we hear our little baby's heart pitter-pattering like a soul that has strapped on tap shoes to dance towards life. The radiologist smiles at us and we grin at each other in awe of our powers of creation.

Two weeks later I am in a hire car, on my way to visit you. Mountainview House, where you've now been living for about a year, is a forty-minute drive along the Logan Motorway, a nice bit of road, as Dad would have said.

'She's having a rest,' Mary says. 'You sit with her. She would like that.'

You are dozing in the fancy wheelchair Val sourced for you. I pull up a stool next to you, one hand in my lap holding a book, one hand in yours. I read out loud to you like I used to do when you were sick in hospital and I still believed the next operation would fix everything.

I hesitate, then lean over and whisper into your ear, 'Annie. I want you to be the first to know. I'm going to have a baby.'

I press your hand. I check your eyes to see if you might open them and see me. I smile at the carer and make myself cups of tea. When she isn't looking, I take photos of you on my phone. 'Annie enjoying my scintillating company.' 'Annie laughing at my hilarious jokes.' 'Annie exchanging droll observations with me about the other residents.' I consider sending them to Val and Brian, but they might not get the joke. I don't feel guilty about taking the pictures, because I think you would have laughed. If you could have, you would have opened your eyes, shaken your head at me and laughed.

That's my Annie, I think fondly. That's my Annie, sleeping through what turned out to be my last visit to you in the world of the living.

I assume that you will know I have been with you because I feel so very much there.

I am standing at the sink in my work staff room, making a cup of tea. I am thinking about a report I have to finish by the end of the day. I am parsing grammar when my waters break and the fluid keeping my baby alive leaks out of me. It turns out that humans are mere fish living on land. We carry the primeval ocean with us, just to survive.

She was a girl, Annie; she was a little girl.

have finally graduated from visitor to patient. The doctor explains my options. A midwife offers to take photos in case I don't want to see it, her, afterwards. They hook me up on one side to a morphine drip, on the other to Syntocinon. Syntocinon bypasses all the pleasantries of mild contractions and takes a woman straight to labour. It is an artificial version of oxytocin, the molecule that humans produce when they love; the molecule with which mothers perfume the air of a birthing suite.

The induced contractions splice me in two, but I refuse to press down on the morphine drip. The pain is a form of justice. It is all I have as proof.

'One last, big push!' the midwife urges. My mind is numb, my body has taken over in a dance I did not even know I knew the steps to. I push with all my remaining strength. I want everything inside of me to fall out with her: my guts, my blood and all my history. I want to be completely empty.

Evan stands next to the midwife. The midwife hands him a wee bundle wrapped in a pink flannelette blanket. Tears stream down his face. The only other time I have seen him cry, I think irrelevantly, was on the day we married.

'She's beautiful,' he says to me. 'She's got your little nose.'

I reach out and he places her in my arms. 'Joy,' I whisper to her. 'It's all right. Mama's got you now.'

They let me have her next to me in the cold crib for three days. No one rushes me. I am allowed to hold her, then put her back, then hold her again. My little baby, my tiny little girl. She does not cry. She does not make a sound.

After the procedure, the hospital gives Evan and me a letter that states, 'This is to certify that Joy Sang-lian Bradley-Lee was born without signs of life before twenty-four weeks.' This letter is more valuable than gold. I keep it close to my chest, which aches from the milk no baby will ever drink. This letter is what will allow us to bury her, rather than have her treated as waste from a medical procedure and destroyed by the hospital along with the cancerous tumours and infected appendices of Sydney's lower north shore..

It's a shining day when Evan and I arrive at the Garden of Remembrance. Evan comes around to my side of the car and opens my door for me. He takes my hand and we walk towards the building.

A funeral director is there to greet us. She shakes our hands and leads us inside. On a table lies our girl. She is the colour of marble. Her eyes are closed although she is not sleeping. I lift her into my arms. The funeral director has brought oils and shows me how to massage my baby's little hands so they feel almost warm in mine. I kiss her little cheek and now it feels like skin rather than the stretched-out icicle that the morticians turned our father into for his funeral.

Evan and I say the things we came to say. I don't want to put her down. Evan doesn't make me. He takes a turn holding her, murmuring words to her that I don't hear, words that are between a father and his daughter.

It's time. I hold out my arms and Evan hands her back to me. The funeral director gestures towards what looks just like a white wicker basket for a baby's naptime, except that it has a lid. I place her on the pretty satin cushions of her little resting place, instinctively thinking, *organic cotton would have breathed better, less risk of heat rash.*

I want her buried, not like Dad, who wanted to be cremated, and not like you, either, whom the family has agreed should also be burnt, your ashes interred next to his. I want my little girl to return to the earth, to become soil and plant and some other form of the life that I could not give her.

The smell of freshly turned dirt fills my nostrils, redolent of spring and flowers and new life. Joy's plot is in the middle, with room for us to go either side of her when the time comes. The undertakers lower her into the ground. Evan and I place flowers on top of the wee box. They wait with heads bowed for us to finish. Then they refill the hole with the waiting earth.

That night as I lie in bed, the doctor's words play over and over again in my mind. A chromosomal abnormality. Not my fault. When she said this to me I had nodded, because that is what we Bradleys have always done when doctors lie to our faces.

I wake with a start before dawn. I am sweating and my lower abdomen feels like needles are sticking into it. I try not to fall back to sleep, but the sedatives take me under. Each time I close my eyes I see her, a little version of me. Each time she tries to gouge out a piece of me, leering at me with such utter disgust that I feel like I am a bin for contaminated sharps, a receptacle for the waste of bodies more important than mine, more worthy of life.

I remain in bed until I can be sure that Evan has gone to the shops, then I get up, open the fridge. There is nothing to eat but dust and ashes. I turn on the TV. Nothing but grey, grey, grey. I think about tomorrow. I think about the day after that.

I get in the car and drive. It is dark by the time I arrive home with five prescriptions from five different medical centres.

* * *

I realise you wouldn't approve, but Annie, I've made a number of very detailed calculations, some of them using weighted variables, and I know that Evan will be better off without me. People say this, but I can categorically demonstrate that he deserves better than what I can give. It might be hard on him for a little while, but he will move on. It will all make a certain kind of sense.

Before I got the call from Val I had it all planned. You and your dying, endlessly getting in the way of my business.

My work in OH&S risk management has taught me one thing: even the best plans can go awry. So I have researched the dosage I need for my body weight. I have tested my sensitivity to a range of sleeping pills and chosen the one that knocked me out the longest and hardest. I used a smoothie blender, one of our wedding presents from Evan's side of the family, to crush the pills into a fine white powder, which will increase absorption and efficacy by up to fourteen per cent. I have packed my kit – the container of pills, my ID, my will, my instructions – in a sealed bag so the moist ground at the Garden of Remembrance will only affect me and not my documents.

I know you wanted me to be happy, Annie. But every time I took a step closer to happiness, I dragged you away from it. All our lives, it felt like only one of us could make it. Darling girl, I am so sorry it wasn't you. You would have been so much better at it.

* * *

In the weeks after we bury our baby, Evan goes back to work and I start a new routine. On Mondays, after my visit to the Garden, I pull down the sun shield over the state-of-the-art stroller and push it to the park, where I see other thirty-something-year-old mums sitting on benches, rocking their prams to and fro with one hand while sipping from takeaway decaf lattes in the other. Tuesdays there is story-time at the library, during which I browse the non-fiction large-print books, nudging the pram backwards and forwards in that universal sign that the resident baby is sleeping. Wednesdays I have to hustle to get from the Garden back to the park for yoga, where I can walk the circumference of the park sixteen times in my post-pregnancy activewear, while the mums do cats' stretches with babies in their arms. I find a group on Facebook for mothers with social anxiety, and I go to their weekly meet-ups on Thursdays. It's perfect, because no one forces you into inane conversation like, how much weight has she put on this week? Honestly Annie, infancy is the only time in a girl's life when their success is determined by actually getting fatter. Fridays I go to a local cafe where mums 'n' bubs converge at 11.05 am after clinic. I nurse a pot of peppermint tea because, like the lactating mothers, I avoid caffeine.

Every day I drive to the Garden of Remembrance and walk along the undulating pathways. Sometimes I sing a lullaby, sometimes I talk, but most of the time I just lie next to her. I wonder about how much her little bones have decayed, and which worms have been lucky enough to nibble at her perfect, tiny toes. This may sound morbid, but to me it does not feel especially melancholic. It's the closest I come to feeling at peace. Other mothers watch for first tooth, first step. I just have a different set of milestones.

On the Monday before you die it is raining lightly. I am out for my regular walk, pushing the pram around the park, considering heading home early because of the weather, when I see a mum carrying a baby, huddled under the Port Jackson fig tree near the playground. A toddler in a bright green raincoat gleefully splashes in puddles.

The sight of this makes me stop for a moment. This is my undoing.

'We're the only brave ones today!' the mum calls and raises her takeaway coffee to me in a gesture of solidarity. Her shoulder-length hair is damp from the rain. 'Come stand with us, there's loads of room.'

I make the universal hand gesture for 'no, I don't want to trouble you', but the toddler has spotted me and runs over in her oversized purple gum boots.

'Come see my, my, my mermaid castle!' she says, tugging at my free hand.

'Mermaid castle,' the mum says, shaking her head and laughing. She and her toddler have the same slightly upturned nose.

I try to smile politely at the same time as extracting myself from the little girl's moist grasp, but I pull too hard and, like a Christmas cracker popping, the toddler lands on her bottom in the wet sand. She immediately starts to cry.

'Oh my God, I'm so sorry!'

The mum reassures me. 'Don't worry, it's fine. She's probably just hungry.'

I lean down to restore the toddler to her feet but as soon as I lay a hand on her, she bawls even louder.

'Mu-u-u-u-ummmy! I want Mu-u-u-u-u-ummmy!'

'Oh, it's not *you,*' the mum apologises. 'She's been like this since,' she indicates the baby in her arms, 'this one came along. Can you just take her for a minute? I better pick her up.'

Before I can protest, the mum has placed the baby in my arms. I leave the pram and drop my own coffee on the ground so as to have two hands for jiggling the baby up and down, up and down. The mum squats and picks up the toddler in a smooth, strong sweep of her arms. The toddler's tears start to subside.

'Are you hungry darling?'

The toddler nods, her sandy thumb making its way into her mouth. The woman peers inside the bag on the back of her stroller. 'Oh, bugger,' she swears. 'I forgot to pack the crackers.' At this, the toddler re-commences wailing.

'God, can you just – hold her while I run to the cafe and grab some banana bread?'

Before I can offer to run over and get it for her myself, she is shouting thanks over her shoulder and hitching the toddler further up on her hip. *Do mothers really do this?* I wonder, stunned. How can they be so trusting?

Just at that moment, the baby wakes up and starts to grizzle. I sway from side to side, but she opens her little mouth to let out a proper bawl. The mum will wonder why I can't handle a baby. I panic. I raise the shield over my pram and place the baby inside, then start to push the pram to and fro. The baby immediately stops crying. She is contemplating the dangling toys I attached to the pram when I first bought it. She swipes at the Lamaze rattle, and coos at Sophie the giraffe. When I peer in to see that she is all right, her face breaks open into a smile.

There is still no sign of the mum. The rain starts coming down even harder. I draw the shield over the baby and start walking.

I am fifty metres from our apartment when a blue-and-white police car pulls up in front of me, another behind me, and another alongside of me, red and blue lights flashing. The mum shrieks from the back seat. 'That's her! The Chinese one! She stole my baby!'

I look around, curious to see the Chinese woman who has kidnapped a child. Then I see where I am and what I have done. I lift my hands from the pram and get in the back of the police vehicle without so much as a murmur.

'I was never planning to steal her,' I say to the policewoman who has climbed in next to me. She shakes her head and begins to read me my rights.

Evan spends more than an hour speaking in a low voice to the police officers while the baby snuggles against her mother and the toddler plays in the corner with the station's Fisher-Price play kitchen set. After half a styrofoam cup of tea, the woman agrees not to press charges as long as the police issue a protection order prohibiting me from coming within two hundred metres of a day care centre, school, playground or other children's facility.

The policewoman waits a decent interval after the mother has left with her children before signing me out. When I emerge from the cell Evan envelopes me in a hug. I start to sweat but he doesn't seem to notice, keeping his arms firmly around me as if I am a balloon and he is afraid I will float away and kill some poor unsuspecting marine animal. When he finally takes his arms from around my shoulders, it is only in order to squeeze my hands.

'Where's the pram?' I ask.

'The police are going to drop it off at Vinnies for us,' he says. 'We can always get another one, further down the track.'

Evan came to the station in such a hurry that he does not have his laptop, his notes, all the other things he will need to work from home for the next few weeks. The same policewoman who arrested me now offers to give me a lift home while Evan ducks back to the office to grab what he needs. Before I can climb into the police car, this time into the front passenger seat, Evan cradles my face, gently but inexorably forcing me to look at him.

'I love you,' he says. 'You're not alone in this. We'll make a plan.'

I nod because I already have a plan.

The policewoman sees me to my door where she hands me a pamphlet for a counselling service. After she leaves, I change out of my new-mother costume of joggers and leggings and don the white shirt and navy trousers.

I am at the Garden of Remembrance and have just opened the container when the phone rings. I ignore it. It rings again. I ignore it again. It keeps ringing. The next time it rings, I can't resist the old familiar anxiety and I answer.

It's the call I have been waiting for since 1983.

'This is it,' Val says. 'Come quickly.'

* * *

'Val found some of your old notebooks at Mountainview.' I stroke your head. 'I read about the Snowys camp. I'm really happy that you had fun.' I don't want you to feel guilty that you were glad I wasn't able to attend.

'Oh,' I say as if it just occurred to me, 'I found the poem you wrote for Jeremy.' I watch your face. Nothing changes but the atmosphere, which becomes refulgent with more than the scent of summer, as if the room is holding its breath with hope on your behalf. 'I was thinking, Annie. I have this idea I want to run past you.'

I get lunch at the servo near Angel Companions. The place almost feels like home now. I pull out the laptop but instead of going to Word, I connect to the servo's wi-fi, open the internet browser and search for a phone number.

'Queensland Cancer Council,' the receptionist answers my call after two rings.

'Hi, I'm wondering if you can put me through to the coordinator for Carpe Diem. I used to be a member and I am looking for the details of some old friends.'

'Sure, just putting you through.'

After lunch I go to Mum's place, the townhouse in Shailer Park near the Hyperdome, where you and Mum moved to after Dad died. The place is cluttered with Mum's usual mess of old race guides and groceries which she does not bother to unpack, extracting what she needs directly from the plastic bags. In a third-year university subject entitled 'Mental Health and Ageing', the lecturer told us that there are three reasons an elderly person (as opposed to someone as young as you) ends up in aged care: mad, bad or sad. Mad explains itself. Bad – they have a fall and can no longer take care of themselves, their bones too brittle to heal. Sad – they are too depressed to bother eating any more. Since you were moved out of her house, Mum has subsisted on complimentary sausage rolls and party pies, courtesy of the pokies.

I leave the car in the visitor's carpark and walk down the narrow brick path to Mum's door. The complex is neatly kept, and although it is in the poorer part of the suburb, there is no graffiti on any of the walls and the neighbours are tradies, young couples and working single mums.

'Yeah, OK Kathy, come in, come in.' Mum opens the door for me. I walk up the ramp that she had installed for you. *It might help Mum as she gets older*, I think, watching her move to the kitchen with the slight limp she has had for years now, caused by osteoporosis of the hip. 'Too many babies' had been the doctor's report. *I could have told you that*, I had thought, and bought her a bottle of calcium supplements.

'Kathy, you want something to eat? I got these biscuits for you, you know, the ones you like.' Mum digs around in a grocery bag and draws out a packet of custard creams.

'I'm not hungry,' I say.

'Oh, you want something else?' She bends to look inside the fridge, and I interrupt before she hurts her back. 'No it's OK, I'll have a biscuit.'

'Oh good, good.'

I chew through the sweetness as Mum bustles about the room. She doesn't love to cook, but she has always been a feeder. When we were growing up, she would scream at me, call me all sorts of names, then place a plate of mince and cabbage on the table. Sometimes I had to return to kneeling after dinner, sometimes not – in this way she had mellowed over the years, since the big kids.

I take my bag upstairs and then, jingling the car keys, I say, 'Come on Mum, let's get those roots done!' She laughs and hurries into a pair of slip-on shoes. 'OK, OK.'

We drive to the Hyperdome where I walk Mum to Mermaids, her usual hairdresser. They accept walk-ins. Our mother does not like appointments; she has never had the patience to wait.

All the girls who work here look young enough to be our mother's grandchildren. I have a word with the hairdresser at the counter. 'My mum is getting her hair done for my sister's funeral. She's a bit fragile, so please take good care of her.' I make sure I speak loudly enough for Mum to hear, so she knows that she does not have to explain, and she knows that I am looking after her.

Mum sits down, smiling at a trainee who puts a towel around her neck and tips Mum's head back over the basin. How often has our mother been touched by other humans, I wonder, since you were moved out? I pat her on the shoulder and tell her I will be back when she is done.

I head to the grocery store and buy frozen dinners, family-size boxes of breakfast cereal, ring-pull cans of tuna and UHT milk. I make sure to pack it all into two bags, so it does not look like I have gone overboard. The last time I bought Mum groceries, she said thank you in the same breath as asking me for cash. I drive back to Officeworks and pick up the books I ordered, before returning to the salon.

When I get there Mum is ready. Her hair looks neat and slightly reddish from a rinse, because at seventy, her hair is too brittle for dyes. I hand over the cash and Mum tells the girl, whom she is now fast friends with, 'This my daughter. She

288

here from Sydney.' My mum has made a habit of introducing me thus to people in taverns and TABs throughout south-east Queensland. You used to tell me it was because Mum was proud of me.

Back at the house, Mum fetches a bowl and clears a space among the newspapers on the dining room table for me to eat my noodles. Afterwards I find a spot on the couch. I know where to sit without making our mother fidgety: at the eastern end of the Queen Anne replica sofa, where Mum's piles of newspapers and cushions thin to a penetrable depth.

The other couch has been permanently extended into a sofa bed where Mum reclines during the day, before limping upstairs to her bedroom at around eight pm every night. She has two televisions downstairs: one set to free-to-air and the other on Foxtel. For a while she experimented with three TVs simultaneously, but that was too much even for her. Of course she has the radio on, set to the races station.

As I focus on the free-to-air TV and relax into the cushions, I feel as though I am sinking into a familiar and not unpleasant somnolence. Mum fetches me a cup of tea between ads. She peers in the cupboard, trying to find something else to offer me to eat.

Mum starts to nod off and I give her a kiss goodnight. 'OK, An— Kathy, OK,' Mum says, pretending she has not been asleep. She lumbers up the stairs, careful to avoid the chair lift tracks and the piles of clothes. The entire house is one giant fall hazard, but there is also a kind of sense to it: if Mum were to stumble, her accumulated mess would break the fall.

She shows me into your old room. I thought I would feel upset being in here, but mostly I feel at home. I make a tour of your small library, which comprises just two shelves next to the bed. People stopped giving you books after you got sick, so the collection includes only the old familiars: *Black Beauty*, Trixie Belden, Enid Blyton, the Bible.

I open this last and come across your handwriting on the pages where a person can write in their family's names. There we all are, the Bradleys, memorialised in your childish hand: Trish, Barb, Val, Bev, Brian, Annie and Kathy. Even Matthew gets a mention – you have squeezed his name above Trish's, eldest first. Then there is a list of our siblings' spouses and children, and at the bottom of the page you have written in your special cursive script: 'Annie Bradley, married to Jeremy Wood, children Michael, Azrael and Gabriel, angels one and all.' I laugh a little at myself for being surprised, and then I take a pen and add Evan and my own sweet baby's name to your list.

PART 6

CLOSING

This is the end of the eulogy. Try to leave mourners with a sense of hope. You may like to select a suitable quote which sums up your message.

How to Write a Eulogy

The day of your funeral is a beautiful, sunny Queensland winter day. I had managed to do a load of washing at Mum's so the pink Kmart top is fresh; I don't need my jacket but I make Mum wear one because she feels the cold in her old age.

We drive to the church. The Bradley family has gathered before the service so we can say our last goodbyes. Val has brought textas so we can scribble our farewells between the paintings on your coffin. Since I saw it yesterday, Val has also attached some of your own drawings along the sides of the casket. I write a message on one side, and I can't stop kissing the box and kissing my hand to the box.

Inside the casket and in the daylight, you look one hundred per cent dead. The clothes that Val bought for you and which I dressed you in have somehow been glued to your body. I place the golden crucifix around your neck. Val asks me if I am going to want it back but I shake my head. You are not wearing glasses because your eyes are shut so I put them in the casket beside you. How will you know where you are going without them? Someone else, probably Val, has placed rosary beads in your hands. I gather up your little holy medals and scapulars and slip them in beside you. It feels like an intimate holiness, a secret between you and me and maybe your God.

The church fills up with people in various shades of pink who must have seen the newspaper notice, who knew you when you were a kid at primary school. People I have not seen in twenty years come up to me, weeping for you, in shock and wonder: wonder that we all still exist and are all grown so old together, and shock that you, the terminally ill child who grew up, have actually died this time. I shake their hands, wanting to tell them that I never really believed it would happen either.

A woman approaches me and for a second I startle, thinking it is the mum from the park come to avenge herself on me. As she draws closer, she looks more and more familiar.

'Jess!' I exclaim. 'What are you doing here?'

'Of course I'm here,' she replies, wiping her eyes. 'You're my best friend.'

Look at all of these people, I think. Annie, you were loved. You loved and you were loved.

'Thank you,' I say to Jess. I move through the crowd and although I am not looking for him, exactly, I don't see Evan. I try to stop feeling so unreasonably disappointed.

We take our seats and the priest commences the service. Barb is wearing what looks like a pink mother-of-the-bride suit and even a hat and matching pumps. Bev, less over the top in a dress with pink flowers printed on a black background, mumbles through her prayers, trying not to open her mouth too wide, forgetting she has good teeth now. Barb simpers and looks as holy as she can.

Trish, Brian and I approach the lectern. Trish is in a smart black suit with a pink silk scarf knotted at her neck. She goes first, her mellifluous doctor voice projecting across the church with an anecdote about you as a bossy little sister who had the nerve to tell Doctor Trish what to do. She gets a few sympathetic laughs. Brian has been dressed, no doubt by his wife, in a tasteful pale-pink business shirt and a dark pink tie. He goes next and tells the chronological tale of your life and death.

It's my turn. 'A few housekeeping matters.' I pull back from the microphone, which has just turned my s's into the hisses of a bingo caller.

'It says on your order of service that after this we will be heading to the Mount Cotton Memorial Gardens. There has been a change of plans. Annie's body will be taken to Yeronga Memorial Garden and interred with Jeremy Wood. You might not have known this, but Annie and Jeremy were in love.'

There is a murmur from the crowd, and Brian half stands as if he is about to pull me away from the microphone. I grip the lectern more firmly.

'I loved Annie. She was a part of me, and she always will be.'

Val tugs Brian back to a seated position.

'It's not what you want me to say, but Annie was sometimes really annoying.' A gasp from the faithful. 'Before she developed dementia, she would talk to herself all the time, not remember what you had told her five minutes ago, and she started wetting herself after Dad died as a sign of *independence*.' I laugh admiringly, but no one else does. Trish sits next to Val with an unreadable look on her face, Bev weeps quietly next to her, while Val places a restraining hand on Brian's arm. I hear Barb ask *sotto voce*, 'Has she been drinking?'

I look out across the sea of pink and I see him. He is wearing a T-shirt that looks like it may have turned pink from being washed with my reds. He smiles and nods, urging me on to whatever it is I am about to say and do.

'This is just the truth, or my version of it, because who knows what Annie would have really thought about her life, or her death, or anything? She couldn't speak for the last three years of her life, and for more than ten years before that she lived in a fantasy land in which she and Jeremy were saving the world from the likes of *us*,' I sweep my hand around the church.

'I used to say, "No Annie, I'm real," but was I? Or was I just playing the game like all of you, pretending to care when actually I just wanted to get out of there as fast as I could, away from her, this girl who made herself so sick to protect me from—' I pause. From up here, I can see white roots through the red rinse in our mother's hair.

I clear my throat and modulate my voice. 'Annie's role models were the female saints of the Church. My role model was Annie, who served as a kind of summary of all the virtues for me, a shortcut to God.

'Annie was my big sister. To you, she was a disabled girl, a tragic story, but to me, she was real. On a deep level, I knew she was always there, a blanket of goodwill, shielding me from the sufferings of the world.

'I have been pondering, even attempting to answer with research, *What does love feel like?* Annie was the one who taught me how to love. It feels like this.'

My voice breaks, but I keep going. 'I read somewhere that there are five things you should say to someone before they die. So, on behalf of all of us who were unable to enjoy the privilege of being with Annie in her final days,' I take a deep breath, 'please, say this with me: Thank you Annie. We love you. We forgive you. We're sorry. Goodbye.'

I repeat the words, and the congregation raises their voices in shared farewell. It sounds just like a prayer.

I direct the funeral cortège to Yeronga, and no one can stop me because I am sitting next to the driver of the hearse. Waiting there for us is Mrs Wood, who bursts into tears when she sees me and wraps me in her arms. 'Thank you,' she says, and cannot stop wringing my hands. I lead her to our mother. I don't think Mum really knows what is going on, but she is gracious and pats the other mother's hand as they limp together to Jeremy's grave.

The Memorial Garden has prepared a temporary placard with the words I gave them.

'Anne Maria Bernadette Bradley, beloved sister, aunty, daughter, friend, lover and mother. May she rest in peace with her beloved Jeremy and their little ones, Michael, Gabriel and Azrael, angels one and all.'

Brian mutters when he reads it, but Trish rubs my back and Val nods through her tears. Mum pats Mrs Wood's hand and says, 'Oh, yeah, *Jeremy*,' and Mrs Wood nods vigorously. The two mothers smile at each other and take a seat on a nearby bench, their hips aching from the weight of bearing so many lives into the world.

The Bradleys gather at Brian's house for the wake. Our siblings pick over your few belongings, selecting mementoes. There are no more surprises in the box: no secret letters or credit card bills, no records or discoveries of a different side to your nature. Your death is a wound that will heal with fresh air and the acknowledgement that such things need tending.

Brian refuses to speak to me, but I get up and hug him. I walk around my circle of siblings, distributing kisses and the small pink books I picked up from Officeworks while Mum was having her hair done. I have included your illustrations alongside your poems, so the pages are adorned with the childlike grace of your texta-drawn flowers, crucifixes and smiling suns. I have addressed each book and added, 'Smile, God loves you! Love Annie.'

Tears spring to Brian's tired eyes and he pats me on the back. Val says, 'Oh,' and gives me a kiss. Trish nods and says, 'Maybe you could do this with her other poems. For Christmas.' Barb flicks through her copy as if looking for her own name – that is unkind but you know it's probably true. Bev's lower lip trembles. She is a good egg, really. Like the rest of us, she just had to find her own way out.

Mum holds the book away from her face so she can see it – she is forever forgetting her reading glasses. 'Oh, oh, this Annie book, is it? Oh, thank you, love! This Annie book!' she says to the gathered masses, her offspring, the people she has made and who now shape and stretch the world beyond what she could ever have imagined when she tripped down the steps to the Starlight Club for the simple pleasure of feeling arms around her waist.

'Oh,' she repeats. 'You got more?'

I point to the pile next to her and laugh. 'Yes, Mum, I got more.' I know she will want to give copies to the sundry strangers she meets at the TAB.

She flicks through the book and says, 'You good person, Kathy.'

You know, there was a missed call on my phone from Mum, just minutes before my baby was delivered, even though I had told no one about what was happening. I like to think it was mother's intuition. I never asked her why she called that day in case it was for money. Maybe it was both. Probably it was.

'Yes, I am.' I give our mother a hug and kiss her on the forehead.

So here we all are, Annie. All together again, united once more by you. But now it is almost time for me to leave this house that is not mine, and this family that always will be, no matter how I try to scrape them from my skin. There is just one last thing I need to do before I go. I head out to the car and reach for the Tupperware container. I raise it like a toast to Dad, who swilled his pills on his last night on Earth, recklessly indifferent or hopeful of an outcome, I will never know. But I do know this: on my wedding night I wept. Not from pain, but from a new memory being created within these walls of shame.

I empty the white powder into the breeze, and it floats away like the ashes of someone much beloved. I tear up the documents and the wind dances away the fragments of my last will and testament.

I walk back into the house, crossing the never-ending tiles of my brother's living room (was this place always so big?). I pat my mother on her red-tinted hair where she sits, deep in conversation with Jeremy's mother. Brian raises a glass to me; two beers and one poetry book have melted his soft old Bradley heart. I sidestep Bev and Barb, who are discussing the relative pros and cons of spas in outdoor living areas, and fend off mini frittatas (Trish) and chocolate brownies (Val). Husbands stand around Brian's pool table discussing real estate, while nieces and nephews slouch on the floor in various positions of competitive sloth.

I pass them all and keep walking until I am within kissing distance of the tall, handsome Chinese-Australian man who has been sipping a soft drink in the corner, watching us Bradleys at our best. Even in mourning we are a loud mob. We are the apes who lit the first flame, becoming human in the flickering glow of sheer excess, the joy of watching things be consumed.

I have travelled across so many years, borders, and acres of Brian's living room to stand before this man, in this moment. The hope and pain in Evan's eyes feels like home. I rise up on tiptoes to meet him there. And I hold out my hand.

HELPLINES IN AUSTRALIA

Lifeline: call 13 11 14,
text 0477 13 11 14, lifeline.org.au

Embrace Multicultural Mental Health:
embracementalhealth.org.au

Switchboard Victoria: switchboard.org.au

Open Minds: openminds.org.au

Search online for **'Our Directory – Mental Health Support
for Mob, Māori and BIPOC'**

RELEVANT RESEARCH

The following articles informed the research mentioned in this manuscript.

American Psychiatric Association (2000), *Diagnostic and Statistical Manual of Mental Disorders, Fourth Edition: DSM-IV-TR*, American Psychiatric Publishing: Washington DC

Felitti, V et al. (1998), 'Relationship of Childhood Abuse and Household Dysfunction to Many of the Leading Causes of Death in Adults', *American Journal of Preventive Medicine* 14(4): 245–258

Herman, J (2015), *Trauma and Recovery: The Aftermath of Violence – From Domestic Abuse to Political Terror*, Basic Books: New York

Kensinger, E (2007), 'Negative Emotion Enhances Memory Accuracy: Behavioural and Neuroimaging Evidence', *Current Directions in Psychological Science* 16(4): 213-218

Van der Kolk, B (2003), *Psychological Trauma*, American Psychiatric Publishing: Washington DC

* * *

The eulogy-writing resource 'quoted' throughout this book is fictional; for advice on how to arrange a funeral and write a eulogy, visit jackiesfunerals.com.au/steps

THANK YOU

I thank my sister Allison for teaching me how to love. My sisters Deborah and Susan for showing me how I could change the narrative we were cast in. My brother David for always doing his best. My mum and dad for teaching me how to be generous.

Thanks to my wonderful editor Emily Hart who transformed my manuscript into a book with her lightness of touch and kindness of heart. Thank you to Rochelle Fernandez and Ali Hiew for fixing everything, to Akiko Chan for your inspired cover design, and to my agent Sarah McKenzie for believing in my work. Thank you to the entire Hardie Grant Books team for making my dream come true.

I thank my doctoral supervisors Anne Brewster and Janet Chan for their encouragement, faith and wisdom at key moments of the process. Thanks to my excellent readers Andy Kissane and Metta Jacobsen who showed me how to think like a writer and to Anne Enright for her masterclass (and not seeming too fazed when I showed her my *slightly* stalkerish spreadsheet analysis of her novel).

I am grateful to my dear friends and readers especially Roanna Gonsalves without whom I would never have thought I could do this thing. Marie Segrave and Julie Lovell gave me their love, patient attention and laughter, Holly Ringland gave me early encouragement, and David Colville gave me hope at a moment when I needed it. Thanks to my Wollongong writer buddies, especially Hayley Scrivenor for her joyous support, Julie Keys for her steady reassurance, Chloe Higgins for her laser-like insight, Friederike Krishnabhakdi-Vasilakis for her intellectual excellence and Belinda Quinn for her gentle nourishment.

I thank my manuscript assessor Susan Paterson who told me to do all the things I had been hoping to avoid and Tricia Dearborn for polishing the work until it shone. My gratitude to Kerri Shying, my sensitivity reader and friend, who speaks truth at all times. Thanks to Dilini Perera for her practical and moral support with my author headshot, and Greg Appel for my author video.

I also thank the Eleanor Dark Foundation, the Australia Council for the Arts and Create NSW for the gift of Varuna, without which my book would be a flea-infested, sorry-looking version of itself, and the staff at Varuna who make it such an oasis for writers, including Veechi, Amy, Vera, Shelagh, Rod and Joan. And thanks to the writers I met, commiserated and celebrated with at Varuna while writing this book – I cannot wait to read your stories.

Thanks to the SBS Emerging Writers Competition team, especially Natalie Hambly and Danielle Teutsch, and judges

Bejamin Law and Melissa Lucashenko. Special thanks to Loran McDougall who edited the *Roots: Home Is Who We Are* anthology and championed my manuscript, and to the Kill Your Darlings Unpublished Manuscript Award team. This book simply would not exist without you all.

Thanks to the community of writers and artists of colour and disability and allies. You are all JEDI (justice, equity diversity and inclusion) warriors. In the moments I thought it was pointless to continue writing you gave me advice on how to keep going and the hope that it was worth it.

Thanks to my daughter Ellie who will always be my little poppet even if she is taller than me. I love you with my whole heart, infinity times infinity to the power of infinity. To my husband Yen, without whom none of this would have been possible. Thank you, my dearest darling man.